Dying Roots

Karen Peradon

Red Feather Publishing

Book Cover by 100 Covers

Designed by Red Feather Publishing

www.redfeather.com.au

Contents

1. Chapter 1 2
2. Chapter 2 9
3. Chapter 3 16
4. Chapter 4 26
5. Chapter 5 31
6. Chapter 6 41
7. Chapter 7 51
8. Chapter 8 60
9. Chapter 9 66
10. Chapter 10 79
11. Chapter 11 86
12. Chapter 12 92
13. Chapter 13 98
14. Chapter 14 108
15. Chapter 15 114
16. Chapter 16 123
17. Chapter 17 131

18. Chapter 18 139
19. Chapter 19 145
20. Chapter 20 149
21. Chapter 21 157
22. Chapter 22 167
23. Chapter 23 180
24. Chapter 24 189
25. Chapter 25 196
26. Chapter 26 208
27. Chapter 27 215
28. Chapter 28 225
29. Chapter 29 235
Epilogue 240
Playlist 241
Reviews for Dying Roots 243
Letter to Mrs Grimshaw, 1987 244
Dear Reader 246
About the Author 247
About High Lights 249

1

Sylvia Scutlash—orphan, virgin, hairdresser—watched the coffin of her husband descend past the weedy grass roots into the hole. The afternoon breeze blew hauntingly through the gum trees that clustered near the grave, their leaves drooping in melancholy as Solomon Scutlash, hairdresser extraordinaire, was laid to rest.

"Ashes to ashes..." the pastor intoned.

Sylvia's uncle Arthur stood by her side. He dropped to his knees and laid a pair of golden scissors on the coffin. Sylvia followed suit and held out her hand to catch his. He gave her a withering look. She pushed her glasses back up her nose and dropped her hand.

"Dust to dust..."

The soft dirt kicked up as the coffin clunked on the bottom. It stung her eyes, caught in her throat.

"May his parting be smooth and straight, may he wash away his sins, may he brush with the angels and style his soul as befitting our Lord. Amen."

Arthur's black quiff had come undone, and it drooped over his thin face. His moustache quivered and his chin wobbled until his face broke. He sobbed. The rest of the mourners tossed combs in the grave. The assembled crowd were mostly strangers, a fitting word to describe the eclectic bunch. Sylvia eyed the hairstyles; a shag, two flick and wings, a surprising four afros and a dozen perms. Her husband had magnetised many with his wit and extravagant personality. It had been his dying wish that no one wear black at his funeral. His friends had responded with peach shirts, rainbow striped flares, red polka dot dresses, whites, yellows and oranges which smeared the dry cemetery with life. Sylvia had opted for a purple frock but wore her mother's onyx brooch, a deep black stone flecked with seams of gold.

"May his follicular fingers rest in peace!" called out a man of indeterminate age. A shock of white hair haloed around his head, he wore silver skin-tight jeans and a white silk shirt unbuttoned to his sternum. He unhooked a hairdryer from his belt, slotted in a battery, and gave it three long blasts. The mourners nodded and dispersed, taking Arthur, her broken uncle, with them to the waiting cars.

But the hairdryer wielding man held back.

"You must be Sylvia," he held out his hand, "I'm Wiz, Wizard Blowave, charmed to meet you."

She shook his hand.

"Pleased to meet you."

He gestured for them to follow the others.

"So sorry for your loss, my dear."

"Thank you." Sylvia shrugged. "But it's Arthur you should be saying this to."

"You were his wife, Sylvia!"

"In name only. I only ended up here looking for my Uncle Arthur after I left the orphanage. They had been together for a couple of years before I came on the scene. I was just a cover for them. Arthur never forgave me for marrying Sol. I hope one day a man can marry a man."

"I know all about that, but Sol told me about *you*, Sylvia, said you were a very promising hairdresser."

"Oh... he did?"

"Said you had a good head for business, quick to learn and tough. You may have been his beard, but he loved you as well."

His words warmed Sylvia's lonely heart. She felt Sol's sunny presence in this man.

"I remember him telling me how you arrived in the salon in... when was it?" he continued.

"1972, I was 16."

"He said he's never seen such a mess—old, ragged, faded dress..."

"That was my best dress!"

"A horrible mess of black wiry hair, broken glasses and the shoes!" Wiz put his hand to his head in mock horror.

"And I smelt shocking!"

They both laughed.

"But he saw something in you then, and he did until the day he died."

"I wish Arthur did."

"Don't mind him. He was just jealous that you got to marry Sol, be his wife for the last two years. He'll come around."

"Maybe. How did you know Sol?"

"Sol and I go back years. He was one of my best agents, you know."

"I didn't know he was a salesman."

Wiz laughed.

"He sold dreams, my dear, but he was more than that. He was an entertainer, a negotiator, a trickster and could see the essence, the goodness in everyone."

"He taught me everything I know." Her nose fizzled with snot, and hot tears gathered. "I really miss him."

"I know, my dear, we all do. He was a big part of the organisation."

She sniffed and wiped her cheeks.

"What organisation?"

"The Guild, of course!"

Before she could ask any more questions, they reached the car, Sol's beloved lilac Cadillac. Arthur waited in the driver's seat, staring out the window. Wiz opened the back door for Sylvia. She slid onto the cream leather seat.

Wiz sat in the front, relieving Sylvia from the need to interact. She took her compact out of her handbag and viewed her blotchy face in the mirror. Her dark brown eyes were magnified in her glasses, a smudge of mascara underlined each one. She tried to dab it away without shifting the false eyelashes Sol had taught her to wear. Her olive skin was prone to greasiness and her forehead was already shiny. She dabbed powder over it and hooked a lock of stray hair behind her ear. She was so different in build to her lean and wiry uncle. From what she remembered of her father, he was similar to Arthur, which made her think she had her mother's looks. She'd given up on the idea of ever finding out. Another wave of tears threatened. She found comfort in her mother's brooch and rubbed her thumb over its cool surface. On the short drive back to the salon, Wiz talked shop with Arthur, who answered with only monosyllables and sighs.

The Wavy Lady hair salon filled up with customers, friends and the large colourful group of what Sylvia assumed were colleagues. Arthur and Sylvia had positioned themselves at the door to greet the guests.

"Artie, darlink! Oh Artie I'm so sorry about Sol." They kissed cheeks. The woman dressed in a bright mustard embroidered caftan threw her arms around him and squeezed his body. She took his shoulders and looked at his face.

"How are you doing?"

Sylvia saw Arthur's back stiffen.

"I'll be OK," he managed.

"Ah! Is this she?" Tatyana caught sight of Sylvia in the doorway. Arthur cleared his throat.

"Tatyana, meet Sylvia. Sylvia, this is Tatyana Streeckz."

Tatyana put her head to one side, as if waiting.

"The best hairdresser in Moscow," Arthur added.

Tatyana smiled. "In Russia, Artie in Russia!"

Arthur gave a tight smile. "You can call her Tatty."

Tatty scooped Sylvia up into her wobbling breast and folded her in. She squished out the little breath Sylvia had, her many bangles digging into her shoulder blades. The musky perfume was about to suffocate her when Tatty released her. For good measure, she took Sylvia's face in her hands and planted a sucking kiss on each cheek.

"Solly told me so much about you. Oh!" She put her hand to her brow, which rested beneath a towering golden turban from which sprouted a mass of auburn curls. The cloth was dripping with jewels and gold chains. Sylvia wondered how her neck could cope with the weight of it.

"I can't believe he's gone." Her green eyes filled with tears, which threatened to dissolve her caked mascara. Sylvia looked at Arthur, who had his fake smile glued to his face.

A woman with braids skipped forward. She wore a denim miniskirt, a checked shirt knotted at the waist and cowboy boots.

"Hey Art." A big tear squeezed out of one of her sky-blue eyes. "I'm sorry, honey." She squeezed both his hands.

"This is Emmy-Lou Bangs from the U S of A," Tatty, who was lingering, said. "Emmy, meet Mrs Scutlash... finally!"

Arthur blew a steam of air through his nostrils.

"Charmed to meet you," she drawled in an accent Sylvia had never heard.

"And Al Fa'rou, he joins us all the way from West Africa."

A man in a rainbow singlet and crocheted flares ducked through the doorway. After shaking Arthur's hand and placing a consoling pat on his shoulder, he towered over Sylvia and shook her hand.

As more guests arrived, the two salon juniors served Asti Spumante and finger food from trays. Sylvia directed and organised them, made sure glasses were filled, food circulated. The party spilled out onto Rosella Street, memories of Sol too many to be contained in the small salon. For Sylvia, the afternoon dragged on through tears and laughter. Tales of brilliance described the largest personality in Hardup, and later, as the bubbles were consumed, in Perth, until the star of Solomon Scutlash rose to that of a god. Finally, in ones, twos and threes, his friends, clients and neighbours wobbled off into the pink sunset that washed over Rosella Street. Sylvia gathered up the glasses and plates scattered throughout while Arthur slumped in one of the salon chairs, a whisky clamped between his hand and chest. Sylvia wished the last few a farewell and closed the salon door with relief. Three short blow-dryer blasts made her jump. Arthur released his glass and raked his hands through his hair. Wiz hooked his blow dryer back into his belt.

"Have they all gone, the minions? They have feasted and left us to pick over the bones! Ah, the sorrows of my heart! Draw up a chair, you two."

Emmy-Lou, Tatty and Al appeared from the back room.

Sylvia rubbed her forehead. Fatigue washed through her. "Oh, I thought everyone had gone!"

She sighed. Sylvia and Arthur had spent the last six months looking after Solomon as the cancer slowly claimed his body whilst still running the business. A daily mixture of being cheerful for Sol and fearful for the future had taken its toll. Now he was in the ground, all she wanted to do was sink into sleep and forgetfulness.

"Sylvia, put down those tear encrusted glasses. We have business to discuss."

Tatty made herself comfortable in Sol's special hairdressing chair in the window. Sylvia pulled up four chairs to join Arthur.

"Today UGH has buried a deeply loved and valuable member of our organisation. As head of the guild and dear friend, Solomon asked me to be the executer of his last will and testament."

He gave a short blast.

Arthur choked on his drink. "You! Executor? What happened to Balls, Ballsup & Son?"

"The solicitors? Bells & Bellson? Sol fell out with him over the correct length of a false eyelash, passed the job onto me." Wiz blasted once more and pulled a thick envelope out of his bag.

2

"I am honoured to be the executor of one of the best-loved hairdressers of our time, Solomon Scutlash."

"May he rest in peace," Emmy-Lou purred.

They nodded and were silent for a moment. Arthur pinched the bridge of his nose and leaned his elbows on his knees, staring at his shoes.

Wiz drew a pair of scissors from a pocket and slit open the envelope. He took his time to unfold the will and cleared his voice.

"Ready?"

Everyone nodded.

"Very well, 'I Solomon Scutlash of fair mind and hair, hereby divest my estate as follows: To my darling, my dear sweet companion in sickness and in health..."

Arthur's face melted. He sighed.

"... Sylvia."

"What?" Arthur and Sylvia spat out in unison.

"... yes, Sylvia..." Wiz confirmed. Arthur folded his arms and huffed, "... to Sylvia, I leave my collection of wigs."

Arthur smirked and swung back on his chair. Sylvia tried to smile.

"To my best friend, soul mate, the light of my life, Arthur..."

Arthur stared at the back of the letter.

"... I leave the Cadillac."

"The car? The freaking purple wagon? What about the salon?"

"Patience, Arthur, I'm coming to that. Arthur, you will also receive a cash deposit Solomon had set aside, which after tax should amount to $20,000."

"The wily old squirrel—he never told me he had dosh!"

"The salon has been doing really well, Arthur. Perhaps if you took more notice of the books instead of..." Sylvia huffed.

"What? Instead of what, Sylvia, brown-nosing the boss? Making him believe you were worth something?"

"Brown-nosing? You were the one sleeping with him! Not me, his wife!"

"No squabbling, my darlinks! Let's continue, shall we?" Tatty interjected, holding her hand between them.

"Now for the salon, an extremely lucrative going concern I believe you *all* worked hard to attain." Wiz blasted a tattoo and continued.

"The Wavy Lady Hair Salon shall go to..." he paused. Everyone held their breath. The florescent light along the mirrors whirred.

"... to whomever can prove their mettle in the hairdressing world."

"What the hell does that mean?" said Arthur, flinging his hands in the air.

"Solomon deliberated long and hard about this, Arthur. As business partner and true love, he wanted you to take over the salon. But you, Sylvia, he adored you, spent hours training you and he saw something special in you. He couldn't make up his mind, so he decided to see who cut the mustard by..."

"By what, Wiz?" asked Sylvia.

He picked up his hair dryer. "By..."

"With all due respect Wiz, but if you blast that thing one more time,

I'll shove..."

Tatty intervened again with a firm hand. "Artie, pipe down. Please continue, Wiz, this is so exciting."

"Whoever cracks the next UGH case will become the rightful owner of the Wavy Lady Hair Salon, Hardup, Perth."

Tatty put her hand to her mouth in shock, Al whistled, Emmy-Lou silently wowed.

"This is a flicking prank, Wiz, who's made this up? You think this is funny? I'll sue your skinny arse to Xanadu and back!"

"Arthur, calm down at once! How dare you speak to Wiz like that." Tatty stood in all her glittering glory and placed a bejewelled hand on his arm.

"UGH?" Sylvia was at a loss.

"Yes, that's right, dear."

"That's it! I've heard enough of this drivel. Let me look at that." Arthur snatched the document out of Wiz's hand and read. "Where's his signature?" He rifled through the pages until, at the end, he found Sol's flourish.

"You bastard, you callous, miserable turd." He scrunched up the paper and threw it at Wiz. "I quit. I don't want this crappy little shop. I never wanted any of this."

Arthur got up, poured himself a large whisky and threw it down his throat.

"Can someone please tell me what UGH is?"

"Bucking bangs, girl! UGH! The United Guild of Hairdressers. Why didn't you tell Sylvia about UGH?" Wiz turned to Arthur, who was propping himself up on the shelf that ran along the wall below the mirrors.

"It's a secret, isn't it?" Arthur mumbled and tapped his nose. "Secret business, for skilled and important and, and beautiful people!"

he yelled and raised his glass. "Isn't that right, Solly? Hey?" He looked up. "I know you're listening. You were always listening, flappy-eared old queen."

"Arthur!" Sylvia reprimanded. His irreverence distressed her.

Wiz sighed and shook his head, "Sylvia, UGH is a, er, let's say, a discreet association that looks after the welfare of hairdressers. Members adhere to certain lores and help comb out any knots in the hairdressing world. For example, our dear Sol undertook many dangerous and top-secret missions for UGH."

"Trannie in six-inch heels with a pair of scissors *is* very dangerous," Arthur slurred.

"Thank you, Arthur. Sol *was* a master of disguise."

"Sometimes I could hardly recognise him. I once thought I was sleeping with Greta Garbo," Arthur stated.

Sylvia glared at the glass of whisky he was refilling.

"Sol has left a big hole for us to fill," continued Wiz as he smoothed his goatee.

"Yes, a big, ugly bald patch on the scalp of Australia!" Arthur started singing the national anthem. "In joyful strains, then let us sing, advance Australia hair." He laughed hysterically until Wiz blasted him right in the face with his hairdryer. Arthur knocked the hairdryer away with his glass and stalked out of the salon, slamming the door.

"I'll go," said Tatty.

She jingled after Arthur, leaving the room stunned into silence.

"I don't understand. What does this mean for the salon?" said Sylvia.

"It is an unusual turn of events, I'll grant you. Nobody expected this, my dear."

"But why didn't Sol leave the salon to Arthur? He's the rightful heir, not me."

"Girl, have you ever seen Arthur lift a pair of scissors?" Al's soft brown eyes peered from under his afro.

"Of course, he... he, well, he washed and talked to the customers."

"But did you ever see him...?" Al snipped his fingers.

"Well, no, not really, but he could still run The Wavy Lady."

"I believe he was here for love, not locks," said Wiz.

"This is better than TV," said Emmy-Lou. "Say, what happens if Arthur throws in the towel and doesn't turn up for the gig?"

"There was a clause for that," exclaimed Wiz with a blast. He put his spectacles on his nose and read. "Sylvia can still accept the mission and, on completion, will inherit the salon."

"But what is the mission? And what if neither of us turns up?"

"Then the business will be sold, and all proceeds will go to the Wigs Preservation Society of Western Australia."

"But Sol worked his whole life building up this business. We can't just let it go to the wigs!"

Tatty and Arthur reappeared.

"Ah, welcome back. How are you feeling, Arthur?" Wiz didn't give Arthur time to reply and continued. "To summarise: The salon will go to whomever successfully solves the next UGH case. Sylvia, are you prepared to take on this challenge?"

Sylvia swept her eyes around the salon. It had been her refuge for the last four years. She loved it, but without Sol...

"I was planning on leaving tomorrow," she whispered. "I'm going to try Sydney. Find some work, maybe travel a bit. Like he said, we all know who belongs here. There's no point me doing this UGH thing, whatever it is."

"There is always a point when you are a hairdresser, Sylvia."

Sylvia glanced at Arthur, who looked wiped out.

"Arthur was Sol's partner in business and life, not me. I was just a wife of convenience, a manager."

Arthur stared at his hands.

"I'm aware of that, but Sol did love you, Sylvia, as a progeny, a successor," he hesitated. "But I'm speaking out of turn. Let me say that a whole world of opportunity may open up for you if you join UGH."

Tatty, Emmy-Lou and Al all looked at her like eager puppies. Arthur sighed. Sylvia shrugged.

"Well, OK then."

They all gave a little round of applause, except for Arthur, who was hitting the whisky again.

"And Arthur? You will take on the mission?"

Arthur raised his eyes to look at Sylvia.

"Yes, this is my salon, mine and Sol's. I can't believe he's done this to me."

Tatty patted his knee.

Wiz cleared his throat. "Well, then it's agreed. Wonderful!" He blasted his hairdryer and Arthur growled. "So in order to continue with proceedings, we will need to initiate young Sylvia into UGH. As you all know, that happens at my headquarters in Kalbarri."

"Kalbarri? I'm not going to that filthy no-hope town!" Arthur shrieked with a look of disgust. "You take her. I'm not going." He folded his arms.

"My car is full, Arthur. Al, Emmy-Lou and Tatyana are all part of the initiation training and will be returning with me to Kalbarri tonight. You can drive down in the Cadillac tomorrow... after a good sleep." Wiz haled the air with a triumphant blast.

"Where's Kalbarri?" Sylvia asked. She had only been to two places in Australia; the orphanage in the southwest and Perth.

"It's about 600 km north of Perth."

Al and Emmy-Lou stood to leave. "It can get cold... at night, so bring some woollies," Emmy advised.

Wiz picked up his case and went to the door. He attached a special nozzle to his hairdryer, which sounded a high-pitched whistle. They all said their goodbyes. A large white car glided along the street. He nodded at Sylvia before they all slid in. She watched the lights until they disappeared around the T-junction. Moths flew in the open door, she locked up and changed the sign to 'closed'. She pulled down the blinds, as she had done nearly every day for the last five years. Arthur, now laid flat in a salon chair, snored. She dislodged the glass from his hand and placed it on the shelf. She straightened a trolley, folded a cape that had slipped onto the floor. Trailing her hand across the basins, she tightened the tap that always dripped. With all ship-shape, she flipped off the lights and headed up the two flights of stairs to her small bedroom where she had planned to spend her final night in the Wavy Lady Hair Salon.

3

Early the next morning, Sylvia sat in Solomon's favourite chair in the salon. It was a 'Hairflet 700', Danish designed, German engineered, manufactured in Japan, owned by a Swiss company and constructed in Russia out of purple Baltic steel with a leather seat from wild Appalachian horses. The inventor had come up with a technology that not only moulded itself to the sitter but also relaxed them deeply by emitting pulses to their meridians, inducing dopamine release. There were only six made in the world, and Sol proudly displayed it in the shop window and waved to passers-by while cutting and styling on his own mini stage. The few international hairdressers visiting Perth always called in to see the chair. Sylvia often wondered if the Hairflet was as much a draw card as the skills of the hairdressers.

She twisted and watched as the sun fingered her rays across Rosella Street, sending strands of light through the jacaranda trees. They were in full bloom, the brazen lilac flowers taking over the tree, the street and covering the same coloured Cadillac. The blossoms screamed Solomon, but the silence in the salon and in her heart was deafening. She twirled the chair away from the window and pulled up her legs. As her head rested against the smooth leather, she caught a faint scent of Sol's cologne. Curled up, embraced by the Hairflet she viewed the little hairdresser shop that had been her refuge. Here she had found friendship, a purpose, a home. She would miss it, but the world awaited her.

A sound made her jump. Arthur lurked at the rear of the shop.

"Couldn't sleep either." It was a statement about himself. Neither had the energy to care much about the other. "You packed?"

"Yes, but I don't want to go. I've decided... I'm going to Sydney."

"But you agreed yesterday, to Wiz."

"Well, he put me on the spot. I didn't have much choice."

"Choice? Ha!" Arthur flared and sneered. "You really think you're something, don't you? Who gets to choose anything? Shit happens, and we are just flushed along the stinking sewage pipes. We can try to make it smell nice, but at the end of the day, it's all shit."

"You could've warned me, at least told me about this UGH thing."

"Look, do you even know who Wiz is?"

Sylvia spun the chair away from his vitriol.

"Well, how would I? Nobody told me anything around here." She flung back around to face him. "I'm just the general dogsbody who's not important enough to be in the nose." She tapped her nose. "In the know."

Her face flushed. She'd already felt like an idiot yesterday. She knew less than half of the mourners, never heard of UGH. What else didn't she know? Irritation bubbled.

"He's the head honcho, founder of UGH."

"And?"

"Well, you know how England has a queen?" He spoke to her as if she was three years old.

"Is he royalty?"

"Oh, for crimp's sake, Sylvia, he's the most important man in the hairdressing world!"

"But that's Vitale Crassoon."

"Oh no, Wiz is bigger than that. Look, if Wiz wants a scented fart, you give him a scented fart. And now he has his fingers on that bloody will; he wants you, us in Kalbarri, so that's where we are going. Got it?"

"How can anyone be higher than Vitale Crassoon?"

"Listen sweetheart, just pack your bloody bag and meet me in the car in an hour. Then once this shitty business is over..." he trailed off.

"What?"

"Then I'll drop you off wherever you want. And you'll get to play the heartbroken widow, and me... just a sad, lonely old queen."

"I loved Sol too, Arthur. I *am* heartbroken. You're not the only one."

She wanted to say more, but the brief flare left her, and grief sucked her energy. She slumped back in the Hairflet as flat as a Teddy boy's buzz cut.

"Well, boo hoo. I want to be on the road early, so get moving," Arthur spat and turned on his heels.

Sylvia sighed and slid out of the familiar comfort of the chair. She went to put the kettle on, her packed bag already by the door.

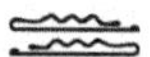

An hour later, the Cadillac roared into life. The psychedelic blinds of the salon were drawn. Someone had laid a wreath on the doorstep. Sylvia and Arthur were not the only ones who would miss Solomon Scutlash. The car turned off Rosella Street. They weaved through the suburbs until the long, straight coastal road took them north. Arthur turned on the radio.

The songstress implored them to not leave her this way. It was too upbeat. Sylvia turned it off. Arthur turned it back on and upped the volume.

I can't exist, the singer belted out, yearning for a tender kiss, the music crescendoed.

Sylvia turned it down to a faint sound.

"Can we just have some peace?"

"Can we just have some NOISE?" Arthur slapped her hand away from the dial and twisted it to full blast.

The song ended, and the DJ's voice boomed throughout the car. Arthur turned it off. Sylvia watched the houses thin out, the West Australian bush rooted in the red earth thickened.

"How long will it take?"

"Are you serious?"

"Yes, how should I know? I've never been to Kalbaggi or wherever."

"Eternity in hell, at this rate."

"Can't you just answer the question?"

"No."

"Why not?"

"Because I don't want to talk to you."

"But you're my uncle."

"A disappointing fact."

"Blast it Arthur! Why do you hate me?"

"I don't."

"You do. From the moment I walked into the shop five years ago, you've detested me."

"I left our so-called family, and I never wanted to see another one of you. The only reason I'm here in Perth is because of Sol. I don't know why he wanted to stay in this back arse of beyond."

Arthur switched the radio back on. They drove in silence, only the music and DJ drivel filling the space. It felt awkward being alone with Arthur. Her mind was full of questions.

"Who are these UGH people? Why didn't Sol ever talk about them?" she said eventually.

"Because you didn't need to know. Nobody except members of the guild know, secret business," he tapped his long nose.

"Well, it's not secret anymore, so you might as well tell me."

"It's a network."

"What does that mean?"

Arthur sighed. "You know? Heard it on the grapevine?"

Sylvia shook her head.

"So Josie Doe comes into the salon for a rinse and blow dry. Tells hairdresser that the salon on Dodgy St is charging double, or has a new manager, or that her neighbour is banging the bank manager. Whatever, it gets fed back to headquarters where it's compiled."

"So?"

"Knowledge, from the street to seat to HEAT."

"The what?"

"Hairdresser Evidence Assessment Team."

"I don't understand."

"Every salon worth its shampoo anywhere in the world has a member of UGH on the team. They all feed back to HEAT in their country and they all feed back to Wiz, in sleepy old Kalbarri."

"Wow."

"Flickin' oath, wow. Wiz knows more than God."

As the enormity of UGH sunk in, Sylvia watched the red dirt smear past the window, as she whizzed through it with no control. Her life had so far been a string of events dictated by others. She had broken free once before, the time she ran away from the Catholic nuns' orphanage, but now it seemed right into the arms of another institution. *She* wanted to be in charge now, to be free as the gulls that spiralled in the sky above her. After an hour, the soft purr of the engine and the generous seat lulled her into a doze. She came to when the engine died.

"Where are we?" she said as she stretched herself out of the car.

Arthur leaned against the bonnet. He took a swig from a hip flask.

"Hangover Bay," he slurred slightly.

"It's beautiful."

"Sol and I used to stop here when we were on the road."

Sylvia noticed a softness in his voice he only used with Sol.

"You two loved your trips." Sylvia had often felt like the poor cousin; left behind to manage the salon. She itched to see the world.

"Yeah, we travelled well together, planned to join the purple rinse brigade when we retired. Except we would have had pink rinses."

A brief smile flickered across his features, but a bleak future hung in the air. Since Sol's death, the idea of 'the future' was dawning on Sylvia. A small flame, puttering for oxygen. From an early age, she had learnt to live in the present, afraid to imagine what a disappointment the future might bring. Perhaps her future lay in the past. The white sand billowed over the vast beach to the Indian Ocean, carrying the colours of its exotic name, bright lapis lazuli to a deep jade. The morning sun heated their backs and silence dropped around them. Years later, she wished she had paused longer in that moment of peace, or at least considered the words that came out of her mouth. But that one shared minute of grief was the only opportunity she had to ask.

"Didn't you ever want to go back to England? See the family?"

"Family!" Arthur spat the word as if laced with venom. "Minds as narrow as a chewed fingernail, morals as skewed as a French plait and hearts as dark as Elvis' hair dye. They hated me, rejected me, as if *they* had the right to be judgemental. I was different from them." He took a long swig. "Thank God."

The air shifted, a breeze blew off the ocean.

"Why?" she dared another question. Arthur drew his eyes from the horizon and looked at Sylvia. His face contorted.

"Because I made them uncomfortable, a deadly British sin; 'Thou shalt not discomfit thy neighbour'. I was never like them, didn't play sport, didn't have a girlfriend, didn't work as a dirty, sweaty labourer with my old man. I left that stinking city as soon as I could get my pretty arse out of there. I met Sol the first day I arrived in Australia and we never spent a second apart. *He* was my family. He was my world."

"Hey, I'm family. *I* never hated you, Arthur."

"'I never hated you'," he imitated her in a high voice, "well woo-flicking-hoo for you. You should. I'm an impossibly handsome loather of any Sprout family members."

"I don't hate you."

"What's wrong with you? Who do you think you are, Saint Sylvia? I hate you even more for not hating me."

She didn't know why she didn't hate him. He had never shown her any kindness, only treated her like a scab he wanted to pick off and throw away. Whilst Sol had adored her, taken her under his wing and cherished her as a part of the family.

"What's it like, London?" she ventured after the bitter words were taken by the breeze.

He threw another slug down his throat and shook his head.

"Ah London; perfect climate for miserable sods, mother tongue Sarcasm and a haven for lunatics and misfits, it would win municipal awards in Hell." The description acted as a set of brakes on the already stilted conversation. Seagulls keened overhead.

"People still judge each other here."

"Not your own family, though. Who cares if a bunch of strangers don't like me or who I go out with? I don't give a fat hoot what those nosy people in Hardup say. Sol did, I didn't. We need to get going."

Sylvia shifted, desperate to get answers. "What was my dad like? You never talk about him."

Arthur sneered, "Your Dad? He was a thieving, drunken drop of mucous..."

"Don't you dare speak ill of the dead. He was your older brother!"

"Brothers don't steal off you, humiliate you, beat you up."

"He beat you up?"

"Look, I don't want to talk about it, you understand? He got what he deserved. I told you, it's history, wiped out."

"But it's not for me, Arthur! I want to know who my family are, were. At least you chose to leave them. I didn't... I'm adrift in this world without anyone."

"Well, you're all grown up now, aren't you, Sylverella. Go and find out for yourself. Go and see if there are any deadbeat cousins, desiccated old skeletons still hanging on in the Sprout family tree. Just don't include me. I never want to see that place again."

"What happened to you, Arthur?"

He looked at her for a moment, took a breath. His lips wobbled and the muscle in his neck tightened.

"You."

"Me? What did I do?"

"You came with your ugly shoes and your ugly glasses. Sol couldn't resist a pet project like you. Doll you up, make you into something. Right little Eliza Doolittle. Worming your way between us."

"You guys would have been run out of town if I hadn't married Sol. I did you a favour. I don't know what Sol saw in you, childish, selfish and vain. You're as bad as them in England..."

She sensed his mood rumbling dangerously, but she couldn't stop.

"Now, Sol's dead too. You probably drove him there with your jealousy and whining..."

Arthur stepped back as if he'd been hit in the stomach and looked at Sylvia with hatred.

"Well, well, well, the church mouse has turned. You know nothing about family. You're no more than a stray, a pet that my soft-hearted Sol played with. Get in the car!"

"No, not until you tell me about my parents. Tell me what happened. I deserve to know."

Tears welled, but she swallowed them back.

"Why? What did they ever do for you, Sylvia, eh? One died the minute you took your first breath. The other shipped you off to the opposite side of the world. Why do you give a damn? I've nothing to say. Now get in."

But she moved away from the car door and advanced on him. Something had taken her over, a desperate wave of curiosity that she couldn't hold in.

"What did she look like, Arthur? Why did she die? Why did he send me away? You have to tell me!"

"I told you, I can't answer your questions and I don't care. I left that all behind me and good riddance. If you ask me, they did you a flicking favour."

"You owe it to me."

He faced her until she could smell his whisky breath on her skin, his lips bared from his teeth.

"I don't owe you anything. The day you married Sol was worse than all the years I spent in that plug hole England. Now get in the car before I abandon you, just like all the others did." He opened the door and pointed.

A power rose in her. "No."

"OK." He slammed the door hard. "I'll tell you why, shall I?" He squeezed her chin in his hand, "because they took one look at your ugly little face, no wonder your mother carked it." He threw her chin away, making her stumble.

"You're right, you *are* selfish and I *do* hate you. I hate you!"

She opened the car door, hitting Arthur square in the torso. He doubled over in pain, gasping. She ran to the lookout, wishing she could fly away, white fury coursing through her. His footsteps crunched behind her.

"You evil witch, I'm telling you one more time to get in or I swear I'll leave you for the dingoes."

"Good, I'd rather get eaten by dingoes than be anywhere near you," her voice rose, and she turned and beat her fists at his chest. But Arthur grabbed her wrists and twisted them, dragging her to the car. He shoved her roughly in the back seat.

Shaking, Sylvia sat up and stared at the back of Arthur's Brylcreemed head, her one and only remaining relative, with the realisation that he too was lost to her.

4

Arthur pulled up on the main street of Kalbarri and cut the engine. A muscle in his jaw quivered. Not a word had passed between them since Hangover Bay. Sylvia looked through the red dust that caked the window in the sudden silence. Pink tinged the buildings as the sun dipped through the ocean they had been driving along for the last eight hours.

"Get your things," he said.

"I'm sorry Sol didn't just leave you the salon."

"Well, he pretty much did, didn't he? You think you're going to crack your first case just like that? This was just Sol's way of getting you into UGH. Just means it'll be a bit longer before the keys are in my hand. That's all. Now get your things."

Arthur released himself and made for the pub that dominated the street. He emptied the last drops from the hip flask into his mouth. The sign announced, 'The Snip and Sip'. Sylvia removed the headscarf she used to keep her hair style intact and took her compact out of her handbag. She applied powder to blot away the sweat that had already pooled above her lips and slathered on a coat of lipstick to detract from the faint bruise on her jaw. Arthur rapped impatiently on her window. Of all the places she could have visited, this shabby town would not have been top of her list. The main street was the only sealed road. She wondered why anyone would come here.

Arthur had disappeared into the pub, letting the door bang behind him. She took a breath and followed him. She waited for her eyes to adjust to the gloomy interior. The bar ran along the right side of the room and high stools and tables held a few hippie surfers seated around a jug of beer and one or two weather worn fisherman sipping pints. A stained lino floor complimented the sandy walls and dun coloured plastic seats. The whole effect did nothing but frame the shiny and glamorous jukebox. It clicked and whirred as one surfer slid in a coin. The barman glanced at Arthur, who said, “Is this saloon a cut above the rest?”

Sylvia frowned, but the barman nodded towards a door at the back that said ‘dunnies’. Arthur pulled himself up straight, puffed out his chest and slicked his fingers across his tightly gelled hair. He pranced a path through the untidy tables and chairs to the door with Sylvia in his wake. The door opened into a dull passageway. They passed the toilets and arrived at another door at the end of the corridor. Arthur knocked a complicated rhythm; a tap tap tappity tap tap responded from within. He knocked in response. Sylvia held her breath. The door swung open.

Tatty welcomed them inside. Sylvia blinked. On one side of the wall was a rundown bar with a dodgy corridor, but this room was like a scene from a movie. Large potted plants flanked the entrance under a glass atrium. Gold flecked marble tiles led to a mosaic path that formed a bridge over a small stream that trickled into a sparkling swimming pool. Tatty grabbed her hand and drew the astonished Sylvia towards Wiz, who stood waiting on the bridge.

“Wiz, they’re here. Arthur and Sylvia have arrived!”

Wiz pulled off his round metal framed sunglasses and stepped towards them with out-stretched hand. Taken aback, Sylvia did not know where to position her eyes. He wore a pair of tight white denim shorts that threatened to slice him in half. White hairs flecked his ridged stomach and chest that stood out from his deeply tanned skin. Off his shoulders flowed a towelling cloak.

"Thank you, Tatyana. Welcome to UGH headquarters." He presented his domain with a sweep of his arms. "This way!"

They walked towards the pool and Wiz went ahead to lead them in single file over the narrow bridge. Large coy swam lazily with the flow among waterlilies. The path led through a garden, lush with hanging plants, to a pergola with sofas decorated in luxurious fabrics.

Emmy-Lou and Al lounged there and jumped up to great the road-weary travellers. Al's afro shadowed Sylvia from the sun that beamed through the wide-open window in the ceiling. Tatty jangled her hands together and said, "You must be exhausted. I'll show you your rooms, then reconvene by the pool for refreshments."

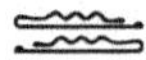

Sylvia put her bag on the bed of the single room that looked out over the dusty main street of Kalbarri. There was a knock at the door.

"Dinner is served!" Tatty called.

At the pool, the table was set. The barman arrived with a tray of food. As a basket of chips and a dish of watery chops were laid on the table. Tatty emerged from the kitchen with an ice bucket in one hand and six flutes clinked between the fingers of the other.

"Let's drink a toast!" she shrilled.

Arthur scowled. Tatty popped the cork, which landed with a plop in the pool. She dribbled the bubbles into each glass.

"To Solomon!"

They all raised their glass, "To Solomon!"

"Memories! Let's each tell a memory we have of Sol," Wiz chuckled, "a memory of his largesse!"

Arthur choked on his champagne.

"I'll go first!" shrieked Tatty. "We were in Russia. Sol was in Moscow buying his precious Hairflet, from which the scoundrel outbid me. He styled the hair of Varula Vladomop, the famed opera singer. So to get him back, I bet him one hundred roubles he couldn't hide a bottle of vodka in her wig. The sneaky man did, but he drank the vodka first, so it wasn't so heavy. I swear he could smuggle an elephant in one of those creations! To Sol, a creative genius," she held up her glass, "Na zdorovie!"

They all clinked glasses.

"I knew him before he knew himself," said Wiz. "He was sixteen and towered over me. All gangly arms and spotty chops. He had eyelashes so long he could have plaited them, and long fingers to match. I knew those hands would work magic on a head of hair. He was the most talented apprentice I've ever had. Watching him style a shag brought tears to my eyes. Such grace." Wiz blew his nose. "To Sol, chin chin!"

"Chin chin!" they all repeated.

"Well," Al Fa'Rou said in his honeyed African accent. "We met in Cairo. He'd got himself in a knotty situation with an Egyptian prince. He wanted to buy his wife's hair, and the prince misunderstood. Thought Sol wanted to bed his wife. Poor Solomon ended up in a prison cell, took all my charms to get him out." A deep, resonating laugh rumbled from his chest. "To Sol, a man who would risk anything for a good wig! Santé!"

"Well, I just fell in love with him the minute he hightailed it into my salon. Oh boy oh boy! He was the cutest darn thang I ever laid my eyes on. Cheers to Sol!" Emmy Lou sang in her melodious voice.

They clinked and sipped. There was silence.

"Arthur, do you want to say anything?" Wiz asked gently.

Arthur unravelled from his hunched position.

"I met him in a movie house in Sydney. I'd only arrived in Australia that morning, didn't know what to do with myself, so I went to see a flick."

Sylvia had never heard Arthur speak about how he'd met Sol, never heard him sound so small.

"The film was called 'They're a Weird Mob', ha! We used to laugh at the irony. Anyway, I was sitting in the row in front of him, thinking I was blubbing to myself in the dark, when he dangled a hankie over my shoulder. It was the kindest thing anyone had ever done for me." Arthur closed his eyes tight and put his head back.

"He was a good man," said Wiz.

Everyone nodded. "To a good man!" said Sylvia.

"To a good man!" they all repeated, raising their glasses high.

5

Chapter Five

As Sylvia opened her curtains on the new morning, it was as if the winter rains of the months before had never been, and summer had arrived with a big fat suitcase of dry dust. She hadn't slept well, thrashing around in the alien bed, wondering what turn her life was taking. It was 5.16 a.m. and UGH training was to begin at 7.00 a.m. sharp. She brushed her black hair into a tyre-like halo that framed her head and sprayed it with a good squirt of hair lacquer.

She opened her suitcase. As she had planned to leave Perth the morning before, the case contained all her possessions. There were two treasured items, one a letter from England dated 1966. It hadn't arrived in the convent until 1968, when she found out she had lost a father but gained an uncle. The second was the onyx brooch that had belonged to her mother. Her Dad had given it to her the day he boarded her on the ship to Australia at the age of seven in 1963. The large, oval black stone nestled in an ornate gold base with a hallmark. The intricately laced edges wove golden strands together, creating a nest that cushioned the grand jewel. She breathed on it, polished it against her top and placed it back in the shabby old box.

She heard voices and peeked out of her door. The waft of coffee lured her out to meet the others who were helping themselves to breakfast in the kitchen.

"Good morning, darlink!" Tatty kissed her cheeks and invited her to an array of breakfast items laid out on the bench. "Did you sleep well?"

"Um, yes, thanks," she lied.

"Hurry and eat your breakfast, darlink. We are ready to begin the training."

After breakfast, they convened. Wiz, Emmy-Lou and Al sat on a circular couch, Sylvia in a hairdressing chair facing them next to a trolley of tools. Tatty stood with a clipboard and pen and explained.

"The initiation process is quite simple. Firstly, full training, then the challenges. You will also need to memorise the Hairdresser Charter and pass the final test. After that, we have the initiation ceremony."

It sounded strange and complicated. They looked at her with expectation.

"Okay," she drawled in trepidation.

"Repeat after me," Wiz said.

"I, Sylvia Scutlash,"

"I, Sylvia Scutlash,"

"Hereby swear by the hairs on my head,"

"Hereby swear by the hairs on my head,"

"To uphold the Charter of UGH."

"To uphold the Charter of UGH."

"To use your scissors wisely, always carry a comb and bring honour to all hairdressers."

She repeated to the end. The small audience clapped politely.

"Now Sylvia, you are to commence the training, which consists of four sections:

1. Gathering of secret information procedure (G.O.S.I.P.)

2. 101 uses of a bobby pin and other tools

3. Survival hacks in tricky situations

4. How to look highly presentable under difficult circumstances.

After this you should be equipped for the challenge."

"What's that?"

"To learn perseverance and resourcefulness, you will be left to your own devices in the bush for three days. You will be provided with a pair of scissors, a hairbrush and a bottle of shampoo."

"In the bush?"

"Yes."

"On my own?"

"Yes, and finally, to show courage and commitment, you will... well, I'll leave those details for later."

"Jiminy clippers, sounds serious," she winced.

"You'll be fine. First lesson is the nine commandments of hairdressing. Please take notes. Ready?"

Sylvia got a pad of paper and pen and nodded.

"Thou shalt:

1. Do hair, not harm, nihil mali capillos. This is the UGH motto which we ensure is stated in every salon in the world.

2. Always keep your mind and your scissors sharp

3. Never let another hairdresser finish your client

4. Never leave a client waiting

5. Always help a hairdresser in need

6. Never leave a client unfinished

7. Always test the water first

8. Always have open ears, open eyes and open mouth

9. Never mess with a hairdresser who's had a bad day."

"Why aren't there ten commandments?"

"To remind God he isn't the only one that makes up the rules."

She nodded wide eyed, could feel her Catholic nun conscience gasping.

"Now, to be a full member of UGH, there is a probation period of one month. In this month you must complete an UGH mission. Any questions?"

"What will the mission be?"

This sounded much more exciting than commandments and training.

"The next mission has not yet been received. In any case, you must first complete the training," Wiz said with finality.

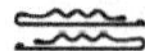

Sylvia spent the following three days manipulating bobby pins to form needles, keys, a frame for glasses, an electrical conductor, a pedicure item, a weapon, a splinter remover, a car starter, a fishing hook, a toothpick and most importantly a hair spray canister nozzle clearer. She learnt how to crochet them into a chain, melt them down, fire them out of a hairdryer and fix a zip. She mastered using them to break into cars, houses, windows and safes.

The UGH motto meant she couldn't use a bobby pin for torture. But she learnt other techniques to extract information out of people. Number one was 'charm'. Tatty and Wiz role played scenario after scenario where Sylvia had to charm the target until he or she dropped their locks and let the chat out of the mag. It was on the fourth afternoon when Wiz was showing Sylvia how to fashion a hairbrush out of a sponge and seventy-five bobby pins that Sylvia passed G.O.S.I.P.

"So Wiz, what about you? Tatty said you are the founder of UGH?"

"Ah Sylvia, it was my poor mother who was at the root of it all.

She was a looker in her day, had half of Kalbarri chasing her, the male half, that is. Eventually she picked one and," he emphasised the word, "*settled* down. Well, she got married, but she was never what you'd call 'settled'. As highly strung as a guitar string on a telegraph pole, my dad used to say. He soon nicked off to live a quieter life in the outback."

"That must have been hard for you. At least you still had her though."

"Yes, we were close. She loved a get-together. We used to paw through the magazines and dream up elaborate parties. Every now and then she'd actually throw one and the townspeople would come. But she'd end up smooching with the doctor, or a teacher, or once or twice the town mayor. Always ended in trouble, wives leaving, scandalous gossip. People stopped coming." He stabbed the sponge with a pin.

"But she always had her friend Wendy, she was the local hairdresser and no matter whose life my mum ruined, Wendy was always there to hear about it. Every Friday morning Mum would get her hair done, ready for the weekend."

"Do you have any photos?"

"No, no one had cameras back then. She was a stunning woman."

"Where did you learn to be a hairdresser?"

"Well, Wendy got married. Her husband was a chef, and he dreamed of working in the city. I was about twelve years old when she left town. The hairdressers shut down and my mum with it. As her hair became wilder, so did she. One day, my teacher looked at the state of me and threatened to call the authorities. That afternoon I got home and I wrestled my mum into the bath, washed her hair, dried and styled it. In the following weeks I blow-dried my mother back to sanity."

"Sounds like you were a natural."

"No, she looked like a dingo's dag after I'd been at it! But it made her feel better. She never recovered, even when a new hairdresser opened. I kept doing her hair until she died a few years later. I was sixteen, and I went to Sydney and learnt all I could."

"Did you open your own place in Sydney?"

"Not straight away. First, I travelled the world on a wing and a hair! I worked Paris, London, Hollywood."

Tatty's bangles announced her presence in the room as she clapped. Wiz laughed. Sylvia looked at them and frowned.

"What?"

"Good work, Sylvia. It usually takes at least two weeks before Wiz tells his story."

"But we were just talking, I didn't..."

"Then you are a natural, my girl!" Wiz blasted his hairdryer, "but your sponge hairbrush still needs work." He blew what looked a hedgehog with alopecia out of her hands.

The days crept along, lesson by lesson. Sylvia paced around the pool memorising the nine commandments, learning how to do her hair and make-up. She practised dressing in the dark, in a confined space, in a fast-moving vehicle, in a monsoon (where they set her up in the shower) and when holding her breath - an unpleasant experience she hoped never to repeat.

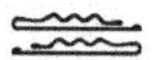

After a week of training, Sylvia joined the others for breakfast as usual. Today, they were in the salon next to the kitchen. It was fully equipped with two chairs, a huge mirror and a machine that resembled a TV. Sylvia wandered in, chewing on a piece of toast.

"I love that idea, a TV in the salon," she said. "I could watch the Young Doctors while cleaning up."

The screen was flickering green with rows of text. Wiz was banging on the keyboard next to it in frustration.

"Can we put it on channel seven?"

The others tittered.

"This isn't a TV, Sylvia."

"What is it then?"

"It's an Alhair 800. A computer."

"What's a comuta? Looks like a dodgy TV to me. Why is the screen all green? You'll need to get that fixed."

Wiz flicked a switch, and the screen died. "Let's not worry about the 'TV' for now, my dear. We have reached a momentous occasion of your initiation. Please take a seat."

He wore a black velvet cloak embossed with tiny scissor stars that made him look like a real wizard. Tatty glowed in a gold brocade kaftan with the usual metal overload, Emmy-Lou, a Las Vegas style suit and Al dark flares, his own ebony skin instead of a shirt. But he also wore rubber gloves. He placed a small case on the table. Sylvia had taken on the training with a little nervousness but now sitting cloaked in a chair with the four UGH members standing around her had the hairs on her neck stand on end.

Wiz blew his dryer and tucked it into his pants. He put both hands on Sylvia's shoulders.

"And now for the ritual shearing of the initiate."

"What?" Sylvia twisted around. "Shearing?"

Tatty swung the chair back so she was facing the mirror.

"Yes, my darlink. It is the final stage. There's no backing out now. And it'll grow back." She smiled.

"Clippers," Wiz held out his hand. Al passed them over and flicked the switch.

"But I like my hair!"

Emmy-Lou snorted. "It sure is unique."

"But why? Isn't it against hairdressers' lore to make someone bald?"

"Yes, but this is to prove you are committed, plus we need to get to your skin for the tattoo."

"Tattoo!" Sylvia jumped up and backed away from the chair. "I'm not having a tattoo!"

"Why not?"

"Because... well, it's not ladylike." She remembered the dark images on her dad's arms, ones he had got in prison. A new one appeared after each visit.

"Is it you saying that, or your nuns?" asked Wiz.

"I... I... It'll hurt."

"Al is a most famous tattooist and snake charmer. He's not a hairdresser, you know."

"No, I didn't know because you didn't tell me." Sylvia was panicking once again. "What's a snake charmer got to do with it?"

"He'll hypnotise you, you won't even feel the pain."

"I don't want to be hypnotised... or charmed or tattooed or shaved. This is not happening."

She tried to whisk off the cape. It got caught around her neck and she wrestled with it, getting more tangled. In the end, she gave up and tucked it into her pants and fled along the corridor and into the bar.

The truth was she didn't want a tattoo because criminals had tattoos. People who did bad things; thieves, murderers, gang members. And bad people went to hell and damnation. She may have spent a night behind bars when she was sixteen, but she hadn't committed a crime. What if a tattoo led to a crime and a fast track into the arms of Satan? She called over the barman.

"Can I have a...?" What did people drink in such a situation?

"Give her a Hairy Wallbanger." Al's deep voice reverberated from the other side of the room.

He slid a coin into the jukebox.

The barman served up the cocktail in the least fancy way possible and stuck in two straws. As David Soul crooned about not giving up, Al took a barstool and placed it next to Sylvia. He turned over a beer mat and took a pencil from out of his afro.

"There's two hundred and seventy-eight members of UGH all over the world. Uruguay, Canada, India, Russia, you name it. I've tattooed every single one." He finished a sketch and slid the mat towards her.

"They've all got this logo on the top of their heads, hidden under their hair."

Sylvia looked at the small drawing of the crossed scissors that Wiz had on his cloak.

"This tattoo means you're part of a special club, Sylvia, an exclusive club that will make you friends everywhere. Now, I can tell that you got the world shining in your eyes. I can see you dancing on the far horizons. This is your ticket, Sylvia. This will get you to places that haven't even made it into the National Geographic. So, you can walk out of this bar and catch a bus to Perth, fly to Sydney and walk the streets finding a job," he paused. "Or you could let me tattoo this little emblem," he tapped the mat with his elegant finger, "for a smooth slide to your dreams."

"Are you snake charming me?"

"You got it. I'm slick, right?"

She nodded.

"So, what's it to be, Cookie? Gonna let me hitch you a ride to your dreams, or you going to take those sticky, tricky streets to Dullsville?"

"And my hair will grow over it?"

"Completely."

"Will it hurt?"

"Not after you drink three more of these." He signalled to the barman.

After Sylvia had slurped the dregs of the third cocktail, she needed Al's arm to guide her through the tables and chairs back to the salon. Emmy Lou and Tatty played cards while they waited. Wiz's TV was back on and he was typing on a keyboard.

"You ready, darlink?" Tatty enveloped Sylvia and led her back to the chair. Sylvia took a breath and nodded.

"Clippers!"

Wiz revved them up and placed the blade on the back of Sylvia's neck. Heavy ribbons of her hair fell to the floor. She couldn't take her eyes away from her reflection as her head shrunk. She was woozy, but knew not whether it was the Hairy Wallbangers or the hairy floor-bangers. Within a few minutes there she was, her head as naked as a nectarine. She had never seen the smooth skin of her scalp. She brushed a palm across it and shivered despite the baking heat of the day. Wiz silenced the clippers, but before long, the sound of the tattooist's needle purred.

It did hurt, but she kept the pain in, not admitting to the agony of the relentless hammering on her skull. Once finished, Al held a mirror up for her to see. The black logo of crossed scissors wept small beads of blood on the back of her head. It throbbed. She felt raw, naked and suddenly tired.

Wiz put his hands on her shoulders and gave them a squeeze.

The others chorused "Nihil mali capillos".

"Nihil mali capillos," Sylvia croaked in response, wondering if she could handle the final challenge.

6

The following morning, Wiz declared Sylvia ready for the outback challenge. They jumped into a jeep parked behind the pub and set off into the flat dry land of low shrubs, dotted with delicate wildflowers but little else. It took half an hour to reach a red rock that emerged from the earth. Wiz stopped.

"This is it. We'll see you back here in three days. Good luck, my dear."

"You really expect me to stay out here on my own for three days?"

"Here's your bottle of shampoo, a pair of scissors and a brush."

In disbelief, she stepped out of the jeep. Wiz gave her a wink and drove off, leaving the dust to settle on her legs. Soon the noise of the engine receded and all she could hear were buzzing flies and her breath. She looked around her. The rocks rose in a wall behind her, the flat plain stretched out beyond her. It reminded her of the day she'd arrived at the convent. It had seemed like nothing could survive there. Why had anyone built a church there, she wondered. Why did the nuns choose to live there? She never worked it out, but the years at the convent taught her some bush skills. She'd learnt that water was always the priority, and she couldn't drink shampoo for three days. If she climbed the rock, she might find pools of water, if not a river once she could see the lay of the land. Wiz had warned her about this challenge at the beginning of the training, and she had prepared herself as best she could. She pulled a cape out of her pants that would do as a primitive shelter for the night, and she had stuffed a towel under her jumper for warmth. She put all her gear into the middle of the cape and folded it up with a knot. A stick nearby served as a carrier and she climbed the warm rocks. Her legs revelled in the climb, her muscles cheering her on. The flat top rewarded her with views that never ended, hundreds of miles of red earth. The world spread at her feet. She felt like a queen. She noticed a gully still running with water from the winter rains on the other side of the climb.

"Bingo," she muttered, "hopefully not dingo!" she joked to herself, and began the descent.

Sylvia found a flattish sandy patch by the gorge. The water tasted clean, and she drank, tossing a handful over her bare scalp. She rigged up the cape into a small tent and gathered twigs and sticks to make a fire. Using the scissors against a rock, she lit the kindling (she had at least learnt one thing at the orphanage) and blew on the flame. Although food might be a problem, she guessed a diet wouldn't kill her for three days. As the evening drew in, she lay next to the fire and thought about her family as she did most nights before she slept. She prayed her parents were resting in peace and tried to recall their faces. She would have sold her soul to the devil to know anything about her mother, what she looked like, her middle name, something. All she had was the onyx brooch that gave her no clues about the woman who birthed her. Sylvia fell asleep.

She woke the next morning shivering. Her headscarf had slipped off, and the fire was out, the dawn air fresh and damp. She washed her face in the stream, feeling her naked scalp, using the scarf to dry her skin before tying it back on her head. Her stomach rumbled. She was desperate for a cup of tea.

A rustling nearby startled her. She froze and looked towards the direction of the noise. There were low bushes which somehow survived on the rock. With breath held tight in her chest, she turned and scanned the ground. As her eyes adjusted to the muted browns of sand and leaves, Sylvia noticed a mouse moving amongst the debris. She gave a sigh of relief and watched the little creature. There was a sudden movement, and the jaws of a snake emerged from behind the mouse and closed around it. Sylvia gasped and retreated as far from the undergrowth as possible. How would she survive for three days with snakes at foot? How could she sleep or walk around with danger lurking under every rock? She huddled under her makeshift camp, holding her stick and fingering a pile of rocks she could throw at a dingo, snake or even human.

Sylvia must have fallen asleep. A shadow formed over her, which woke her up. As she opened her eyes, her gaze fell on a pair of feet. A young woman as still as a tree stood in the coarse bushes. She was about the same age as Sylvia, wearing a loose, faded skirt over her bare dark brown legs and an old jumper. For a moment, their eyes locked.

"Be careful, there are snakes!"

"Whatcho white fella doing here?"

"Um, camping."

"This my country, black fella country, you go home."

The girl backed away. Her mass of knotted curls bobbed across her eyes.

"Wait, can you help me? I have no food."

The girl shrugged.

"You'll be food. Go home."

With that cheering news, the girl disappeared.

The sun crawled across the sky. Sylvia brushed flies from her face and listened to the dry scraping of the cicadas. She didn't dare move away from the stream where the walls of the gully gave shade, terrified the snake would reappear to turn her into food. She dozed and dreamt she was born out of a shampoo bottle, her father waiting with a pair of clippers as she fell out. Solomon stood close by in a nun's habit, praying to God.

A noise brought her to wakefulness. Sylvia rubbed her eyes. The heat had addled her brain, the lack of food sending waves of delirium through her senses. The same girl was back, hovering over her, blocking the intense sunlight. Sylvia wasn't sure if she was an apparition. A piece of bread and a bar of chocolate landed at Sylvia's feet. She bit into the damper—it was dry but her teeth were grateful to chew on something other than grit.

"Thanks dove, that's so decent of you."

The girl crouched and watched her.

"I'm Sylvia," she mumbled with a mouthful of bread. "What's your name?"

"Madge."

Sylvia peeled the foil off the chocolate. It had melted into the cracks. "Would you like some, Madge?"Madge shook her head."Do you live near here?"

"At the back of town."Sylvia finished the chocolate and scrambled to the water's edge to drink and wash her fingers."This is women's place here, special," Madge said.

"Is it OK for me to stay?"

Madge shrugged.

"You wanna come with me? My auntie said OK."

"That would be flicking great."

The thought of another night here scared her. It wasn't even the snakes or dingoes or mosquitoes; it was the loneliness she feared most.

The one comforting thing about the convent was the dormitories, the sound of breathing, the creak of bedsprings, even the snoring acted as a lullaby for Sylvia. With relief, she gathered up her meagre possessions and followed Madge for the long walk towards the town. Eventually, they came to a stand of trees around a clearing. Scattered within the trees, basic houses spilled out mattresses and crates. Madge's people sat on mats passing the day with dogs sniffing, and toddlers circling from arm to arm. Madge introduced Sylvia to an old woman called Auntie May. Sylvia shook her hand, and the auntie gestured her to sit with the raise of her chin. They sat in silence for a while, the old lady sizing Sylvia up, Madge hovering nearby. At last, May spoke.

"What you got in there?" May tossed her head toward the cape.

"Not much." She unfolded it.

"Is that grog in there?"

"No," Sylvia laughed, "shampoo."

May guffawed, "what sorta camping is that? Ay! White fellas!" She sucked her teeth. "This is a dry station, but we take shampoo."

Sylvia passed her the bottle. May sniffed it, nodding.

"Why don't I wash your hair for you? I'm a hairdresser."

It didn't take long for Sylvia to set up a crude salon. They filled an old steel bath with water, the children fetching refills with glee and pouring it in and over themselves, making their skin shine. The women took it in turns to come to the sink, and Madge brushed their hair afterwards. Sylvia styled and pinned, plaited and primped. As the sun went down, they showed off, looking fine, and ate the food the women had cooked. As the evening drew in, some men played guitars and sang. Madge pulled a mattress up to the fireside for Sylvia and they swayed to the music.

In the morning, Madge took Sylvia out and they collected roots and berries. The men roared to town in a smoking ute with two women to buy bread and cigarettes. The aunties showed Sylvia how to weave a basket and she listened to their stories spoken in half English and half Aboriginal.

"What about you, skinny? What country you from?"

The question left her speechless. No one ever asked her where she came from. She stammered and slipped over her story, but bit by bit, she told how her dad had sent her away from her home country to live with nuns. The women listened in silence with pain in their eyes. They knew that story.

"You go back to old country, you find your dreaming."

Sylvia sighed. "My old country is thousands of miles away. I'm not sure if I can get there."

"You start with one footprint, then two, then three. You get there." The auntie nodded. "Come here." She pulled Sylvia into her shoulder and patted her head. "What happened to this?"

"I got initiated."

"What's that?"

"It's like I joined a club, a tribe."

"Sylvia, you welcome here anytime, to this tribe. If you need a feed, a friend, a fire, this is your country now, we your family."

She hugged the old lady tight and said goodnight. She settled down by the embers of the fire and listened to the talk, scraps of indigenous words and white fella words, fragments of guitar chords, spikes of laughter. That night, she had the best night's sleep since Sol died.

In the morning, Sylvia helped cook breakfast. She swept the leaves away from the gathering area and brushed Auntie May's hair one more time. "You're right, Auntie May. I will go back to my old country. It's time to find my ancestors."Auntie May's old face creased into a smile."Take this," she handed her a woven necklace. Sylvia tied it around her neck and hugged her."Thank you, Auntie."In return, she presented her with the hairbrush, scissors and what was left of the shampoo. May put her fingers to her mouth and gave a long whistle. She told the men who were preparing to go to Kalbarri to give Sylvia a lift. The ute took her away in a cloud of exhaust, but she waved goodbye to Madge and the women until they were specks in the dust.

The barman was mopping the floor when she entered the Snip and Sip. He nodded to her. She strode along the corridor and let herself into Wiz's domain. No one was up yet. She made herself a strong cup of coffee and dipped her dusty legs in the pool.

Sylvia thought about Auntie May and her mob, how close and easy they were with each other. She imagined, as she had many times, what her life would have been like if her dad hadn't sent her to Australia. Would she, could she, have some half-siblings? How would she ever get to England to find out? Voices brought her back to the present. Someone was in the kitchen. She could hear Tatty.

"Darlink, she is a 21-year-old country girl. She knows nothing about the world."

A man's voice muffled a reply.

"Think about it. It might be just what you need. As we say in Russia; You bring vodka, I bring tea and no one sad or thirsty."

She let herself out of the kitchen and saw Sylvia perched on the edge of the pool.

"*Moy bog*!" she screeched. "My God, where did you come from? I thought I saw a ghost." Tatty's hand clattered to her chest.

"Sorry, Tatty, I got a lift home. Hope that's OK. I survived." Sylvia raised her hands with a shrug.

"Yes, I can see that. Very well done, my girl. I think you will go far. Sol was right about you," she pronounced with a serious look. She hurried off to wake the others.

When they emerged for breakfast, she described her night by the gorge and how she met her new friends. She pleaded with Wiz to keep an eye out for them, make sure they had enough shampoo after she left.

"Well done, my dear. I will make sure the store gives them enough. Your resourcefulness is to be congratulated. So now, to finish. Gather round everyone."

The team put down their mugs. Arthur sidled in and leaned on the wall, watching with arms crossed. He had spent the week at the end of the bar in the Snip and Sip. The UGH committee had noted his frostiness towards Sylvia, but his grief wore a prickly suit and not even Tatty could persuade him to be a part of the training. Wiz guided Sylvia to the salon chair and swirled her to the mirror.

"With this golden cape, I now declare Sylvia Scutlash..." Wiz placed a shimmering cape around her shoulders, "a full-blown member of the hair-archy of the United Guild of Hairdressers."

Tatty, Al and Emmy-Lou clapped and kissed her on the cheek. Despite her bald head, mild sunburn, stiff back and tiredness, Sylvia smiled at her reflection and the group of people celebrating her. It was the same warm feeling she had got the night before at the fireside, singing songs and sharing food. And she liked it, as if a hole in herself had been plugged and she was contained, held, safe.

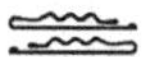

That night was time to celebrate. The group held a party and feasted on prawn cocktail, devils on horseback and chicken vol-au-vents. The evening ended in the swimming pool, Wiz lounging on a lilo singing while Tatty sung along in Russian. At midnight Al retired to call Africa, and Emmy-Lou had snapped a guitar string and never returned from her room. Wiz snored on the lilo. Tatty was telling Sylvia of yet another of Solomon's adventures, but she'd lost the thread of her story with a hiccup and declared the night over. She hugged Sylvia and staggered along the pathway, waking Wiz and sending him off to bed too. But Sylvia was wired. She wouldn't be able to sleep and so sat on the edge of the pool, enjoying the slosh of cool water on her ankles. In two weeks she had left the graveside of her husband and found herself in the outback with a raft of skills she had no idea how she'd use, a bald head and a tattoo. She wondered how much further a girl from east London could travel when she heard a noise. Her scalp tingled, and she ran her hand over it.

"So, Little Miss Sylverella has finally got her crown, a real-life rags-to-riches, if ever I've seen one." Arthur slurred and staggered towards her. Sylvia started and stood to face him.

"I didn't think you were talking to me?"

"I want the ring. That's it."

Sylvia glanced down at the wedding ring Sol had placed on her finger. She had loved him, and he her, but not as husband and wife. They both knew Arthur was the real widow. She slipped the plain gold band off her finger and held it in her fist.

"It doesn't have to be this way, Arthur, we could..."

"Take, take, take. First my man, then my business, now my friends. It has to be this way because of you, you manipulative little cow. But you can't take away my memories. Now give me the bleeding ring."

"You might still get the salon, if you stop drinking for long enough!"

"I'm not playing this game. UGH, the salon, everyone can go stuff a hairbrush up their arse. Hand it over."

Arthur grabbed her wrist and prised her fingers open.

"Stop it, Arthur. I just wanted a family, people to love. Sol was the only one who ever gave me that. It's my ring."

She gave him a shove, but he held her firm, and they tumbled into the pool, Sylvia crashing under the weight of him. She twisted out of his grip and made for the edge, gasping for air.

"Bitch!" Arthur screamed and lurched toward her. He grabbed and pulled her head back under the water, but there was no hair to hold. As bubbles escaped from her mouth, she opened her hand and the ring fell to the bottom. He released her, and she bobbed up, heaving in deep breaths.

"What is wrong with you? You nearly drowned me!"

"Shut your whingeing mouth, you're pathetic, little miss goody-two shoes, you make me sick."

Sylvia sobbed and kicked out of the pool. His manic tone and dead eyes scared her. The pool light shone through the turquoise water, the ring reflecting the light as it balanced on the edge of a drainage hole. Arthur took a breath and dived toward it, but the ring shifted in the swell and in slow motion it tilted and slipped over the lip, disappearing into the hole. Arthur tried to get his fingers through the slots, but running out of breath, he shot to the top and out of the water.

"You'll pay for this Queen cow-face Sylvia, you will pay," he spluttered between coughs. He crouched down on the floor and cried. Sylvia held her hand on her mouth, watching her broken uncle weep. She ran from the garden, shivering in her bikini and hairless head, a sudden cold blast of loneliness that reminded her of her childhood.

7

A few hours later, Tatty banged at Sylvia's door.

"Rise and shine, darlink, the plane leaves in two hours!"

Sylvia took a moment to remember where she was and ran a hand over her bald head, which she now realised ached. Her tongue stuck to her dry lips. The fight with Arthur had inhabited her dreams all night, and she felt a knot in the pit of her stomach.

"What plane?" she croaked.

Tatyana stuck her head in the door.

"One to Perth and then onto a jumbo jet for London."

"What? London? Why?"

"Your mission..." Tatty's bangles jangled with glee. "A new mission has come in. It's show time!"

"London," she whispered, "I'm going to London?"

Sylvia pumped her fist and mouthed 'wow'. She swung her legs out of bed but noticed her feet, cracked varnish and toes ragged from the bush. In the mirror, her face was blotchy and her bald head only magnified the effect. And clothes! She had nothing to wear in London, especially in winter.

"Tatty, help!"

An hour later, Sylvia was ready. Emmy-Lou, the girl guide of the hairdressing world, owned an array of outfits that fitted Sylvia. Tatty and Wiz yayed or nayed until they all agreed. They trimmed, buffed and polished her nails mauve. Emmy-Lou chose the colour to match her outfit. She then produced a long silk cloth. Tatty and Emmy-Lou plonked her in the hairdressing chair in front of the mirror.

"Now, watch closely. Ya start here, hold this end and turn and turn and turn, pin, twist, turn, turn, pin, figure of eight, turn, pin, twist, twist, repeat. The end will be right... here, now don't let go, ya hear me, and remember to have the brooch on your sleeve ready to fasten. There. Ya look cooking hot, honeybee!"

Sylvia assessed herself in the mirror. Her white and yellow pant suit swirled with mauve highlights, picking up the purples of her turban and nails, yet she looked businesslike. The fabric didn't crease and felt as comfortable as a pair of pyjamas.

"Fit for a king, Sylvie, even Vitale Crassoon," said Tatty.

"What?" Sylvia's eyes widened. Vitale Crassoon *was* the king... of the hairdressing world. He owned the London fashion week catwalks.

Tatty nodded. "Oh yes, the man himself needs our help!"

"I... I... can't help Vitale Crassoon! I, I'm not ready!"

"Nonsense, my dear. You have always been ready. You're fresh from training, you have everything you need. If you are half of what Sol said you are, well, you'll pin this case down in no time." Wiz appeared in the mirror reflection holding a piece of paper.

"But what's the case? What do I have to do?" Panic set in.

"It's a serious matter, I'm afraid. If Crassoon loses his credibility, it could put the whole hairdressing world in a bad light." Wiz waved the telegram in the air.

"Why? What's happened?"

"Vitale's hair colour has been malfunctioning. Word is spreading, and to make matters worse, his oldest client died in the chair last week.

The coroner says she died of old age, but the papers are saying she died of shock. Things are not looking good."

"Hang on there! Is this a murder investigation?" Sylvia was freaking out.

"No, no. No charges have been made, but if Vitale's career is damaged from this, all our reputations are at stake."

"The plane is ready, Wiz." Al arrived with a dark leather case. "Now, here is your kit. All the details are in there. Everything you could possibly need. And your tickets."

She took the case and ran her palm over the shiny lid.

"But I need help. I can't do this on my own."

She glanced beyond the group to see if Arthur was there.

"He's not going," said Wiz, "don't you worry about him."

"But the salon, doesn't he want it?"

"It's down to you, my dear girl. If you can solve the case, the salon is yours."

"And if I don't?"

"We don't believe that is a scenario we have to worry about." Wiz smiled and patted her on the shoulder. Emmy-Lou and Al nodded in agreement. Tatty smiled broadly and spluttered, "Come on now, time to leave. I can hear the pilot revving up his engines!"

They walked her out to the hangar behind the pub where a bi-plane shuddered in readiness to get moving. Wiz gave her his hand as she stepped up into the cockpit. He kissed it before letting go. Emmy-Lou blew kisses, Al a tight bow.

Sylvia leaned out of the plane. "Thank you, all of you."

"Good luck, darlink, send our love to Vitale!" Tatty jangled her wrists in the air.

"Remember our motto - Nihil mali capillos! Bon voyage, sweet Sylvie, call me when you arrive!" Wiz waved a hankie and dabbed his eyes. Al's afro blew back as the pilot cranked up the blades. The plane trundled away from the hangar and picked up speed on the runway. Sylvia watched the huddle of hairdressers waving as the world she knew fell away. On the main street of Kalbarri, Sylvia saw the purple roof of the Cadillac head south out of the town. The plane circled and she lost sight of it. By the time they had banked around, Sylvia was too mesmerised by the views to find it again. She was leaving Australia. She looked to the brown horizon that curved against the true-blue sky.

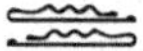

Sylvia's stomach lurched as the rattling plane skimmed over thermals and buffeted in the wind. But after ten minutes, the steady blast of the engine and vibrating seat lulled her into a hypnotic daze. She marvelled at the wispy clouds and the swirling patterns of the dry earth below them. An hour later, the jolt of tyres on tarmac returned her to the hard reality of solid ground. She could barely wait for her next foray into the heavens. Sydney's airport jostled with more people than she'd ever seen. She collected her luggage and checked in for the international flight. Sylvia queued at security, watching passengers step through a portal that would occasionally beep. When it was her turn, she took a deep breath and stepped through. It squawked repeatedly. The security guard looked her up and down.

"Can you take the brooch off your, er... headpiece please, madam."

Sylvia obliged, and the guard let her go back through the portal. It beeped again, accusing her of being a security risk.

"Are there any more metal objects in there, madam?"

"Yes, some bobby pins."

She felt around and extricated three pins. She went back through. The queuers huffed and looked at the ceiling.

The detector screeched again.

"Anymore, madam?"

"Maybe."

She unwound the top few layers and five bobby pins flew out of the fabric.

"That should be it."

She stepped through. Beep!

"Perhaps you should remove the entire arrangement and put it through the x-ray?"

"I'd really rather not, dove."

"I suggest you do as I request, young lady. You're holding up the queue, see?"

Sylvia turned and looked at the long line of waiting passengers, watching unhappily.

"Rightio."

She undid the turban, which had a surprisingly large amount of fabric as pins pinged out in every direction. As she removed the last layer, the crowd gasped and winced. She sensed the crowd stare at the scabby tattoo on the back of her head as she went back through the portal. The silent machine finally released her to collect the pile of fabric on the other side of the x-ray machine.

The security guard handed her the pile of pins and the brooch.

"Strewth, you could do a bit of damage with that arsenal, love," he laughed.

"You don't know the half of it," she said under her breath and hot-footed it to the toilets to cover up her head once more.

The jumbo jet that took her to London offered not only clouds but food, cocktails and time. They had been flying over the ocean for a while, so Sylvia drew her attention to the case they had given her. She cleaned her glasses, retrieved it from the overhead locker and snapped open the clasps. It opened into compartments like a small portmanteau. Deep purple velvet lined the interior. In the lid, silk pockets held a set of golden scissors and combs, stamped with the UGH logo. She pulled out a pair of shears, weighing them in her hand. The main body housed a gold-plated hairdryer. It was a cordless state-of-the-art model with six settings. Underneath the hairdryer, drawers housed clips, bobby pins, rollers, hair ties, shampoo, conditioner and setting gels.

A note was tucked into the shaft of the hairdryer with instructions on how to open a hidden compartment. One pair of scissors was also a key that, when inserted into one clasp, pinged open a secret chamber. An envelope lay in the drawer, sealed with the same UGH logo. She took a deep breath and slipped her purple fingernail under the seal. It read:

Operation root dye

Client:Vitale Crassoon

Place:55 Carnaby Street, London

Style notes:Unusual colour results have caused clients to withdraw colouring services in his salon.

Mission:Find the root of dye malfunction and resurrect colouration services

She read the name again - Vitale Crassoon. It gave her a fluttering in her stomach to think she would meet the legend. Of all famous hairdressers, he was the first, and like Adam in the Garden of Eden, he had named many styles and colours. He was the most sought-after hairdresser for fashion week, and travelled the world styling and primping the lords and ladies of LA, London and Paris. Did he know they were sending a novice like her to solve the case? What if she failed? She would lose the salon and all credibility. Then what? Would she stay in London and find her family? She'd always dreamed of going back.

She thought about the Wavy Lady on Rosella St. She did love that place. Imagine if it was hers? Her own business, just like a grown-up! She looked out of the window saw the sky disappear into infinity.

She had no idea what time it was anywhere in the world, but had been too excited to sleep. In the last six hours of the flight, Sylvia's eyelids finally gave up, her hands draped over the closed case in her lap. When the sun shook her mane above the horizon, Sylvia woke with dried spit encrusted lips. Her turban tilted from leaning against the window and her glasses were angled across her face. The cabin crew moved through the aisles, bringing up seats and waking passengers. The pilot announced they were flying over London and that they would land in half an hour. Sylvia's heart lurched as through light clouds she saw the Thames curling amongst the roofs of London town. It was her birth town, both strange and familiar, like the blood coursing through her veins she could sense but never see.

As she emerged from customs, Sylvia was overwhelmed by the number of bodies crowding the halls. Wiz had booked her accommodation at a guesthouse in south London. She wheeled her trolley through the barriers and looked for the exit. There were people holding signs up when her own name surprised her. A woman with long blond hair swished back in a Farrah Fawcett flick locked eyes with her and barged through the throng.

"Sylvia?"

"Yes, hello, I'm her, Sylvia," she pointed at the sign.

"Hi there, welcome to England. I'm Amanda Makepeace, Mandy," she held out her arm. Sylvia shook Mandy's limp hand.

"I wasn't expecting anyone to meet me."

"Monsieur asked me to, he said to get you settled at your digs and tell you to come to the salon tomorrow morning."

"Monsieur?"

"Vitale Crassoon."

"Isn't he a good bloke?"

Mandy gave Sylvia a sideways, judgemental glance.

"Yes. He is. A *gentleman*, I think you could call the Monsieur."

Sylvia, feeling admonished, changed the subject.

"Rightio, dove, which way?"

Mandy raised her arm toward the doors. A brisk wind hit Sylvia's face. It curled under her turban and sent shivers down her neck. She was glad to get into the car waiting outside. The driver loaded Sylvia's cases into the boot and they pulled away.

"Strewth, it's bloody freezing out there! It's nearly summer back home. But I was born here, you know. Hoping to find some family, if I have time. Are you a hairdresser, Mandy?"

"No, I'm his receptionist."

"I can't wait to meet him. What's he like? What time is it, by the way? I feel completely upside down, which I suppose I am since I'm from Down Under!" She laughed at her joke.

Mandy filed her nails and gave a tight smile.

Stop talking, Sylvia, she said to herself. It had been around thirty hours since she'd had a proper conversation with anyone, the longest time for her. She was used to people chatting all day. But the greenery of England soon caught her attention. Lush fields hurt her eyes and the raw, rain-drenched aroma of dark soil took her back to her childhood. Too soon, they approached the urban walls of London. The old buildings towered above them, fat with memories of generations, unlike the houses in Perth that were low and flimsy in comparison. The road joined the Thames and they drove alongside. It looked less romantic up close, a sludgy brown, so unlike the Swan river of Perth that gleamed in the endless days of sunshine.

The car pulled up to the Come Again Guesthouse. It was settled comfortably on Crimpton St, shouldered by similar houses with wide steps leading up to a shiny painted door. Sylvia was unfamiliar with buildings being joined together and she wondered how they could breathe. The driver helped her unpack the bags from the boot and Mandy reminded her of the address of the salon before winding up her window. A woman opened the door a few minutes after Sylvia rang the bell and hustled her in with a loud flurry of flat vowels.

"You must be Sylvia. Come in. Hurry up, you're letting the heat out. Come on, quick sticks."

8

Sylvia's lodgings were in the strangely named Elephant & Castle in a guesthouse owned by a Nancy Grimshaw. The air in the hall smelt of sausages and rubber. An upright vacuum cleaner with a cord leading along the hallway sat on the bottom step of a staircase. The carpet was a nauseating swirl of mustard coloured flowers and piled with large cases. A hall tree held jackets and hats and had a sign stuck on the mirror. Mrs Grimshaw continued before Sylvia had a chance to speak.

"Please note the house rules." She pointed to the long list on the sign and carried on. "Breakfast at 7.00 a.m. sharp, lights out at 11.00 p.m. No visitors, no noise. Ey upsy daisy! Excuse the luggage."

They squeezed past several large cases. "I have the Tuba Tuners' Association staying here for the weekend. There's no space for the cases in the bedrooms, besides they can't resist blowing on their tubas once everyone's gone to bed, keeps the whole street awake," she tut-tutted.

"Dining room in here, no plates, cups or dishes to be removed."

She ushered Sylvia up the stairs. Sylvia's suitcase could barely squeeze past the vacuum cleaner, which wobbled precariously.

"Mind me hoover, lass! It's on its last legs as it is," Mrs Grimshaw huffed. At the top of the stairs, she led them along the corridor and opened a door.

"You share the bathroom, so be considerate of other guests, baths between 7 o'clock and 9 o'clock in the morning only. Don't waste the hot water and rinse the bath and sink when you're done. No one likes a scummy bath."

Mrs Grimshaw showed her to her room.

"Right, this is you." She folded her arms and looked at Sylvia.

Waves of exhaustion washed through her, her ears ringing, teeth aching and body longing for the horizontal plane. She managed to thank Mrs Grimshaw, who pursed her lips with a 'hmm' and left the room. Sylvia dumped her luggage by the door, dragged herself the short distance through the soupy heated air and crumpled onto the bed.

What felt like a few minutes later, Sylvia opened her eyes. She pressed the button on her alarm clock, 6.00 am. Her body clock was still in Australian night-time, but she could hear the street stirring, a low hum of distant traffic, chirpy birds competing with a clattering milkman, though the sky was still dark. Water shuddered in the pipes. She rubbed her grainy eyes, and it took a moment to remember where she was. The smell of bacon wafted under her door along with the sounds of Mrs Grimshaw clinking crockery and cutlery in the dining room. Like a flash of scissors, a memory seared through her. She was a small child, waking to the sound of her father whistling while he fried up a monster breakfast. On those rare happy days, her dad burst into her bedroom and scooped her out of bed, smelling of sweat, tobacco and beery breath. He sat her at the head of the cramped kitchen table, crowded with his mates. The living room piled with boxes of video recorders, kettles or jewellery. Someone knocked. The men tensed, suddenly looked serious, a sheet thrown over the goods. Her dad sniffing the air for trouble. A real knock came, breaking through the memory.

"It's a quarter past six, your morning wake-up call. Brekkie is served from seven. Don't be late." The Yorkshire twang of Mrs Grimshaw made Sylvia smile with relief.

"Ta, I'll be down in a tick," she called out.

Sylvia threw back the heavy bedspread and retrieved her suitcase from the rack by the door. From the inner pocket, she extracted the envelope and drew out the letter. She unfolded it and read the notice of her father's death. She imagined her life as a ribbon, a loose end that started with her father, threaded through her Uncle Arthur, marrying Sol, burying Sol, to this place where she was born, London, hoping it would come full circle into a neat bow. She would start by visiting her father's grave, say hello and goodbye to her foolish old man. And then, perhaps, find her mum's grave. If she knew little of her father, her mother was a blank page, not one memory, image or aroma. She dreamed of meeting her family, a cousin, an auntie, maybe even a grandparent.

Mumbled voices of other residents drifted through the walls. She selected an outfit and ventured to the bathroom along the landing to wash. The low tones of a tuba escaped from the shared bathroom. She waited outside. Eventually, the door opened and a round man exited, looking guilty. "Just, er, warming my tuba up," he said as he scurried away.

The chunky radiator heated the bathroom, and she luxuriated in a steaming bath. Back in her room, she dressed in a pair of purple nylon flares and matching jacket that Emmy-Lou had donated. She noticed tiny pricks of hairs breaking through her scalp and she wound on the turban as Emmy-Lou had showed her fastening with her onyx brooch.

In the dining room, Mrs Grimshaw placed a stainless-steel pot of tea for one, a tiny jug of milk and a rack of toast on her table in the bay window. There followed a plate overflowing with swimming food, three eggs stacked between long strips of bacon topped with sliced bread fried to a crisp. Two tomato halves bled on the edge of the plate. She never dreamed she'd reach the bottom, but the strong hot tea helped it along. Before she knew it, she was wiping the last ribbons of oil up with the bread crusts. Mrs Grimshaw looked at her empty plate with surprised satisfaction.

"Aye, a good Aussie girl who can eat, not like the rest of the slimpicks in London. Gunna see the sights today, then?"

"Well, sort of, I'm actually here on business ... mainly."

"Too young for business, lass, you should be out enjoying yerself!"

"That's the good thing. I enjoy what I do."

"And what is it you do?"

"I'm in the hair industry, nihil mali capillos."

Mrs Grimshaw looked perplexed and caught the sight of a gentleman waving for her from table 2.

"Oh, before you go... what's the best way to get a birth certificate?" Sylvia asked.

Mrs Grimshaw raised her chin with interest.

"You need the General Register Office on Kingsway. Not too far from here. Tube to Temple. I suppose I can give you a map. Just let me see what Mr Brown wants."

Mrs Grimshaw returned with a map of London and the Underground.

"The tubes are easy enough to catch, all colour coordinated. Keep these and you'll get around easy."

"That's ace of you, Mrs Grimshaw."

"Well, that's what I'm here for; never let my guests want for anything."

She folded her arms and glanced out the window. "Make sure you wrap up warm. Temperatures are said to drop today." She gave a tight nod. Sylvia couldn't imagine any more of a drop in the frigid blast she experienced yesterday. She sighed as a barrage of rain smashed against the window, washing any colour out of the world. Even in dusty Australia, the blue sky cheered everyone up. That reminded her. Wiz had made her promise to call him as soon as she arrived in London. Fourth commandment of UGH: never keep a hairdresser waiting.

"Thanks. Do you have a telephone I can use?"

"Are you calling Australia?"

Sylvia nodded.

"Then you have to use the phone box down the road. Out the 'ouse, turn right."

Sylvia lingered over her tea, safe in the warm, dry dining room. She studied the map and noted where the office and the salon on Carnaby Street were located. Even though she wanted to get to Crassoon's as soon as possible, she had her own personal quest and with only three weeks in London; she had no time to waste. As she could squeeze no more tea out of the pot, she took a deep breath and prepared to embark the cold soggy streets of London.

Once she battled the oncoming sleet, she was relieved to find the red phone box. It smelt of spicy food and sweat. She shook the raindrops from her shoulders. The noticeboard inside displayed an array of ads; masseuses, escorts, taxis, and a hairdresser called Wiggles on Clipper Street. No appointment needed, call 01 733 437.

She dialled the number Tatty had jotted on a beer mat and as a voice answered; she fed the slot with two ten pence coins.

"Wiz?"

"Sylvia! Thank the Lord! Where have you been?"

"I'm sorry. I arrived yesterday afternoon and just slept."

Beep, beep. The money was disappearing fast. She shoved in more coins.

"I was worried about you."

"I'm fine! The guesthouse is nice, I'm going to..." *beep beep beep.*

She scrambled with the coins in her hand, clenching the receiver between her shoulder and ear.

"Yes, yes, my dear. Now listen, there's something I need to tell you. R..."

Beep, beep, beep, beep, the last coin fell into the box. Her palm was empty of coinage.

"I don't have any more change," Sylvia said into the silent receiver. Someone knocked on the glass door. "You finished?"

Sylvia replaced the phone on to the cradle and let herself out of the booth, wondering what Wiz was going to tell her.

9

The General Register Office was a grand old building on the corner of a whole street of grand old buildings. Its white bricks and many windows housed the yellowing paper bones of thousands of people in the form of birth, marriage and death certificates. The painstaking process of finding where her father's actual bones lay was like looking for a blond hair in a haystack. While she waited, she wandered the streets of London, searching for recognition, for the word 'home' to feel right here.

The hospital where she was born was gone, now a block of flats disappearing into the grey sky, the address on the letter she cherished, a condemned building. When her father had shipped her off to Australia at the age of seven, the great blue sky of the southern hemisphere had erased every memory of this place. A pang of homesickness for Australia hit her; this dishevelled city was far from a home. She retreated to the offices and flicked through *Blather* magazine on a rickety wooden chair in the waiting room.

After a long time, the clerk arrived with the location of the grave, the address scrawled on a piece of paper. Sylvia put on her glasses and read it—Hackney Cemetery. Hackney was where she was born and the address on the letter she received. Her father seemed to have lived and died all within a square mile of this corner of London. With a sense of triumph, Sylvia set out for Crassoon's by the London Underground. She wrangled on to the carriage, the other passengers taking up too much space with their giant newspapers. Sylvia read the headlines 'Fighting in the Streets', 'Heavy Metal Show on River', 'Pensioner Nails Hand to...', she couldn't read the rest as the tube stopped and spilled her and her fellow commuters off at Oxford Circus. Honestly, these places had odd names!

The hip strip of Carnaby Street housed a mix of high-end fashion boutiques and second-hand shops. People unlike those she'd ever seen milled along its pedestrianised pavements at leisure. Wispy girls stopped at shop windows in chunky platforms. Bohemians in flowing skirts and hundreds of clanking bracelets sipped coffee at the café tables. Even the ground was a splash of colour and patterns. Groups of punks leered at anyone who dared to stare. A couple of Teddy boys yelled abuse at them from the other side of the street. Two stiff bobbies slowed their pace and put a hand on their truncheons. Pedestrians looked nervous for a moment and slowed.

At last, she reached the salon. There it was, the grand entrance of Vitale Crassoon, the most famous hairdresser in the world. She peered in through the window. Shiny hairdressing gowns, extravagant light fittings, and the heavy silver framed mirrors made the room resemble the inside of a disco ball. The black-and-white striped curtains fell to the floor, held back by thick silver cords. Vitale Crassoon ran his business like an orchestra conductor. He swept around his salon armed with batons of gold scissor and comb encrusted with diamonds. He directed his trembling staff, bending on one knee to beloved clients and ceasing the entire proceedings with a whip of his arms and "*Arrêtez*!" if anything displeased him.

It was at one such moment that Sylvia entered his shop. His

staff suspended scissors, towels, combs and hairdryers in mid action. Vitale's moustache quivered in frustration, a tirade threatening to tumble from his shapely pink lips in a French plait of Gallic and English. The bell tinkled, and Vitale closed his mouth as Sylvia stepped across the threshold. A dozen pairs of eyes swivelled in her direction; bored clients, nervous hairdressers, relieved trainees, shaking juniors and the penetrating green stare of Vitale. She smiled.

"Mademoiselle! Welcome, *bienvenue, entrez, entrez*!"

He bustled over and took her hand.

"'Ow may I 'elp you?'

"G'day!" she uttered.

Sylvia looked down on Vitale, who, while wearing heeled boots, still only reached her shoulder.

"Nihil mali capillos," she stuttered.

"Ah! Mademoiselle! Oui, oui, ah! So very..." He kissed the back of her hand fervently with baby soft, wet lips, and looked up, straight at her breasts, "young, for an..." He stood on his toes and whispered in her ear, "agent of UGH!"

"Ronaldo!" he suddenly screeched. He turned on his heels and marched to a sweating young man standing behind a client.

"You must never, ever, ever, ever use zee scissors at that angle, or zee 'air will not sit right. Zut alors! You cannot get a decent trainee these days."

He yanked the man's wrist sideways.

"Like this," and rolled his eyes at Sylvia.

"Mandy, keep your eyes on them. I have a *rendez vous* with...?"

"This is Sylvia, Monsieur," Mandy interjected.

With a mixture of irritation and awe, Sylvia gave a small bow. "It's an honour to meet you Monsieur Crassoon."

"Ah oui, oui, Sylvia, ma cherie. Please call me Vitale. Come this way."

He took her firmly by the elbow and steered her towards his huge office. Sylvia had never seen a salon so large and so sumptuously decorated. Basins shone whilst the chairs were sleek black leather. A chandelier occupied all the ceiling space. It was elegant, orderly and gleaming.

"Entrez, entrez. 'Ere we are. Oh, Sylvia, I'm so sorry about Sol. 'E was an extraordinary man."

Vitale's office was chaos. It was full of furniture—a teardrop shaped conference table took up the middle of the room. It was scattered with trade magazines, catalogues, invitations and sketches. In the centre a gold statue gleamed, of what Sylvia presumed was Vitale's hands, as they were now, holding a pair of scissors and a comb. A huge portrait of a poodle primped with ribbons and bows hung on the wall. The rest of the room contained a large bar, bulbous sofas and onion shaped seats.

"Please, take a seat, make yourself comfortable." He draped himself onto a sofa and patted the seat for her to sit beside him. Being both overwhelmed and repelled, Sylvia took the onion seat opposite him. She lowered herself onto the pointy end of the seat, which was indeed comfortable as she sank into it.

"Oh!" she gasped as the nib settled itself in a delicate spot that sent delicious shivers through her body.

"Wiz telephoned to say that I am in very safe 'ands."

She wiggled to release the protruding nib, which only intensified the sensation.

"'Ow was your flight?"

"Mmmm!"

"This weather 'as been getting worse, so cold..."

A hot wave went through her and she tried to look casual by

crossing her legs, but "oh, oh!" she yelped.

"I'm sure you will get used to it."

"Ayayayay... I'm. Sure. I. Will," she squeaked.

"You like my chairs? They are relaxing, no? I am developing them for the salon for zee ultimate 'airdressing experience for my clients."

"I oh, oh, ah! It will certainly be the, ah! Climax... oho... of... aha.. their... mmmmngh... day." Sylvia tried to extricate herself from the onion which absorbed her body and mind. Vitale popped a cork from a champagne bottle and handed her a glass.

"Salut, Sylvia! I am excited to work with you."

"Oh, yes, er, ME TOO," in a shrill, "b-b-bottoms up!" she flung her buttocks to the right to release her from its grip, but the nib held fast. As Vitale chattered on, she couldn't concentrate as the onion top tickled her in places she never knew were ticklish. The more she struggled, the deeper the chair engulfed her. She sipped the champagne, but the bubbles fizzed in her head and her body tingled. Waves of panic and ecstasy flowed through her until the glass slipped from her hold and smashed on the floor. That got Vitale's attention at last.

"Ah, oui, I'm sorry ma cherie, we are still working on some of zee design faults. Zee exit of the chair is *un petit* tricky."

He handed her his comb hand and yanked her out. She stood and panted, her gusset pulsating, and took a deep breath.

Vitale again patted the benign flat sofa where he sat. Sylvia straightened her turban, pushed up her glasses and dabbed at the sweat on her upper lip. A junior rushed in with her broom and expertly swept away the broken glass. Vitale handed her another. She let out a satisfied sigh.

"I'm sorry, you were saying?"

"Wiz 'as telephoned me and explained zee conditions. I am to report to him once zee case 'as been solved. It is a shame that Arzur is not able to be here. We are old friends, but, between tu et moi, he 'asn't got zee skills for an UGH agent."

Sylvia regained her composure. "Well, it's an honour for me to be here to help you. Where shall we begin?"

"As usual, Vitale Crassoon is styling for Winter fashion week. I only 'av seven days to sort it out. Zee label are launching their latest line 'Striped'. First, zee designer, she wanted big hair, an explosion of curls, then a day later she changes her mind to a more structured look. Today I get a message that she wants me to make my models look like zebras! She is showcasing a range of zebra skin fashion. Zee woman is so cutting edge she makes me bleed. Every year she gets 'arder to work with. Next year she will want me to produce unicorns!"

"What are you going to do?"

"I will give them stripes, of course; what Karla wants, Karla gets." He shrugged. "But I am 'aving these problems with zee hair dye."

"Tell me what's been happening."

"A few weeks ago, some of my clients were not happy with zee outcome. Oui, zee colours were a petit dull, perhaps. But then it just got worse and worse."

"How did it get worse?" Sylvia asked.

"Zee colours—they are coming out in some terrible shades."

"And there was a client that..."

"Ah non, non, please do not speak of it! It was terrible, zee poor old girl. Baroness Camelia Spoke, she was my oldest client. I mean, she was zee oldest at 96 years. But it wasn't zee dye that killed her."

"But she was unhappy with her do?" Sylvia could see he was upset but pressed for more.

"It was a petit brassy, but you know she didn't have a lot of hair to work with!" he shouted in exasperation.

"Is there an investigation?" she asked.

"Non, zee coroner said she died of natural causes."

"Have you contacted the manufacturers?"

"Naturally, it was zee first place I went. They say there is nothing wrong with it, they tested it and they 'ave no other complaints. It is my own formula. I 'ave been using it for years."

"So, someone is tampering with it?"

"That is zee only explanation."

"Do you have any enemies?"

"I 'ave many friends who do not like me, but no enemies."

"Is there anybody who wants to upset you? Have you fallen out with anyone?"

Vitale paused. He glanced at the picture of the dog.

"Non, non, non."

He took a gulp of champagne. A suspicious silence filled the space. For years, Sylvia observed clients passing through the Wavy Lady, listening to and making conversations with them. As scissors flashed through the air between her and the clients, she had sharpened her senses. She could tell when they dodged a question, spun a tale, or coloured their story to appear a certain way.

"In seven days, it is fashion week," he continued. "This is terrible timing. Zee designer is not happy to hear of these disasters. She is already une très difficile woman," Vitale complained.

Mandy poked her head in the door. "Monsieur, Mrs Kreeper is here."

"Oh, mon Dieu, talk of zee devil!" he groaned. "She is here to go over zee designs. Sylvia, please excuse me, I 'ave to speak with Karla about zee fashion show."

Sylvia looked wide-eyed.

"Karla Kreeper? The fashion designer? Of the KKK label?"

She hadn't realised it was *that* Karla.

"Oh, you've heard of her in Australia, then?" Mandy said condescendingly.

Karla was well known in all European cities and any wealthy places afflicted with a cold winter. Her fashion house specialised in fur couture, which the rich and famous would kill for. Magazines, talk-shows and movie stars raved about her shows and every year they became more extravagant. Of course Sylvia had heard of her.

"Anyway, reports have reached Karla about the hair dye fiasco and she's threatening to give the job to Humphrey Lebonne at Hairtastic," continued Mandy. "Come on, she doesn't like to be kept waiting."

Sylvia nodded and left Vitale's office. As she stepped out, a small woman with towering heels marched through the salon. Her aura of attitude made her appear much larger and Sylvia automatically gave her trajectory a wide berth. Karla shrugged off her fur coat and trailed a hand out behind her before dropping the priceless jacket off her fingers. A man ran to swoop it up before it hit the floor and came face to face with Sylvia.

"Morning, miss," he winked.

He was cute in a wiry sort of way. His cheeky grin made dimples that pointed to sparkling eyes.

"Morning, mate," she replied.

His face creased into a grin.

"Where are you from?"

"Australia."

"Whoa, one place I 'av never been. Always fancied it. What's it like?"

"It's ace, well, I like it anyway."

He continued to smile at her.

"Well, I better get on with some work, I guess," she stammered.

She had only just recovered from the onion chair, and some very odd sensations still skittered through her body.

"I'm Sammy," he held out his free hand, which she took. It was warm and dry, safe. "I hope we meet again... mate!" he laughed.

Sylvia nodded, smiling, and extricated herself from his grip. She pushed her glasses back up her nose.

"Sammy!" Karla screeched from inside Vitale's office. Sammy touched his fingers to his forehead and ran inside.

Sylvia shook her head, still feeling the touch of his hand in hers. She approached Mandy, who was confirming bookings at the imitation baroque front desk.

"Do you have anyone in for a colour treatment today?"

"Yes, Lalula Von Crump. She's the wife of the Ambassador of Lithuania. She never cuts her hair more than a 'soupcon', as Monsieur says. We call her Rapunzel. She books in for five hours every four weeks to have it coloured."

"What colour does she have?"

"'Velvet black hole', not Monsieur's favourite. It's very messy, and she has a lot of hair."

"What if it fails, like the others?"

Mandy shook her head. "He won't fail."

Sylvia hoped he wouldn't.

After fifteen minutes, Vitale's door crashed open. Sammy followed as Karla marched through without a backward glance and barrelled through the salon. He grinned at Sylvia and winked. She giggled and winked back. Karla clicked her fingers at him, and he slipped on her fur coat and left the salon, much to everyone's relief.

"We better check on Monsieur," said Mandy.

Mandy led Sylvia to his office and peeked around the door. Vitale was sitting at his enormous table, looking lost in its vastness. Karla's stringent perfume lingered in the room. He looked up and waved them in.

"What did she say?"

"I am ruined. She say I am one hair away from losing zee job, she say she has memorised that beast 'Umphrey's telephone number. If there is one more disaster at this salon, I am done like a duchess dumpling."

"What are you going to do?"

"I 'ave to convince Karla I can do the job before she calls that murderous little shit."

He dismissed them and held his comb to his forehead, channelling inspiration.

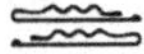

The staff in the salon quietly went about their business. Ronaldo briefed the team, who polished mirrors, folded towels and arranged the trolleys. Mandy scribbled notes in the booking diary.

Vitale emerged from his office with a bottle of Perevian. He poured himself a glass and gulped the French sparkling water from the Alps. He offered one to Sylvia, but she politely declined. She was unsure of the bottled water, preferring good old tap water with no bubbles. The bell tinkled, and a chauffeur opened the door for a woman who entered the salon with her head in the air. Mandy chucked the nail file onto the counter.

"Mrs Von Crump, how are you? Can I take your coat?"

A figure-hugging black satin dress clung to the tiny frame of Lalula Von Crump. Her legs struck out like bolts of lightning into a pair of lethal stilettos that threatened to drill holes in the floor. Mandy removed her heavy fur coat and the lady herself took off a matching hat. It contained a massive swirl of fat locks that tumbled down her back to the floor. It was an impressive sight and Sylvia leaned in to see. Vitale arrived and kissed her hand."Come with me, mademoiselle."He snapped his fingers at Ronaldo, who picked up the hair. They led her to the chair in a private booth, screened off for the privacy for those clients in the public eye.

Lalula's hair swamped her pale face. A thin streak of mousy brown showed at the roots. Vitale brushed out the long swathe of hair and trimmed the ends, showing the quarter of an inch to Lalula, who nodded her agreement. Sylvia followed Vitale to the storeroom where he selected a box of Velvet Black Hole hair dye. They both checked the box was unopened, the seal intact. An eerie silence washed over the salon, no one daring to break the maestro's concentration. He mixed the developer into the dye and the applied the mixture with the greatest of care, combing each lock and painting the roots with the sticky goo. After an hour, he had finished the pelt and left her with magazines and a glass of champagne. Every ten minutes, he peeked at her roots and sighed with relief.

At last, a timer went off.

"Mademoiselle, would you accompany me to the basin?" Vitale took her hand and Ronaldo helped balance the towering towel. Lalula made herself comfortable and a hum of normality returned to the salon.

"Is zee temperature OK?"

"Ya, is good. I vould like a massage Monsieur, don't forget!"

"Bien sur, mademoiselle, of course, I never forget my fave..."

Vitale took a sudden intake of breath, a scream in reverse. His eyes were as wide as the black hole he was trying to replicate.

"Mon Dieu, mon Dieu, mon Dieu!" he muttered, "Sylvia! Come here, non, non, non, non, non!"

Sylvia rushed to the basin. Lalula's hair was turning a sludgy grey, the black sheen disappearing down the plughole, leaving washed-out lifeless hair, yards of it.

"Vitale, vot is the matter? Why have you stopped?"

"Madame Von Crump, please relax, there 'as been a slight colour adjustment from our usual tint."

"Vot are you talking about? I vant black, deep black to match my soul, Monsieur, and if I do not get vot I vant I vill get my husband to kill you."

"Mademoiselle, it is just a petit, a tiny difference, I..."

"Let me see." She felt for a piece of her hair.

Sylvia threw a towel at Vitale and in a flash, he wrapped the mountain of grey ash-like hair.

"I said let me see."

"Certainment, let me help you to the chair."

Lalula struggled to lift her head with the weight of wet hair, and they helped her back to an upright position. She tottered to the mirror and unwrapped the towel. Vitale held on to Sylvia's shoulder as they watched from a safe distance.

Lalula screamed at her reflection, her fingers clutching the once glossy locks. Looking deranged, she turned and advanced on Vitale. He spoke in French, imploring her, backing away as she grabbed a pair of scissors.

"Kvailas! žmogus, velnio vėmimas, jūs esate miręs!"[1] she threw the scissors at Vitale who ducked behind a chair. She continued to swear and spit. The staff fled to the corners. Vitale ran for the door and disappeared down the street.

"*Mažas nenaudingas bailys*![2]" she screamed, picked up a trolley and hurled it at a mirror which shattered.

"I will sue the riebalinis asilas off each and every one of you!"[3]

She coiled her damp hair into the hat, snatched her fur coat off the hook and stalked out of the salon.

The quivering staff cleaned up the mess. Vitale crept back into the salon and motioned Sylvia to join him in his office.

"Strewth Monsieur, that was hairy. What are you going to do?"

"Sylvia, what are *you* going to do? This is your job! You are 'ere to save me. You saw zee bottle was sealed. What went wrong?"

"Search me, Monsieur, but you're right. I'm here on a mission. I won't let you down."

Sylvia smiled and swallowed her nervousness away. A new respect for Sol, Wiz and the UGH members arose in Sylvia. No wonder it was an elite operation. This wasn't going to be easy. Her only experience was cutting hair and running a small salon. So far, she had played along with UGH and its commandments. She had memorised them and shown her ability in the training, but this was real life. Vitale was relying on her to solve the mystery and save his business and his reputation. This was her mission and if she succeeded, she would be her own boss, owner of the Wavy Lady and connected to the most famous hairdresser in the world.

---

1. . "Dumb man, devil's vomit, you are dead!"

2. . "Little useless coward!"

3. . "I will sue the fat arse off each and every one of you!"

10

Church bells heralded in Sunday morning, replacing the street noise from the day before. The salon was closed, and Sylvia was not meeting Vitale until later in the afternoon. Mrs Grimshaw served breakfast at 8.00 am on Sundays, so guests could 'go to church or sleep off the headache', though Sylvia couldn't tell if she was joking or not. Anyway, Sylvia did neither, but she was glad of a more leisurely morning. Over breakfast, she checked her map and worked out her route to the cemetery.

"How's your business trip going?"

"I've still got a lot to do, early days."

"And do you get a day of rest on a Sunday?"

"Yes, I'm visiting my father's grave."

"Oh, I'm sorry to hear that, pet." Mrs Grimshaw softened and put a hand on Sylvia's shoulder.

"It's OK, I didn't really know him. Both my parents died when I was very young."

"Well, no child deserves that." Mrs Grimshaw took a deep breath through her nose and scurried off to Mr Brown from table 2, who clicked his fingers.

Sylvia shrugged on her coat and picked up her bag. She stood on the steps of the guesthouse and looked to the sky. The morning sun had given up on providing any heat for the day and retreated, beaten by the whips of chilled fog that descended on the city. The front door opened behind her and Mrs Grimshaw thrust a flask at her.

"To keep you warm, that's all." And the door closed before Sylvia could open her mouth to reply. She put the flask in her bag and set off.

A bus delivered her to the elaborate wrought-iron gates of Hackney Cemetery. Sylvia entered and read a sign stating that it was no longer accepting the dead into its overgrown earth. The clerk said her father was one of the last to rest here. Frozen feathers of wind brushed against her face. She flicked up her collar and felt glad of the turban keeping her naked head warm. A path led to an old chapel; graffiti smeared across the door and broken glass from the windows crunched beneath her feet. The woman at the General Register Office said the latest internments were in the western part of the graveyard. Remembering the trick Al had taught her, she unzipped the front pocket of her bag and pulled out her special UGH scissors. She loosened the screw and held the handle with the finger rest. The free scissor blade wobbled and spun, finally settling on north. She turned left and headed west.

The headstones lined up through a dark path. They were covered in moss and lichen, sloping and slanting into the leafy ground. As she walked through the woods, the mist hung lower, and droplets from the trees slid down her neck. A clearing appeared in the trees, and newer 20th century headstone officers watched over their cadaver cadets. Sylvia slowed and scrutinised the lettering.

At last, with a jolt, she saw his name—'Alfred Frank Sprout 1926 - 1966'. Tears sprung hot and fast. She placed a hand on the headstone and knelt, tracing the carved words which read:

"Not in vain did he taketh for we can reapeth from his endeavours."

She stared at the stone, wondering what to do next, if she should kiss it, or speak to it.

"Dad," she croaked into the thick air, "it's flicking freezing here, a bucket load warmer than ho..." she stopped herself, "... Australia."

She wondered who had chosen the headstone, the epitaph. Who had stood here whilst they lowered his body into the ground? She recalled the colourful array of people at Solomon's funeral, the terrible sorrow of him gone, just gone. Where once existed a solid person, rooted in the world, connecting so many. And those left; the mourners scattered on the ground like snipped hair, no longer connected to their head, now in the heavens. She stood with her hand on the headstone. The solid rock was impassive beneath her hand, as cold as the memory of her father whose bones lay below.

"Why did you send me away, Dad? Why didn't you write me?"

Silence, adding to the years she waited for word from him.

"Why didn't you want me?"

Silence, like the days, weeks and years of silence she endured at the orphanage. Every time the postman came, which wasn't often, she expected something; a postcard, a telegram. And with each fruitless delivery, her hope sloshed out of the teacup. At first it lost the handle, then faded, and then chipped. But it could still hold tea. After time, it cracked and fell apart and hope had no vessel, it abandoned her too.

"God damn you!"

Anger reared.

"I'm sorry."

Guilt retaliated. Silence ensued. She changed tack.

"Where's my Mum?"

Loss welled.

"There's so much I don't know. Where am I supposed to start?"

Frustration reigned.

"... down the Lively Lady," a voice said. Sylvia jumped.

"What? I beg your pardon?"

"He'll have what you're after, guarantee."

Sylvia knelt and put her ear to the ground next to the headstone.

"Dad? Can you hear me?"

There was a thumping sound, like a heartbeat. "Dad?" The beating got louder. Sylvia listened harder.

"Mornin'," a voice said.Sylvia looked up to see two pairs of legs moving past the grave. The two men touched their caps at her and kept walking. She stood flustered and adjusted her coat, berating her gullibility.

Although she wanted to stay, to sit awhile, the ground was chill and damp. She crouched by the headstone and combed her mind for memories. They were thin and wispy. Her father's face appeared for a moment and then faded like a ghost. Her legs cramped. She pulled a cape from her bag and folded it under her bottom. Mrs Grimshaw's hot chocolate warmed her insides, calming her beating heart. She sat there for a while, sipping on the warm sugary drink and thinking about her life. Wondering how else it could have played out. Pins and needles caused her to shift.

"Well then, bye Dad." She stood and gazed at the grave. The dark shadow of a cloud seeped through the trees. The gravestones took on a creepy look. She shuddered and hurried out onto the street.

The bus wove its way along the busy London street, steam from the damp bodies misted up the windows. It stopped and started, lurching her back and forth into a hypnotic state. She wiped a hole in the window, nervous she might miss her stop for the Underground. Passengers emptied onto the street and she watched several cross the road and enter the door of a pub. 'The Lively Lady' was swinging on the sign, a queenly portrait of a woman with hair piled high. She recognised the name from the men in the cemetery. The bus pulled away. Sylvia twisted around to see the image for longer. There was something in it that looked familiar, but the fogged windows trundled her away.

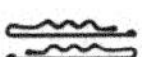

Carnaby Street was quiet on a Sunday afternoon. She knocked on the salon door and Vitale let her in.

She settled on the sofa, giving the onion seats a wide berth.

"So, let's start from the beginning. When was the first incident?"

"It 'as been a terrible time, Sylvia. About one month ago I was colouring one of my best clients, Lady Bagshaw-Jones."

Sylvia's eyes widened.

"Not Maggie Baggie? The one married to Brick Cool, who had the affair with all five members of the Grease Jets and then set fire to a hotel room in Las Vegas after ordering a burger and chips, because the chips were too fat?"Sylvia was up to date on all the celebrity magazines; Tittle Tattle, Dish and Blather.

"*Oui, oui*, but you know she only slept with three of zee Jets, honestly these magazines exaggerate everything!"

"Really?"

"*Bien sur.* Anyway, it was a disaster. I was highlighting 'er 'air as usual,"

"The plum?"

"That is right, Sylvia, it is called 'Aubergine Dream'. But when it was washed off, it came out blue! Blue 'air, who could imagine such a thing? It was 'orrible!"

"What did you do?"

"I 'ad to make her promise she wouldn't set fire to zee salon! It is lucky I know zee dirty secrets of my clients. They wouldn't dare, but they talk. I can feel the deadly trickle of humiliation spreading through phone lines and then zee clubs."

He touched his fingers to his temple and heaved a deep breath.

"Did you use the dye again?"

"Non, I cannot even look at an aubergine ever again! Then Orlana Macrame came in for her roots..."

"Orlana! The Bulgarian princess who owns a mansion in every city that begins with an 'L'?"

"That's zee one," he leaned in close, "did you know she is completely grey? And she's not twenty-one years old, like she tells everyone!"

"Oh, I didn't think she could be—you can tell by the hands," said Sylvia. They both nodded in agreement.

"Anyway, I put on her usual colour—'Summer Corn' but it came out orange! Like a carrot on acid, she screamed and screamed."

Tears welled in Vitale's eyes. "I 'ave never 'ad such an experience. My nerves are in tatters."

"How awful!"

"I am zee most famous colourist in London. I 'ad a wait list of 'undreds, but now, none, zero, zilch. Since zee first casualty, I 'ave been zee only one with keys to the cupboard. I cannot understand 'ow anyone is tampering with zee dye."

"And you need to dye the models' hair for the show?"

"Oui, as I said, Karla wants stripes, black and white. I 'ave to use zee 'Velvet Black Hole' and zee 'Snow Leopard White'."

"Can you risk it?"

"Non, that is why I 'ave arranged for the dyes to come straight from zee manufacturer on Thursday. I will lock them up. That way no one can interfere."

"That's a good plan. Do you mind if I talk to the staff tomorrow?"

"Of course, do what you 'ave to, I just want this problem to go away."

11

Sylvia arrived at the salon on Monday morning as it ramped up for the day's work.

"*Bonjour ma cherie! Comment allez vous?*"

Vitale rushed to the door as she entered. Sylvia had no idea what he was saying, so smiled and nodded politely.

She sat down on the sofa in his office and pictured herself with a client. How did she tackle a new customer? Firstly, she looked at the hair, running her fingers through it, getting a feel for its thickness, health, weight. Then she viewed the client from behind and in front. She talked to them, listened to them.

"Can you show me the dye? I'd like to test some samples. I need the invoices and the address of the manufacturer. I'll visit them. Also, a list of the victims and dates. And, as I said, I'll need to chat to the staff."

"*Bien sur*, of course, but they know nothing. I 'ave already interviewed them all myself."

"Oh well, won't do any harm." She hoped her G.O.S.I.P. training would get some more information out of them than Vitale did.

Vitale called Mandy in and instructed her to give Sylvia everything requested. Mandy showed her into the storeroom. The rows of exotic sounding tints thrilled her. The Wavy Lady only stocked boring shades; ash blonde, brunette, or strawberry red. Here there was coffee cream, burnished gold, crackling chocolate, frosted jet, sun-kissed blonde and the aubergine dream that malfunctioned so badly on Lady Bagshaw.

"How long have you worked for Monsieur, Mandy?"

"About two years. Why? Am I a suspect?" She looked down her long nose at Sylvia. Sylvia took her glasses off and polished them.

"I don't know yet. Have to wait and see. Do you know of anyone that bears a grudge against Monsieur?"

"No, he is very popular." Mandy tidied the already neat boxes on the shelf. There was a moment's silence.

"Okey dokey," said Sylvia. "I'll take one of each."

She dropped the bottles into her bag. "And where does he keep the paperwork?"

"In his office, follow me."

They let themselves into his office again.

"He's a very private man, you know. I wouldn't do too much digging," said Mandy.

"If I have to dig back to Australia, I will."

"Just come and talk to me if you need anything. Don't bother Monsieur."

"Thanks for your cooperation, Mands. Perhaps we can meet for a cuppa across the road sometime?"

Then Sylvia sought out Ronaldo in the towel cupboard. She'd heard the way Vitale had screamed at him.

"How you going, mate?"

"I'm OK." He flicked the towels with verve before folding them and adding them to the tidy stacks.

"Can I ask you a few questions about the colour problems?"

"Sure, but I don't think I can help. He won't let me near the colours."

"Why not?"

"Because I'm a lowly apprentice. You have to train for a year before you move on to colouring."

"How long is an apprenticeship under Vitale?"

"Two years, if you manage it."

"Why? Is it hard?"

"Yes, it's hard! Have you heard him?"

"So why do you stay?"

"Because he's the greatest. I was lucky to get in—thought I'd have to wait another year. If I finish my training with him, I can work anywhere. They say there's a secret association that the crème de la crème can join. No one knows how to get in. You get asked."

"Really? That's interesting," said Sylvia with raised eyebrows.

Crème de la crème? UGH was an organisation that hairdressers aspired to and yet she had fallen into it by default. Ronaldo shook out another towel.

"Do you have any idea why anyone would tamper with the hair dyes?" she continued.

"No, he knows too much. No one would dare upset him."

"Even if they did it anonymously?"

"Look, his clients love him, their husbands love him, the rich and famous love him. He might as well walk around on a red carpet," he said.

"What about his competition? There must be hairdressers out there who want the fashion week gig?"

"No one would risk it. If they ever got found out, their business would be..." he drew his finger across his neck. "... metaphorically speaking, of course. What he doesn't know about hairdressers in London isn't worth knowing."

“What about Humphrey Lebonne?”

“Look, Sylvia, I don’t know anything about Humphrey. Best ask Mandy about him.” Ronaldo waved his hands and shrugged.

This wasn’t going to be easy. But then an entire salon was the prize if she solved the case. Sol would have wanted her to work for it.

“OK, thanks, Ronaldo. Let me know if you think of anything.”

She left the cupboard and approached one of the stylists who was filing her nails.

“Hey, Val, busy day?”

“Nah, there aren’t many bookings today. Things have gone pretty quiet since the hair dye disasters.”

“Is there anyone who might be upset with Vitale?”

“No one I can think of.”

“Has he fired anyone recently?”

Val shrugged. “Staff come and go.”

“It’s a bit delicate, but does he have a love life? Any heartbroken lovers?”

“No, he’s single, he had his dog, but...” Val trailed off and looked around nervously.

“Is that the pooch in the pic in Monsieur’s office?”

“Yes, but we don’t mention the dog,” she whispered.

“Why not?”

“Mimi died last year. Someone murdered her. Monsieur won’t speak of it.”

“Murdered her? That’s terrible. Why?”

“No idea, love. All I know is it was hell around here for a long time.” Val shrugged.

Sylvia sighed. Even if she found the culprit, Vitale would need a publicity miracle to recover from this disaster. Why would someone sabotage the great salon maestro? Why murder a poor defenceless dog?

If he had enemies, she would have to do some digging to unearth them. And now fashion week was around the corner with the designer Karla breathing down his neck. She joined Mandy at her desk.

"So, Monsieur doesn't seem to like Humphrey Lebonne. Ronaldo said you knew him?"

Sylvia had read about Humphrey too. He had made his name by inventing a hairstyle that involved weaving buttons, chains, pencils and even zips into his clients' hair. This cumbersome style soon lost its shine when the clients found it impossible to wash their hair and ended up with heads of matted junk yards. In the end, they had to return to the salon to have it cut out. His notoriety and innovation made him famous, and he continued to be a favourite of the punks and rebellious.

"Er, no. He. Does. Not."

"But you said he had no enemies?"

"It's a long story."

"Well, out with it then. Do you think he is a suspect? Perhaps he's trying to steal the contract for Karla?"

"Oh no, I don't think so," Mandy hesitated. "Humphrey was Vitale's apprentice."

"He worked here? When?"

"Before Ronaldo."

"Did he finish his training? Ronaldo said he was lucky to get in," Sylvia probed.

"He left rather suddenly and, er, set up his own place."

"Is that why Monsieur doesn't like him? Because he left?"

"Maybe." Mandy shrugged.

"There's something you're not telling me, Mands. If I don't solve this case, Monsieur will go out of business. No one in their right mind will come here to get their hair done. You'll be out of a job and probably not going to get another one if Karla has anything to do with it. Come on, what do you know?"

Mandy sighed and leaned into Sylvia's ear.

"It was Humphrey who killed Mimi. I wouldn't ask Monsieur about it if I were you," she whispered. "It's got nothing to do with the hair dyes."

"Humphrey killed the dog? Strewth! Where does he work now? I need to talk to him."

"Shhh, his salon is around the corner on Blade St. But don't let Monsieur know."

"If you won't tell neither will I, Mando, I'll be back later."

12

Blade St was a too short walk from Crassoon's. Sylvia barely had time to formulate her plan of attack before she was walking through the door. Where Crassoon was spacious, white and ornate, Lebonne's looked more like a grandma's front parlour. People lounged on old, comfy sofas smoking aromatic cigarettes and drinking tea out of chipped cups. Humphrey saw Sylvia enter.

"Greetings, come in, make yourself at home." He gestured to the seats by the window. "I'll be with you in a jiffy."

Sylvia joined the lounging bohemians. She wasn't sure if they were there for a haircut, were employees or just to enjoy the laid-back, social vibe.

"How's it hanging, chickadee?"

Sylvia looked in the mirror above the sofa, thinking the end of her turban had dropped out of its place.

"I *am* a bit loose," she replied, tucking it in tighter.

"Aieee, just our vibe, sister, we as loose as my granny's false teeth! Take a pew."

She didn't understand what he was saying, but sat down as they shuffled up to make room.

"Where are you from, sister? Can't place your accent."

"I'm from Perth, in Oz."

"Ah, the fair maid of Perth! What's brought you to old Londinium?"

Sylvia eyed the magazines strewn across the coffee table.

"I'm a journalist, for an Aussie mag. Doing a heap of interviews for fashion week."

"Cool, man. What's your angle?"

"Well, I'm going for the behind-the-scenes lowdown, taking the focus away from the designers."

The man on the other side nudged her and waved one of the aromatic hand-rolled cigarettes at her. The scent took her back to the time she hitched a ride to Perth from the convent. She got a lift with a group of surfers coming back up from the coast. She had shared one of those cigarettes with them, and although it had been tremendous fun, she'd ended up getting arrested.

"Is that cannabis?"

The man nodded with saggy eyes.

"No thanks, need to keep sharp. You go ahead." She waved her hand in the air.

He shrugged and passed it to the chatty one on the other side of her. He took it and dragged.

"Go on," he said, holding a lungful of smoke. He exhaled with a long grunt and aromatic smoke wafted in Sylvia's face.

"Well, hair stylists rarely get a mention." She waved the smoke away and coughed. "They put weeks of work into the designer's brief and yet every show it's all about the clothes. No one reports on the hair. I mean, imagine if they were all bald, like mannequins?"

Humphrey approached, wiping his hands on a towel.

"Sorry to keep you. I see you've met my merry band of men and women. What can I do for you today? I'm intrigued to find out what you're hiding under that turban."

"G'day Mr Lebonne, I'm S... Susan Sprout." She held out her hand. Lebonne gave a firm handshake.

"Please, call me Humphrey."

"She's a journalist, Hump."

"A journalist? For who?" He narrowed his eyes at her.

"It's an Aussie mag." She searched her mind for a name. "Fair Dinkum."

"Never heard of it, but then why would I? I'm not really au fait with what's happening in the colonies."

"It's a fashion mag that tries to report truthfully, to see what's going on underneath the gloss and glamour."

"Interesting. Why me? Lebonne eschews gloss and glamour. We're a *grass* roots sort of place." He winked at his party, and they guffawed at his joke.

"What you see is what you get." He whirled around the shabby salon.

"Do you mind if we sit and have a yarn?"

Humphrey laughed. "How quaint! Yes, a yarn, I'd love to. Come into my den."

They sat at the back of the shop, where it was quieter.

"OK, fire away."

"Let's start at the beginning. How did you get into the hairdressing business?" she asked.

"My father was in the foreign embassy and we lived in dozens of different countries. Great for life experience, but I bombed at school. I loved art but never had the patience to sit and draw or paint."

"Hairdressing is bit of a leap from art."

"Yeah, for a laugh, I took a hairdressing traineeship, just to piss my father off. Turns out I was quite good at it."

"Where did you do your training?"

Humphrey's enthusiasm dropped by just a hair's breadth.

"Crassoon's."

"Wow, straight to the top. How did you land that gig?"

"Just a lucky break, I guess."

"How was working under the world's most famous hairdresser?"

Sylvia scrutinized Humphrey's face.

"Great," Humphrey rushed on. "But then I opened my own place 'Hairtastic', as you can see, ta da!"

"Yes, I see. And how long were you with Vitale?"

"About a year and a half. Actually, I'm about to take on my own apprentice."

So Lebonne hadn't quite made the two-year apprenticeship. Sylvia thought that perhaps there was something to Mandy's story.

"I thought it was two year's training with Crassoon?"

Humphrey hesitated.

"When you're an artiste like me, you need freedom. I wanted to create, to innovate. Crassoon is too conservative for me."

"Any under the glamour and gloss titbits from your time with Vitale?"

Humphrey folded his arms. "Is this interview about him or me?"

"Crickey, it's about you, Humphrey! All about you. Now, next question, I read that some women are having their, er pets styled to match their look. Are you an animal lover, Humphrey?"

"Yes, I am. But I'm not interested in styling dogs."

"So, the coutured poodle is a dog that you're not so keen on?"

"If it's about that spoilt little rat of his. It was nothing to do with me," he squawked and jumped up, as if to leave.

She'd pushed too far but had touched a nerve.

"I'm sorry Humphrey, I have no idea about rats. I was referring to dogs mainly. Please sit down. Whose little rat? This sounds like a under the gloss and glamour titbit to me." She smiled.

"Look, I don't want this in your magazine. But I'm innocent."

"Innocent of what? I promise I won't use it."

"Crassoon accused me of killing his poodle."

Sylvia shook her head with a shocked expression on her face. Things were falling into place.

"How awful!"

"Yes, I was saving its miserable little life, not killing it. All he fed it was fillet mignon and that sparking Perevian water. The poor dog couldn't drink it with all the bubbles."

"I know how it feels."

"I just gave it some proper dog food and tap water. But it got sick and died. I would never harm an animal. I'm practically vegetarian."

"So, what killed her?"

"The vet said she was poisoned, but it wasn't anything to do with me. Crassoon didn't believe me. He terminated my contract and withdrew his patronage. He was going to help me set up my own place. Anyway, I did it myself on the cheap, and I'm happy here, getting more business, doing my own thing."

"Someone mentioned Vitale is having some problems at the moment. Do you know anything about that?"

"Why would I know anything? Only what I've heard on the grapevine, people talk. Look, maybe you should go down the street and talk to him yourself. You seem incredibly interested."

"I was just wondering if you've gained any clients from him after the colouring incidents?"

"His clientele don't like my style. Hairtastic has a different vibe, experimental, innovative, laid back, you dig?"

"There's a rumour that Karla Kreeper is keeping you in mind for fashion week."

"My, my, my. You are a well-informed little hack, aren't you?"

Sylvia sensed hostility.

"Just doing my job!" she said brightly. "Now, what I really want you to tell me about is how you developed your style and where do you get your inspiration?"

Humphrey relaxed. He talked for over an hour. Even when a client arrived, he cut and told his story at the same time. Sylvia filled a pad with pages of notes. Humphrey certainly had a motive, and he was touchy when she probed him about Vitale. There were no hard facts, but it was enough for her to add him to her list of possible suspects. A list that so far totalled one. And perhaps whoever killed poor Mimi was also responsible for tampering with the hair dyes. At dusk she bade Humphrey and his friends goodbye with a hug, promising to send them a copy of Fair Dinkum when the article was published.

13

Sylvia awoke out of her dream where she ran along a street with a pack of poodles each tied to a lock of her long hair. The milkman whistled under her window and the hot water creaked in the pipes. She rolled out of bed feeling like her body had at last arrived in London and she prepared for the day. Once more, she pleased Mrs Grimshaw at the dining table, managing a piece of toast and marmalade on top of the pile of fried food. Armed and loaded with breakfast, she headed outside. Snow floated through the air. She caught a snowflake in wonder as it drifted to earth.

She hadn't seen snow since... since? And again, a memory flared across her mind. She remembered sitting on a narrow windowsill which looked onto the street. Snowflakes fell in a thick pelt and she watched the children catching them in their open mouths, snowballs streaking at each other. A makeshift sledge was hauled by boys in shorts, their blue legs oblivious to the freezing air, intent on jumping on and flying between the parked cars. Drifts had formed on the car tyres. No one was going anywhere today, including Sylvia, who couldn't even go outside. Once again, her dad had not come home, and he had locked her in until a neighbour got a call to fetch her.

"Excuse me madam, do you mind? I wouldn't advise standing

around in this weather." Mr Brown from table 2 tutted, and she stepped aside for him to pass down the steps. She picked up her case and caught a taxi to the manufacturer's lab to drop off the dyes for testing. The process of making hair dyes interested her. She asked so many questions that the manager hustled her off to the canteen and filled her with tea and cakes so she couldn't talk anymore.

Sylvia was glad to arrive back at the salon. The initial glory of snow had deteriorated into a grey sludge that was both ugly and slippery and reminded her of Lalula's disastrous hair colour. A dark sky threatened the scurrying pedestrians on the streets. The mood in the salon wasn't any brighter. Mandy greeted her.

"Hello Sylvia. Terrible weather today."

The British, she realised, always started off with the weather, and whilst it was stating the obvious, it was a pretty good icebreaker. She made a note to use it in the future.

"Yeah, it's flicking freezing out there. Had a busy morning?"

"For the first time in the two years I've been working here, we have no bookings. We had several cancellations yesterday after Mrs Von Crump, um, left. Vitale is so crabby and to make things worse, Karla dropped in again."

"Oh no, is she still here?" Sylvia asked, a little flutter in her tummy.

"Mmm hmm," replied Mandy.

"With her minder? Sammy?"

"Yes, of course. He never leaves her side, like a dog."

"He seems nice."

The door opened and the subject of their conversation appeared.

"Hello, hello! Just who I needed to see to brighten up my morning. It's Sylvia, isn't it? Never forget the name of a beautiful face!"

"Oh! Hi Sammy! Fancy meeting you here again. Bloody bad weather we're having."

"Since I saw you yesterday, I've felt the sun has done nothing but shine!"

This weather thing worked, she thought. Now what?"But still, very chilly out there."

"Yet you warm the cockles of my heart," he countered.

Mandy rolled her eyes.

"Um, the forecast said rain." Sylvia was on a roll.

"Let's share an umbrella!"

"Sammy!" Karla barked from Vitale's doorway.

"Yes, madam, I'm on my way!" he said, lifting her coat off the hook.

As he walked past Sylvia, he quickly whispered in her ear, "Meet me tonight, Ram's Head, Old Kent Road, 7pm." He winked at her and scooted to Karla, who drummed her fingers on the doorjamb.

"Coat!" she demanded, and he slipped it onto her shoulders.

But Sylvia paid no attention. She just gazed at Sammy's smooth moves and his tight butt as they left the salon.

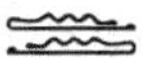

There was nothing happening at the salon that afternoon. Vitale was sulking, and the staff swept and re-swept the floor. Sylvia couldn't take her mind off Sammy's hot breath in her ear and whether she should go to the Ram's Head that evening. She decided another trip to her old man's grave was in order. Perhaps he'd have some ideas for her. At least get some fresh air, cold or not. A cab pulled up to her outstretched arm.

"Hackney cemetery, please."

The taxi navigated the back lanes of London, and Sylvia allowed the ride to relax her. Through her daydreams, she saw a sign outside a pub; 'The Lively Lady', there was something familiar about it.

"Excuse me, I've changed my mind. Can you stop here, please?"

She hopped out and crossed the road. Her stomach lurched as she realised the image of the women wore an onyx brooch exactly like hers. Inside the pub, a fire burned in a huge old fireplace. The warmth embraced her as an old friend would. For a moment, the room spun. A memory flitted through her mind. Voices shouting, a woman behind the bar screaming, a packet of pork scratchings strewn on the floor as someone yanked her away from the yeasty sweetness of the room. She closed her eyes and shook her head back to the present. The barman chatted to an ancient fellow ensconced at the corner of the bar, a fossil that would have to be chipped out of his stool. Sylvia approached.

"Afternoon. What can I get you, love?"

"Er, brandy, I think I need a brandy."

"Straight up?"

"Brandy and black," she replied, not even knowing what she ordered.

He served her the drink and took her money.

"Same again for you, George?"

George looked up from his empty pint, throwing a furtive glance at Sylvia.

"G'day," she smiled.

His rheumy eyes paled and he flinched away.

"E... E... Evie, I did like you said. It wasn't me that called the cops."

The man's hand shook. He reached for the packet of cigarettes, which fell on the floor.

"This ain't Evie, George, steady yourself, mate."

"Who's Evie?" asked Sylvia as she bent down to retrieve them.

George winced as she passed them back to him. The barman placed George's pint in front of him.

"Evie Fraughton, she used to own this pub, ran it for forty years until Bucketmouth's Brewery bought her out. Quite a few folks around here owed her money, and most folks hated her. Had her finger in a lot of pies, not tasty ones neither. Evie lost the plot when her daughter died in childbirth. She was tough before Angie died, but afterwards, well, no one was safe. She went loco. She tried to kidnap the little girl when the father was in prison."

"*Angie,* you said that was her daughter?"

"Yep, may she rest in peace." He arranged his face to look solemn.

"Is that her picture, Evie's, on the sign outside?"

"Yeah, here she is, look."

The barman retrieved a framed photo from behind a row of bottles and cleaned it with his cloth. It showed Evie, posing behind the counter, her hands resting on a shiny bar tap with perfect black hair swirled and piled up high. She wore a low-cut dress with lace edging held together with a large onyx brooch. Sylvia rummaged in her bag and pulled out her brooch. It was identical.

"Well, would you look at that!" exclaimed the barman. "Come to think of it, you do look like her."

"I'm pretty sure I've just found my grandmother. I think the little girl she tried to kidnap was me."

The barman poured her another brandy and black and slid it across the shiny surface. "On the house, love."

"Do you know how old the child was when she tried to take her?"

"No idea, George might. Here, George, can you remember when Evie had that trouble?"

"I ain't saying nothing, shtum."

"George, mate, this girl here might be Evie's granddaughter. Can you remember when she snatched the little girl?"

He took a cigarette from the packet with trembling fingers. The barman lit a match for him and George inhaled.

"Be early 60s, I think. Yeah, it was that cold winter, bloody arctic, it was. Snowed for months. 1963. She dumped the kid by the fire over there, dressed all flimsy, bare legs. The wife wasn't happy 'bout it, said she'd catch her death."

George disappeared back into his pint.

"Where did she go after here?" Sylvia asked gently.

"Evie? Don't know, to the grave I expect," the barman replied.

"I suppose she has. And the kid? What did they say happened to her?"

"Someone said she got sent away," George offered. "The wife was right sad."

Sylvia slumped onto the bar

"Look miss, if you can prove that this here is your grandmother, you can have the picture."

"Really? I can?"

By the time she left the pub, the streets were busy with people wending their way back to supper and to put feet up in front of the TV. The General Registry Office would be closed, and she couldn't bear the thought of sitting in her room waiting for the next day. She had two hours before her potential rendezvous, enough time to go back to Mrs Grimshaw's and freshen up. Her stomach fizzed.

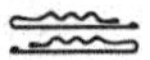

Sammy was already seated on a barstool when she arrived at the pub. She couldn't believe how cosmopolitan she was now, visiting two pubs in one day! He kissed her on the cheek and handed her a drink.

"Got you a Babycham, 'cos it's sparkles, like you."

They clinked glasses.

"Australia, hey? I knew you were from some exotic far off land." He gazed into her eyes. She slurped her Babycham through the straw.

"And what far off land are you from?" she asked.

"Southend-on-Sea," he said bluntly.

"Sounds nice."

"It has its moments."

"Tell me about it."

"Not much to say, really. It's by the sea. I grew up there with my four brothers and mum in a council flat. Sometimes me older two brothers' Dads came to visit but me and me younger brother never knew our own Dad. When I was sixteen, I got into the Teddy boy scene. My mates and the music saved my life."

He took a swig of beer. "Enough about me. How did you end up with the gig at Vitale Crassoon?"

A complicated answer she couldn't go into here.

"Just luck, I guess. What do you do for Karla?"

"Hah, what don't I do! I'm at the bidding of her majesty Karla. I scored the job a couple of years back. I'm her bodyguard and general assistant, even babysit her kid. But I get to travel all over the world and she pays me a tidy sum. Bought my Mum a house. It's just long hours. And she can be a right cow, but I'm letting the good times roll, for now," he finished.

The barman yelled last orders and with only four packets of crisps and several Babychams, Sylvia's head spun. Sammy took control with his strong arm firmly around her shoulder and guided her to the kebab shop. Sylvia devoured her first ever kebab, laughing as sauce and juice squirted down her chin.

"You up for a boogie?"

"Why not? I've never been dancing."

He looked at her agog.

"I know, not much happening in Perth."

It wasn't quite true. Sol and Arthur used to go to a club back home. She was just never invited. She'd listened to the radio in the salon and itched to move her body. Occasionally, she'd wiggle her tush as she cleaned up, but then she'd catch sight of herself in one of the mirrors and feel foolish. There was no doubt, she was definitely up for a boogie, and she needed a distraction from her mission at the salon and the discovery of her possible grandmother at the Lively Lady. The Babycham and Sammy were a perfect foil for Sylvia's busy mind.

"Ho no! Never been dancing? Well, knock me down with a drumstick. Com' on, little lady, I'll teach you the moves!"

They walked a short distance to a club. A live band pumped out music that reverberated onto the street. Sammy whipped his comb from his back pocket and slicked his hair left and right into the floppy quiff that hung over his side-burned face. He grinned at Sylvia and grabbed her hand. They pushed past the kids queuing against the brick wall of the building covered with the remains of posters.

Sammy nodded at the bouncer, and he let them through into a dingy corridor lined with blokes smoking. Most of the clubbers were dressed in Sammy's style; drainpipe pants, colourful waistcoat, a long jacket with a velvet collar. Sammy wore a crisp lilac shirt with raised collars. The corridor opened out into a packed bar. The band on a cramped stage thumped out piano and double bass. The singer's deep voice rolled across the dance floor where couples flung themselves raucously around each other's heads. Sylvia beamed. She breathed in the smoky, wet air. Sweat rained down on the dance floor but the dancers were oblivious, caught up with air under their heels, flying in arcs under legs. Sammy looked at her. 'You ready?' his expression said. Wide-eyed, she shook her head, terrified.

"Com' on I'll teach yer."

He had to shout through the thick noise. She nodded and mouthed

'OK'. He pulled her into the mass and flicked her tight to his body.

"Take my lead, right, left, right hop, right and spin," he whirled her around then before she caught her breath, he had her tight in his arms again.

"Let the music take you!" he yelled. "Relax, OK, that's it, Queenie, you got it, now add a bit of heel toe, heel toe."

He spun her around and around. She picked up the footwork and let her body take over. The music came to a drum rolling stop as the guitar player dramatically played the last chords.

"Thank you, guys and gals. Woooo! What a great crowd! We're taking a short beer break. See you in five! Woooohoooooo!"

The band downed tools and jumped into the audience to get to the bar. Recorded music, somewhat quieter, took over, and Sammy and Sylvia also went to get a drink.

A group of Sammy's friends interrupted their conversation. They crowded on top of him, ruffling his hair and mock fighting. After about half an hour, the musicians leapfrogged back onto the stage and belted out another furious tune that had Sylvia tapping her toes. By the time the band played their encore, Sylvia had mastered the basic steps of swing. She'd never had such an exhilarating night, and she'd never been on a date before. Her feet tingled, her ears buzzed, her heart thumped and the kiss Sammy had daringly implanted danced a tango on her lips.

The club closed at 3 a.m. They meandered hand in hand to the river and settled on a bench under the miraculously cloudless sky. Sylvia stared at the unfamiliar constellations. She could feel Sammy's breath on her cheek. She turned to face him and he leaned in. His lips met hers. She kissed him nervously and pulled away. Sammy took her face in his hands, touched nose to nose and gently nibbled her mouth. Neither noticed nor felt the cold. Sylvia soon got the hang of it and they embraced until the heavens lost its infinite blackness to a deep blue rinse. Then an orange glow tinted the wispy clouds that loitered low in the sky. With her tucked between his shoulder and chin, they watched the naked sun rise and dress itself in cumulus.

"Better get you home, Queenie, or else your Mrs G will pop a sausage."

Sammy dropped her home in a taxi. He leaned out the window and shouted, "I'll call you!"

14

Sylvia woke with a furry mouth and fuzzy head and a rushing in her heart. Memories of the previous night flooded back; the smell of Sammy's aftershave, the taste of his smoky lips, his hand on the small of her back. His soft lips, sharp bristles against her skin, making her feel alive, the taste of tobacco on his tongue, oh, his tongue! She floated to the bathroom and bathed in the silky water and dressed her tingling body. She looked forward to Mrs Grimshaw's hearty breakfast, especially after her night out. So she was disappointed when a rack of toast appeared with a little pat of butter and a jar of Robinson's marmalade.

"Where's the fry-up, Mrs G?"

"Sorry, pet. I've got the Alchemists' Association coming in today. They have their AGM and Award ceremony this weekend and they use the kitchen as a lab. Always going for gold, they are."

"What are alchemists?"

"Sort of scientists, experimenting with things. They leave a right mess, but I'm probably making something out of nothing."

Sylvia nodded.

"Don't let on, but I'll make you a ham butty for lunch."

She gave Sylvia a sly wink and went to the kitchen. Mr Brown from table 2 looked over and huffily slopped a large blob of marmalade on his toast. Sylvia was grateful; she'd need some sustenance; she had a busy morning planned on only a few hours' sleep.

First, she went to the manufacturers with the hair dye samples she had taken from the salon. She was interested in seeing the workings of the mixing lab. The chief of operations assured her the dyes weren't faulty, and the results left her with the only conclusion that someone was tampering with the bottles in the salon. Humphrey was a suspect, but she'd really warmed to him the day before.

Next, she visited the General Registry Office. This time she applied for her own birth certificate, her parents' marriage certificate, and both her mother and grandmother's death certificates. If she could prove Evie was her grandmother, she could get the photo—one more clue to her family tree. The clerk took her phone number and said she would call as soon as they were available.

Back on Carnaby Street, the salon heaved with the tasks of preparation for the fashion parade. Sylvia loved the buzz, the smell of product, the happy chatter and soothing drone of hairdryers. She poured herself a glass of water from the tap and tipped it down her throat, but spat it out immediately. It tasted disgusting. She let the tap run for a while and tasted another. It was vile. No wonder they all drank the Perevian, another good reason not to live in London. Her head prickled under the turban and she gave it a scratch. Must be her new hairs pricking through. She rapped on Vitale's door, ready with a smile for his reverence.

"C'est moi!" she trilled as the door swung open. But Vitale was not alone in his office.

"Christ, Sylvia, what time do you call this? We've been here waiting for hours," said a familiar voice that stopped her in her tracks.

Arthur sat on the conference table with one leg draped over the other. He laughed shrilly. Sylvia breathed in sharply as if she had been slapped.

"Arthur, what are you doing here?"

"Nihil mali capillos? Maybe you don't recall our motto? Do hair not harm. I'm just here to help uphold the law, ma cherie," he replied.

"Oh, look at her dear little face! Sylvia, Sylvia, Sylvia!" he sighed. He wiggled his fingers at her. "Give your uncle a hug."

Sylvia looked at Vitale, who beamed at the family reunion.

"*Quelle surprise, non*? We are so lucky to have Arzur to help us."

She opened and closed her mouth.

"Stop acting like a bleeding guppy and say something. Come on, give me a squeeze."

Arthur grinned and held out his arms. She walked into them as if she was walking into the jaws of a lion, and Vitale, the ringmaster. As she stepped up to Arthur, she turned her head and braced herself, but he plonked a large kiss on her cheek and pulled her close. Vitale held a beatific expression.

"Champagne!" he squealed.

Arthur released Sylvia. Her head spun.

"I thought you weren't coming. I thought you hated London."

"I wasn't and then I thought of you, all alone here in England..."

"I'm doing fine. Does this mean...?"

"Salut, salut!" Vitale handed them glasses of fizzing champagne. "Let us drink to family, friends and good fortune! Salut!"

Sylvia found it hard to swallow, her breath caught in her chest, questions rising like the bubbles in the glass.

"Tell her your idea, Arzur!"

But Mandy interrupted.

"Monsieur, your client has arrived."

"*Bon, bon*, I will leave you two to catch up."

Arthur swung on his heels and flopped onto the sofa.

"Come and sit down, Sylverella, your loitering is so uncouth... wait, I apologise, I promised Tatty I'd be nice. Sylvia, please take a seat. I have something I want to say to you."

Sylvia eyed him with suspicion.

"Look, I know I've acted like a dirt-bag, but I've done some hard thinking. I've been spending a lot of time by Sol's grave these last few days. You know how loud he was. I could still hear him shrieking from the other side. He's having a blast up there with Garbo, Marilyn and Elvis, God rest his soul."

Sylvia smiled despite herself, the image of Sol cavorting in heaven, piling up the hair of angels, giving the saints a short back and sides.

"I've come with a proposal."

"A what?"

"A business proposal."

She narrowed her eyes.

"What are you up to, Arthur?"

"Look darling, I understand why you wouldn't trust me. But I've had a fabulous idea."

"Go on..."

"We can solve this case together and share the salon."

"Share? How would we do that? I don't think we'd be able to work with each other, what with you hating me and all that." Sylvia couldn't keep the sharpness from her voice.

She stood up, though not sure where she would go. She couldn't believe he was here, crashing in on her mission, wanting to partner up.

"Sylvia, stop... you'd get to keep the salon and I'll leave you alone.

You can run it, do what you want, complete creative control."

"And you'd take half the profits. For doing nothing?"

"Details, details, my dear girl. I just need a place to stay once in a while, somewhere to remind me of Sol and our life together."

"I don't think the terms of the will allows..."

"I have discussed it with Wiz, he said it was a splendid idea."

"Did he?"

"Yes. What do you think?" He looked at her eagerly.

"I'll have to think about it."

"I'd love to tell you to take your time, but there's a fashion show in three days and the reputation of the great Vitale Crassoon to uphold. You need to decide right now."

"And what if I say no, Arthur?"

"I don't want to sound big-headed, but I've been at this game a lot longer than you, my dear. I don't think it will take long for me to solve this case. It's in your best interests, Sylvia. I'm doing this for you, my niece, to try to make amends for the beast I've been."

"For your own conscience."

"Sylvia, if we put our heads together as family, we are both winners. You bring vodka, I bring tea and no one is sad or thirsty. You get the salon, I get my freedom and a clean conscience. And more than that, Sylvia, we get each other."

Something Arthur said rang a bell, but she couldn't put her finger on it. Sylvia gazed at the huge portrait of the poodle. She eyed Arthur, who looked at her with intent, with pleading eyes and hands tightly clasped in his lap. His knees jiggled up and down, loosening a black curl from his jelled head. It wiggled in the middle of his forehead. She saw the young boy she imagined he once was, needing love and validation.

"But it's not fair. I've been on this case for days and you just turn up out of the blue and expect us to work it out together?"

"It's always me, me, me, isn't it?" The snide tone she was familiar with crept back in.

"Oh Arthur, don't get upset with me. What does Vitale say about this arrangement?"

"He is fine with it. It's no hair off his chin." Arthur shuffled his feet.

"And you really want to do this? Give up the salon. Everything you and Sol worked for."

Arthur nodded. "For you, my sweet niece." He smiled at her.

Sylvia went into the toilet. She looked at her reflection. Surely, this was the best outcome. She and Arthur would work the case, she'd get the salon and, most importantly, they would be friends. It seemed crazy to go against Arthur now, didn't it? She tidied up her turban and secured her mother's brooch back on. She reapplied her lippy and nodded at herself, ignoring a small nugget of uneasiness in her stomach. She stepped back into the office.

"OK, you're on. Let's do this together."

Arthur jumped up and hugged her so tightly her back cracked. She smiled and felt warmth in her heart. Vitale re-entered.

"*Tres bien*! Zee team is back together, non?"

15

Sylvia tossed and turned in the night. The next morning, she let Mrs Grimshaw down for the first time in the dining room. She pushed the toast to the side and drank the strong tea. Luckily, Mrs Grimshaw was too busy with the Alchemists' Association to worry. Sylvia left for the salon and jiggled along in the Underground, the same dead expression now on her face as all the other commuters.

Arthur had declared himself too tired to start the joint investigation the previous afternoon and had retired to his hotel. Now the two of them sat at Vitale's conference table.

"So, my little Agatha Christie, what have you got so far?"

"Well, I've been to the manufacturer with samples which they tested. Nothing wrong there. I've interviewed Ronaldo, Mandy and Humphrey Lebonne."

"Humphrey Lebonne? He's quite the celebrity these days, I hear. What made him a suspect?"

Sylvia told him the story about Mimi and how Karla was threatening to use him instead of Vitale.

"Sounds like he's our man. Let's bring him in."

"Hold your hairdos for a second, Arthur. We've got no proof and I don't think he's guilty. I mean, he runs his own successful salon."

"Well, go and find the proof, then."

"Me?"

"Yes, this is your theory. You need to ascertain his guilt or innocence."

"And how am I supposed to do that?"

She put the kettle on and scooped two large teaspoons of tea leaves into the pot. She thought it was the English in her, constantly drinking it.

"Fingerprints!"

"Fingerprints?"

"Yes, if he's infiltrating the salon and tampering with the dyes, then he must have left a clue. Come on, Wiz must have put a magnifying glass in that case of yours."

"Can you please take this seriously, Arthur. Honestly. So, what are you going to work on?"

"Ugh, work. I do so hate that word. Is it elevenses yet?"

"I'm making tea."

"Can't stand the stuff, I'm thinking a little drinkie."

He dived into Vitale's bar fridge and uncorked a bottle of wine and sniffed it.

"That'll do for now."

Sylvia shook her head. The nugget in her stomach was growing. She poured the dark tea into a cup and stirred in milk.

"OK, so I'll work on Humphrey. What will you do today?"

"I, er, I'll talk to Vitale," he said, flapping his hand in the air.

She sat back on the sofa and took a sip of tea.

"Bleh!" She spat it out back in the cup, pulling a face. "That milk must be off." She replaced the cup on the saucer and pushed it away. "I've already talked to him. He doesn't have any enemies. His clients love him."

Arthur sighed. "To be honest, I'm still a little jet lagged. I'll be more useful after a teeny nap. You don't mind, do you, sweetie?" Arthur yawned and gave her a sad smile.

"No, of course, Arthur. I've got this," she said, though her teeth tried to keep the words in.

"I tell you what, Vitale did give me a list of clients that haven't re-booked in the last six months. You could start doing a little digging for me?"

He handed her a list of names. She refrained from snatching it from his hand.

"OK, toodle-oo," he trilled.

"Oh, bye then," she responded as he sprung up and dashed out the door.

"Why am I such an idiot?" Sylvia reprimanded herself after he left. "Work together, ha! What was I thinking?" She stamped her feet in frustration and squealed. "Family, more trouble than they're..."

"Everything alright, Sylvia?"

"Yes, Vitale, just, er, doing my morning exercise."

"I am so happy you and Arzur are helping me."

"Yes, me too. Well, I better get on with the investigation. Oh, by the way, the milk's off."

"Mandy!" he yelled.

"Yes, Monsieur?" Mandy poked her head in the door.

"More milk, this is off."

"I only bought it this morning. Give it here." She sniffed it. "It's fine."

"Huh, my tea tasted foul," said Sylvia.

"Pah, I will leave this women's business to you. I 'ave work to do! We are colouring zee girls' 'air today. I 'ave ordered zee colours direct from zee factory."

Mandy shrugged and put the milk back in the fridge.

Vitale poked his head back into the office. "Don't forget to pick up zee dye for this afternoon, Mandy, ma cherie. My driver will be 'ere at two o'clock."

"Yes Monsieur, of course."

Vitale disappeared and Mandy turned to Sylvia.

"Actually, Sylvia? Would you mind getting the dyes? I have so much to do in prep for the weekend. It would be a huge help."

"No worries, Mands. I'm going out, anyway. Perhaps the driver can come now and I can follow up some of these leads?"

"I don't see why not. I'll call him for you."

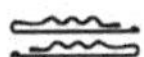

Sylvia had hours before they were due to collect the dye. She asked the driver to take her to the addresses of the past clients on the list. Some weren't home. Two women said their husbands thought Crassoon was too expensive. Although Sylvia disagreed with doing what husbands said, she thanked them and moved on. Another woman was already busy with an Avon lady. By midday, she was dying for a cup of tea. She knew the only place she could get a decent cup was back at the guesthouse. It was worth risking the wrath of Mrs Grimshaw. When she arrived, there were two men carting in boxes of chemist-ware, tubing, retort stands and bottles of many coloured liquids.

"What are you doing here, lass? Can't you see we're up to our eyebrows getting the alchemists settled?"

"I'm sorry, Mrs Grimshaw, but I'm desperate for a cuppa."

"Can't Mr Crassoon afford a kettle?"

"Yes, but it tastes rank, sour, like twopence coins have been brewed instead of tea."

"Blimey, I'd ask him to get that checked if I was you. What tea bags is he using?"

"Same as yours. I still feel like I'm rearranging my face after tasting it."

"Alright, pet, I'm not one to stand between a girl and a decent cup. You know where the tea and coffee making station is. Oh, by the way, the Registry Office called, said they have your certificates, all but one."

"All but one?" Sylvia asked. Mrs Grimshaw nodded. "All but one."

Ten minutes later, Sylvia sat in her usual spot with a perfectly strong brew and watched out of the window as more equipment was coming in. The driver sat on the bonnet, smoking. Her mind drifted to Wiz and that she might phone him again to check the whole Arthur situation.

"How's your tea?" Mrs Grimshaw poked her head in.

"Perfect, thanks. Where do you get your water from?"

Mrs Grimshaw laughed. "The tap! I don't go and collect it from the Thames, you know!" She left, shaking her head.

So then why did Vitale's water taste so different? An ice-cold realisation washed over her. UGH commandment number seven; Always test the water first. She berated herself for overlooking such a fundamental law of hairdressing. In the kitchen, two men in white coats flicked through papers and attached bits and pieces to the equipment. She approached one.

"Excuse me, sir."

"Yes, young lady."

"Would you be able to answer a question about possible contamination in water?"

He removed his glasses. "I'd be happy to—go on."

"If there were something in the tap water, could it affect the colouration of hair dye?"

"Hmm, that's a very good question. It would depend on the chemicals in the water and the dye. Hair dye normally contains ammonia, peroxide, p-phenylenediamine..." he rattled off a list of long words. He consulted his colleague and a long conversation ensued that might as well have been Chinese to Sylvia's ears. After a lengthy discussion, they concluded that yes, indeed, some contaminants could lead to a process that could alter the intended outcome of the dye. Sylvia thanked them and ran out the door. Five minutes later, the car headed back to the salon.

She would take a sample of his water to Thames House for testing.

"Where is Monsieur?" she breathlessly asked Mandy.

"He went out to lunch with Arthur. Why? What's the matter?"

"I have a hunch, Mando."

"Whatever that means. You going to get the dyes now?"

"Yes, yes. Just got to grab some water samples first."

"What for?"

"To get it tested, I think it's the water that's affecting the colours."

Sylvia emptied a bottle of Perevian down the sink and filled it with tap water.

"See ya!" she called and jumped into the car.

The driver was already grumpy from extra driving that day, so it took considerable persuasion to make him go via Thames Water. After promising him a free haircut and a car detail, they arrived. A young woman sat behind a reception desk.

"Good afternoon, I have to report a case of contaminated water in Carnaby Street. Can you test this sample for me?"

"I'm sorry, madam, but one of our officers has to collect the sample, and it takes at least a week for results to come back."

"But it's an emergency!"

"Do you have reason to believe people's health is at risk?"

"People's reputations are at risk! People's hair is at risk."

"Hair?"

"Yes, this water is responsible for bad hair."

"I'm afraid unless it's a risk to health, we cannot carry out testing."

"But that's just it. I drank it this morning and I'm feeling very unwell."

"You look OK."

She didn't want to do it, but Sylvia had to pull a trick she hadn't done since childhood. She conjured up a vision that always induced severe retching, if not a full vomit. She was hoping for the former, but these things aren't always certain. She looked at a spot on the wooden table in front of her and recalled the image of the mother superior's gnarled yellow toenails. Sylvia's shoulders heaved. The girl jumped up and backed away in alarm.

"I'll find my manager."

A man hurried out and asked Sylvia to take a seat. He took notes while she gave him the details, imagining the toenails every now and then for good measure.

"When will you have the results?"

"It takes a week to complete testing. I advise you to refrain from drinking the water until an officer can visit the premises."

"That's too late! This needs to be sorted today!"

The man laughed. "Even if the tests were done today, and results were positive, it could take days for us to identify the problem and rectify it."

Sylvia now really felt like vomiting. She left dejected and desperate.

Sylvia looked at her watch. She still had to collect the dyes, but if her hunch was correct, it wouldn't make any difference. It was early afternoon, and she needed to blow away some time. Plus, there was another pressing thing she wanted to do–collect her certificates from the General Registry Office. After considerable persuasion, she got the driver to take her there.

The clerk handed Sylvia a manila envelope. She slid the papers out and read her name on the certificate. It made her feel real in a way she had not felt before, reading the evidence of her own birth with both her parents' names in black and white. The death notices confirmed what she already knew. But the marriage certificate undid her utterly. She sat weeping like a trampled piece of confetti, the remnant of a love that didn't last because she, her birth, was what destroyed it. Through a lens of tears, Sylvia checked the date of the wedding. Was it a hot summer's day or did they dodge the rain for photos? Eighth of June 1956, the early summer days, she imagined flowers and sunshine, laughter and joy. She smiled. But then an evil streak of maths had her counting the six months forward on her fingers to the date she was born, 5th of December 1956. The marriage certificate now furnished her with a new piece of information. She was conceived out of wedlock. Did this mean they had to get married because of a night of passion? To save her mother's reputation? A forced, unwanted marriage? Her shoulders slumped as self-loathing emptied out of her brain and through her body. It was her fault, everything. The nuns were right. She had been one big sin from beginning to end. To end... she thought about the murky waters of the Thames, one last final rinse.

The clerk coughed. "Excuse me?"

Sylvia wiped the back of her hand under her nose and the heel to clear the tears.

"You may have noticed that your grandmother's death certificate is not there. It appears there is no record of her death." She handed Sylvia a tissue. Sylvia took it.

"Thanks," she sniffed. "Are you saying that my grandmother Evie is still alive?"

"It does sometimes happen that a death is not recorded, but it's rare. Did someone tell you she had died?"

Sylvia thought about the conversation with the barman at the Lively Lady.

"I think so, maybe I'll go back and check."

"Well, good luck." The clerk nodded her farewell as another customer approached the desk.

Dare she dream that a blood relative still existed in this world? Her grandmother? It was enough of a hope to recede from the idea of the chilly embrace of the Thames. There was no time to think about that now. Back in the car, the driver could barely contain his frustration.

"Sorry, I know we've been around the houses this arvo, but we can go and pick up those dyes now."

The next question was how would she convince Vitale not to dye the models' hair that afternoon.

16

They drove out of central London and across the river, back to the manufacturer. The receptionist assured her that the batch had been freshly mixed under the supervision of the manager and thoroughly tested. But Sylvia was sure the dye would still malfunction using the water from the salon.

Outside, she noticed a phone box. It was the middle of the night in Australia, but she had to talk to Wiz. It must have been what he was trying to tell her, that Arthur was arriving. The phone rang and rang, but nobody picked up. She swore and threw the receiver back on its bracket. The car waited. She tried the salon. Maybe she could talk to Vitale on the phone. It was engaged. She gnawed her cheek and cleaned her glasses. Maybe, if she delayed returning to the salon, then it would be too late to colour the models today. That was the only thing she could do.

"You comin'?" The driver sat on the bonnet of the car, arms crossed, shaking his head.

"Yes, just give me a moment, I'm not feeling well." It wasn't a lie; her world was crumbling under her. Her head was spinning. She went to get in the back of the car, searching for a way to delay.

"I need to go to the lady's room. I'll be back in five."

Think, Sylvia think, she willed her reflection in the mirror. She felt around in her bag for her lipstick and her hand connected with something cold and sharp; nail scissors. The driver was smoking a cigarette. He flicked it away when he saw her re-emerge and moved to get into the driver's seat. Sylvia chose the back door on the other side of the car and swooped down, wedging the open scissors under the tyre. As the car moved off, she listened out for the pop, and sure enough, the wheel ground against the tarmac.

"Bloody hell, what now?" The driver pulled over and went to investigate. "You've got to be joking! Got a flat," he said through the window.

"Jiminy clippers, we need to get back to the salon," Sylvia said, faking a worried look.

"That might be so, but I'm gonna have to change this first. I'll be as quick as I can."

It didn't take long for him to replace the tyre. Sylvia glanced at her watch. It was 4.30 p.m., she wracked her brain. They set off again. They passed a couple of nuns walking along the pavement. Again, she conjured up the mother superior's toes, with their raised yellowing nail beds, framed by black wiry hairs and her calloused feet. She was never a lover of feet, but these were the most revolting. The old reflex held strong and Sylvia retched. The driver looked at her in his rear vision mirror with concern.

"Pull over, please." She recalled the toes again, and her stomach convulsed. "I'm going to be sick."

They stopped and Sylvia fell out of the car and dry-retched into a bush. The driver hovered nearby, unwilling to get too close.

"Must have been that dodgy egg sarnie I had for lunch," she groaned. She thought of the toes again for good measure and doubled over again.

“It’s alright love, I’ll fetch you some water.”

He disappeared into a corner shop and returned with a polystyrene cup of water. She thanked him.

“I might have to sit for a bit, wouldn’t want to get your car messed up.”

“Take as long as you like.”

She did. It was past five o’clock when they finally arrived at the salon. Vitale had sent the models home and shouted at his staff. Everyone was quiet as he paced up and down. Arthur was the only one looking unfazed as he swivelled around in one of the chairs.

“I’m sorry Vitale,” Sylvia panted. “We got here as fast as we could. Is it too late?”

She handed the box of dyes to Mandy.

“Mon Dieu, Sylvia, where ‘ave you been? I cannot believe you ‘ave let me down.”

“But Monsieur, if you just listen... I can explain.”

“Enough, I cannot talk to you, I cannot look at your face Sylvia, the disappointment is blunting my scissors. Tomorrow we start at 7.00 a.m. You will assist Ronaldo.”

Sylvia stared at him. White noise rushed through her ears and she felt her heart drop like a stone. She had been demoted to the apprentice’s assistant. Arthur smirked in his chair.

“But Vitale, I’ve worked it out...”

“Arretez!” Vitale put his hand up and though only five-foot one inch tall, he commanded like an emperor. But so could Sylvia.

“Arretez yourself! Now you listen to me Monsieur, sixth commandment of UGH—never leave a client unfinished, and I have not finished!”

Vitale opened and closed his mouth. Ronaldo and Mandy clung to each other, the staff shrunk away. Arthur raised his eyebrows, his lips holding back a smile.

"I think the water here at the salon is causing the dyes to fail. A simple experiment will prove if I am right or wrong. Ronaldo, can I have a private word?"

"Me?" Ronaldo quivered.

She took him to one side.

"Will you be the guinea pig?"

"For what?"

"For the hair dye, it'll mean that half your hair will go wrong, and half right."

"What? No!"

"I would do it myself, but I don't have enough hair."

Sylvia slid off the turban. Ronaldo gasped.

"What happened? Are you sick?"

"No, I'm fine. It's to do with that secret association you heard about. It's true, it does exist, and I'm a member. If you do this, Ronaldo, I'll make sure you get in."

"You will? Wait, how do I know you aren't lying?"

"Look." She turned around and showed him the tattoo on the back of her head. "The United Guild of Hairdressers logo."

Ronaldo's eyes widened.

"You'll get me in?"

"I will."

"Well, in that case, I'm in!"

"Vitale, get Ronaldo gowned up. Mandy prepare the Velvet Black Hole dye from the batch I picked up today. I'm going to get some water."

Sylvia ran around the corner to Hairtastic.

At Hairtastic, Humphrey and two of his crew drank tea and watched the world go by.

"Susan! You're back! What can I do for you today? You still haven't shown me what's under that curtain on your head. Come on, give Humphrey a peek."

He fingered her turban, picking for the end.

"Agh! Maybe some other time." She dodged his hands. "Actually, I have a big favour to ask you."

"What could I possibly do for a reporter of Fair Dinkum on a..." he looked at the ceiling, "... ah yes, Thursday afternoon?"

"About that. OK, very quickly, my name is Sylvia and I'm not a reporter."

"I told you, dude, I knew it," the chatty guy piped up. He clicked his finger and punched the air. Humphrey stuck out his chest and crossed his arms.

"Oh yes? What are you then, cloth head?"

"You're not a copper, are you?" the friend said. He shoved the spliff behind his back.

"No!"

"You're definitely not a model," said chatty guy.

Sylvia looked at him with barely suppressed annoyance.

"No offence, but you ain't got the legs."

She turned on him, but Humphrey interjected.

"Come on, let it loose fabric-face. Who are you and what do you want?"

"I'm, well, you see, er..."

"Hmm mmm, go on..."

"Nihil mali capillos?"

Humphrey raised his eyebrows in wonder. He cocked his head for her to follow to the back of the salon.

"Alright sister, give it to me. How can I help?"

"It's Vitale..."

"No, no, no, no, na, na, na, na, nah, uh-uh, uh-uh." Humphrey spun around with his hands to his head. "I'm not doing anything for that son of a bitch."

"Listen, Humphrey. I found out that the water in his salon is contaminated, that's what's screwing up the colours."

"Well done, Susan/Sylvia whoever you are, congratulations."

"I need to prove it to him."

"Not my problemo, sweet cheeks. Goodbye!"

"Humphrey, you did kill Mimi."

"I told you I had nothing to do with the demise of that fat, ugly fluff ball. Who do you think you are? Waltzing in here..."

"But you didn't mean to. I think the water is poisonous. When you gave Mimi that tap water, you accidentally killed her. This is your chance to make amends. If you help Vitale now, we can explain what happened, then you two could be friends again."

"I killed her? Because of the water?"

"Yes, I'm sure of it. Thames Water is testing it. But in the meantime, I need to borrow some of your water."

"I suppose..."

"Always help a hairdresser in need..."

"Alright, go ahead and take it."

Sylvia hugged him. They filled two buckets of water, and she carefully carted them back to Crassoon's.

Ronaldo was seated and ready.

"First, part his hair and apply the dye to one side. We will start with the salon water, then we'll do the other half and use this water to rinse the dye."

She pointed to the buckets.

As Vitale worked, there was silence. Arthur paced up and down with folded arms.

When the first rinse left Ronaldo's hair ash grey, they were all as sombre as a funeral party. Vitale applied the black paste to the other side, and they waited for it to process. At last, Vitale led him to the sink. Sylvia held the bucket while Vitale poured cupfuls of the fresh water over the dye. As it washed away, Ronaldo's once blonde hair was left a deep black.

"*Mon Dieu*! Sylvia, you are right! You are right! It is zee water! You 'ave saved me!"

Despite Ronaldo resembling an ageing badger, there was celebration.

"You 'ave solved zee case. I will telephone Wiz tonight. I am sorry, Arzur, but this was Sylvia's work. Congratulations, ma cherie, I do not know 'ow to thank you!"

"Just doing my job!"

By the time Sylvia returned to the 'Come Again Guesthouse' she barely had the strength to open the front door. Mrs Grimshaw listened to Sylvia who had sought her out at once, boldly flouting 'No Guest Entry' sign on the kitchen door. She had to tell Mrs Grimshaw about her discovery of the water and about Evie. She itched to begin the search. As she told the landlady all about it, Mrs Grimshaw looked proudly at Sylvia, saying things like, 'That's my girl' and 'I always knew you were a bright one'. Mrs Grimshaw fetched the Yellow Pages and thudded the four volumes onto Sylvia's regular table in the bay window. There were over 50 retirement homes in London. Sylvia copied each one down on a sheet of paper. She picked up her handbag to leave for the phone box.

"Where are you off to at this time of night?" Mrs Grimshaw caught Sylvia as she headed towards the front door.

"I'm going to the phone box to call the homes."

"Don't be daft, pet. You can use our phone out the back."

She smiled and reached out her hand. Sylvia took it as a sob of gratitude rose in her throat and her eyes filled with tears. She made a mental note that she should really compose herself whenever someone was helping her. And so began a task of many hours and many red lines through an endless list of possibilities. The search of retirement homes resulted in many 'no's' and 'never heard of's'. Mrs Grimshaw asked Sylvia to tell her everything the barman had said.

"Perhaps she had to leave London if she wasn't liked."

"Where else do people go to retire?"

The women stared at the corkboard in the stuffy office. It was filled with supplier details, invoices and a postcard of a long pier stretching out from a wide sweep of beach against an impossibly blue sky.

"The seaside." Mrs Grimshaw unpinned the postcard. "Mr Grimshaw and I went to the English Riviera for our honeymoon. It's full of oldies."

Sylvia looked up in surprise. "There's a Mr Grimshaw?"

"Of course, who do you think cooks the breakfasts?"

"And does dishes, mops the floor and is the chambermaid." A plump man in a flowery apron had poked his head through the door. "Very nice to meet you lass, Nancy's been telling me about you."

"Oh! Nice to meet you too, Mr Grimshaw."The Yellow Pages for Dorset meant a trip to the post office. But the sun had gone down a long time ago and at last Sylvia hit the sheets. She dozed off with a smile on her lips. It was not because tomorrow would be her first fashion show, or because she may find a living relative, or even because she had cracked the case and had earned her inheritance, but because tomorrow she would see Sammy again.

17

It was Friday morning, twenty-four hours before fashion week opened with Karla's show, and the models were waiting to be to be prepared. Sylvia arrived at the salon early and had organised buckets of water from Humphrey and lined them up by the sinks. She had briefed staff to refill them secretly at Hairtastic. Vitale addressed his crew.

"I need these girls ready by lunchtime or Karla will kill me. They are booked in for their fittings at 1.00 p.m. Ronaldo, get them gowned up and mix the colours. Let's get on with it."

"Me, Monsieur?" Ronaldo said.

"Bien sur, you have been promoted."

"Thank you, Monsieur, thank you. OK, come on girls, let's prep. Mandy, get the dyes."

"Yes, on to it, just looking for the key." Mandy rummaged in the drawers and under the booking diary when the door jingled and Arthur made an entrance, looking bleary-eyed. He shook the rain from his jacket and handed it to Mandy with a nod. Spotting Sylvia, he bowed low.

"There she is, Sylvia the victorious! Currently, proud owner of the Wavy Lady Hair Salon, Hardup."

"I'm surprised you are still here Arthur, thought you would have fled with your tail up your backside."

"Thought I'd stay and watch the show; should be entertaining."

"Well, you can help then. There's ten models waiting to be zebras."

"Champagne first! After all, we are celebrating, are we not?"

"But we are already behind schedule." Sylvia couldn't keep the irritation from her voice. Her head prickled.

Arthur made a beeline for Vitale's office.

"Relax, ma cherie, I am feeling so good about this now. What could possibly go wrong?" said Vitale. "Ronaldo, oversee zee dye application and let me know when it's processed."

They joined Arthur, who popped the cork and poured them all a glass.

"To the United Guild of Hairdressers! Nihil mali capillos!"

Arthur and Vitale lounged on the sofa, laughing and retelling anecdotes. Sylvia was desperate to be back in the salon, where she felt comfortable and useful, not trapped here being caught up in idle chatter. Her scalp threw a wave of shivers from the back of her neck to her eyebrows. Something wasn't right. There was a sudden rise of voices in the salon, and Mandy burst through the door.

"Monsieur Crassoon, come quick, something terrible is happening!"

"What is going on?"

"Just come!"

Vitale fled through to the salon, followed by Sylvia. There was a commotion of squeals and screams but before Sylvia could venture further, she felt a breath in her ear and a voice.

"Queenie queen Sylvia is about to lose her crown," hissed Arthur. "Don't think you will get your hands on the Wavy Lady. It's mine. You can rot here in the gutters of this filthy shit-hole with the rats."

He shoved past her. "Vitale, let me help, JESUS!"

As Sylvia stung from the words, she looked up to see an unforgettable sight.

The ten models were groping their heads and rushing to the mirrors in horror. Where the stylists had applied the streaks of dye to the hair, it had instead fallen out, leaving lank ribbons of hair and strips of bald patches.

Vitale grabbed a bowl of dye and sniffed it. "Depilatory cream! Who did this? Who is responsible for this disaster? *Mon Dieu*!"

Ronaldo shook with horror. Mandy ran from girl to girl. Vitale collapsed on a chair, models sobbed, hairdressers ran around trying to console them. Arthur's mouth twitched at the corners. He turned away to scull his champagne and retreated to the office.

Sylvia surveyed the chaos as only an outsider could. She opened her case and pulled out a spray of lavender essential oil and let puffs out around the salon. This at least masked the pungent pong of hair remover cream. She passed the broom to an assistant and asked her to sweep up the decapitated hair. She ushered the models to the sinks and away from the mirrors and instructed the hairdressers to wash the patchy scalps.

"My life is over, Karla will chop me into dog meat!" Vitale moaned and keened as if he were the one losing his hair. She steered him into his office and lay him on the chaise longue, dabbing champagne on his temples.

"It's OK, we'll think of something."

"But zee show is tomorrow, I cannot grow 'air overnight! I cannot send my models out looking like that! I am an 'airdresser, I cannot work without zee goddamn 'air!" Vitale placed his head in his hands and sobbed. Next door, the girls were wailing.

"Wigs, darling!"

Sylvia and Vitale looked at Arthur, who was pouring himself a drink at the bar.

“Wigs? Ah oui, wigs!”

“Solomon and I were experts with them. I’ll have your girls fixed up in no time. Leave it to me.” Arthur slid from behind the bar, sloshing his whisky on ice over the lip of the full glass.

“Oh Arzur, you are a saviour, what would I do without you?”

“It’s what any member of UGH would do for another. We’re like family, aren’t we?” He shot a malicious glance at Sylvia.

“Well, what are you waiting for Sylvia? Run along to the wig shop while I take care of Vitale and the salon.”

“But I don’t know where the wig shop is, or who to contact.”

Arthur huffed and stomped over to the table. He rummaged around and found a thick book, which he tossed at Sylvia. The Yellow Pages, again. This book was like an oracle!

“Run along and get it sorted. Vitale’s reputation depends on it, as does yours.” He put his arm around Vitale’s jumping shoulders.

“Arthur, why are you even here? You were going to Las Vegas?”

“Well, if you must know, two little beardies in Kalbarri had a word in my ear, wanted me to keep an eye on you. Clearly you can’t be trusted.”

“Do you mean Wiz and Tatty? They sent you to spy on me?”

“So dramatic! ‘Spy on me?’” he imitated her in a high whiny voice. “You hear that Vitale? Sylvia thinks I’m spying on her!” he cackled. “Darling Sylvia, if you are not able to solve a simple case like this and serve the great Vitale Crassoon, then you’re certainly not capable of running a suburban hairdresser in the arse end of Australia.”

“I did solve the case, remember? Yesterday? Or were you too drunk to remember?”

“Well, it looks like the case is still open. Off you go, I’ll take care of Vitale.”

"I knew it was too good to be true. You just tricked me into working together. How could you, Arthur? We are family!"

Blood rose to her cheeks, but she caught her quivering lips and ran out.

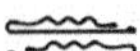

Sylvia spent the rest of the morning searching for wig shops in metropolitan London. She found four. The first specialised in afros, which wouldn't work on the ten white models that Karla wanted, the second was a fancy-dress shop. A shop assistant showed her a range of clown wigs and acid orange bobs. Third, she went to Wigwag, a cool little shop tucked away in Soho. This was exactly what she was looking for, but the owner said that someone had booked out all his stock the day before. He said he was always busy prior to fashion week. Finally, she visited a bespoke wig maker who supplied the lawyers' bar and a few wealthy dames whose vaults of money could not stop alopecia, but could buy other people's hair. She soon came to the gloomy conclusion that wigs would not save the day. She trudged to the salon, terrified of Vitale's harsh words.

When she returned, the models huddled in the salon and slouched in the rows of chairs. Half were catatonic with shock, others still weeping. Ronaldo had trimmed the strips of hair between the bald sections. It didn't lessen the effect, and so Sylvia had instructed the hairdressers to put towels over their heads.

"Where are Monsieur and Arthur?" she asked Mandy.

"Arthur took him out to lunch. He was a nervous wreck. Every time he looked at the models, he burst into tears, which set the girls off again. Did you sort out the wigs?"

"No, not unless we want them to look like clowns or barristers."

"They have to go for their fittings in an hour. What are we going to do?" Mandy looked as pale and shaken as the models.

"Just let me think a minute, dove."

The word had tumbled from her mouth naturally. It was what Solomon always called her. He would know what to do in a situation like this. She closed her eyes and prayed. "Dear Sol, please send me inspiration, help me!" She opened her eyes and surveyed the scene. Vitale had taped a sketch of the planned hairstyle to a mirror. She cleaned her glasses to study it.

"Zebras," she mumbled.

Her eyes drifted towards the window as if trying to escape, but the rain looked as depressing as the salon. She closed the curtains, not wanting passers-by to see the state of the models. As she grasped the fabric, she let out a squeak. "Mandy, pass me the scissors!"

Mandy grabbed a pair.

"Come here, hold this stool steady for me."

Sylvia climbed up and hacked a strip of curtain from hem to hoops and ripped it free with a short sharp yank. She clambered over Mandy and stepped behind the nearest model. With reassuring hands, she unwound the towel. Tears sprung into the girl's eyes.

"Don't fret, it'll grow back and in the meantime..." she wound the black-and-white striped fabric around her head, just as Emmy-Lou had taught her. Within a minute, she created a zebra print turban fit for a safari queen.

The stylists clapped their hands in agreement and came to inspect. The model's neck appeared longer. She had gained an air of royalty.

"What do you reckon?"

"That's genius, Sylvia. Show us how."

The hairdressers ripped the curtains into even strips and Sylvia taught them how to wrap the turbans.

"What are they going to say to Karla this afternoon?"

"Put headscarves on, tell Karla it's a surprise and don't let her look underneath. You got that, ladies?"

The models agreed.

Sylvia and Mandy locked up the shop.

"Do you think this will work, Mands?"

"We'll know tomorrow, I guess, but I reckon we might just pull it off. Thanks for your help, Sylvia."

"Always help a hairdresser in need!"

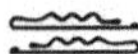

There was nothing more to be done at the salon, and the free afternoon would give her some time to look for Evie. Once back at the guesthouse, Mrs Grimshaw let her use the phone to call around more retirement homes. She tried Bognor Regis, Eastbourne, the Isle of Wight. Nothing. Mrs Grimshaw bought her a cup of tea and some fruit toast. Norfolk drew a blank, Oxford a series of posh 'no's', Torquay failed to deliver. It was like finding an eyelash on a fur coat. She pushed her chair back in exasperation and stormed out of the guesthouse. Maybe seeing the image of her grandmother again would help. She stopped a cab and told him where to go.

Sylvia struggled to get from the door to the bar of the Lively Lady. Fans of the local football team attempted to guzzle every barrel of beer the pub had. This was no moment to interrogate a barman knee high in dirty glasses and overflowing ashtrays. But she was determined to get the only photo of a blood relative. To her relief, the barman recognised her. After a yelled conversation and half a pint of ale spilt over her, Sylvia managed to procure the photo. For once, she yearned for some solitude and decided to visit her father's grave.

The cemetery had a serene beauty in the crisp evening air. The sounds of the city faded, replaced with the hoot of a dove and Sylvia could hear her own breath, her own heartbeat, her own blood coursing through her veins. She stood at the foot of her father's grave and tried to recall his face. She herself had an uncanny resemblance to the woman in the photo, her grandmother Evie. And who was her grandfather? A brave man, perhaps, to be paired with her formidable grandmother. Who were her paternal grandparents? These strangers who anchored her to this earth, yet didn't exist. She wandered deeper into the graveyard and found a bench. There must be one thin strand to her past somewhere, tucked away in an old people's home or hospital. She had a name, Evie Fraughton, and she resolved to phone every care home in England to find her. With a sense of renewed determination, she stood up and marched to the gates of the cemetery.

18

The next morning, Sylvia was the first to arrive at the salon. Mandy had bought her mum's sewing machine, and they hemmed the turbans. Vitale arrived dressed in black with grey hollows under his eyes and moustache drooping. His scissors and comb peeked from his top pocket, not jangling in readiness to snip and smooth as usual.

"I will be the laughingstock! No one has ever sent out bald models before! Karla will tear my skin off with her own hands and make me into next season's couture."

He collapsed onto a chair and buried his face into a hot towel with an audible sob.

"It may not be that bad, Maestro," consoled Mandy. "Sylvia is not sending them out bald. Come on, monsieur, we should go now. The crew are waiting at the venue."

They hauled him out of his seat, picked up the equipment, and jumped into the waiting car.

Backstage was a chaos of clothes racks and semi-naked bodies. Karla Kreeper ran the show. She whirled her arms and words to an army that spun around her. Her assistants with furs and skins, swatches of colour, backstage staff with questions, management offering bowls of olives, sparkling water, and phone messages. She dealt each one with barked commands or a disdainful response. Vitale was swept up in the maelstrom and delivered to Karla, who kissed the air by each of his cheeks.

"Madam, we 'ave been working on zee design day and night, it has been, er, tweaked..." he pinched his fingers together. "... just a little bit, and they look amazing!"

He gulped while his moustache held his mouth in a wide grin.

"Darling, you know I have the greatest of trust in you..." She glared at him. "And therefore, I trust you to follow my directive. And then we will be, how do you say? 'Jolie'?"

He soon got bumped by Karla's set designer, who needed lighting advice. Sylvia greeted him.

"What did she say?"

"She s... s... say we do what she wants, or else."

"Well, unless we paint their heads black and white, we don't have a lot of choice."

The models were dressed in zebra skin bikinis, mini-skirts and boob tubes with zebra skin jackets. Once the makeup artists finished applying long eyelashes, highlighting cheekbones and painting lips black, Sylvia and the team got to work. They removed the head-scarves she had instructed the girls to wear and wound on the turbans. Sylvia had been so busy she didn't notice Sammy leaning against the doorway, watching. Vitale hovered and touched up the turbans as one by one they were piled onto the models' heads. To finish, he inserted ostrich feathers giving an extra exoticism to the look, combing and trimming them at last with his tools.

"This fabric looks so familiar," he muttered.

The stage manager, clutching a clipboard, rushed in.

"You're on, three, two, one..." He held a walkie talkie to his ear. "Go go go!"

The Amazonian models sashayed towards the stage, the lights dimmed, then strobed black and white as they entered the catwalk. The audience clapped and snapped cameras. Then, the goddesses launched their flanks and tossed their heads, their mane of feathers shining. At the end, they glared at the crowd and dropped the jackets off their shoulders before turning with a shake of their turbaned heads to march off the platform. Karla, whose mouth had dropped at first sight, now smiled as she greedily accepted the compliments from her peers and customers, claiming the stroke of genius of the hairdresser's as her own. Arthur, who was seated in the crowd, scowled.

Sylvia perched on a chair in the makeup room chewing her nails, waiting in trepidation.

"That was a sweet move, baby."

Sylvia saw the loiterer reflected in the mirror.

"Oh, Sammy, I didn't see you there!" Her stomach did a tumble. "Thanks. Did it go OK?"

"I haven't seen Karla that pleased since she scored the tail of an albino mountain cat in 1975."

"Phew, thanks for letting me know, dove."

The models came running into the room clutching at Sylvia, gushing and gaggling. Apart from one girl losing an eyelash, the show went as smoothly as leave-in conditioner, and Karla received a standing ovation. Vitale arrived and kissed each model on the lips and then squeezed Sylvia in an embrace so tight it left his moustache imprinted on her décolletage. Arthur arrived backstage.

"Arzur! Can you believe it? This girl is a mastermind! Of course, zee turban! This is what we call thinking outside zee beehive!"

Arthur managed a tight smile. Everyone else chattered and packed away. The party moved to the Ritz and after several crates of champagne, the story of how the turbans came to be spread like gossip under the dryer. At midnight, after Sammy put Karla into her limo, he tapped Sylvia from behind on her right shoulder and appeared around her left.

"You ready to dance, Queenie?"

Sylvia giggled and allowed herself to be led from the glamour of the Ritz to the same sweaty hole in Camden. Fuelled by success and joie de vivre, Sylvia and Sammy hit the dance floor. Her mouth ached with smiling, her feet were sore from dancing and her body throbbed with a desire for Sammy that would a make a nun's habit curl. The band slowed down and Sammy pulled Sylvia's willing body in close to him, and this time, he did not let go. She let her cheek rest against his damp shoulder and then glanced at him. Their lips met like long-lost lovers, devouring each other, oblivious that the final song had ended and the lights were now switched on full beam.

"Sammy!" A screech cut the air that made the smooching dancers jump. "Samuel Lock, I did not give you the night off. I have been looking for you everywhere. Guessed I might find you in this dive with another trollop."

"Karla, you... you said you didn't need me tonight, you went home, I..."

"I said no such thing, you stupid boy. Let go of her right now and get in the car."

"But Karla, this is Sylvia, she..."

"I don't give a devil's testicle who tonight's hussy is. I order you to get into the car or I'll thread a needle through your prick and drag you there myself."

All the men on the floor winced.

"I'm sorry, I'll telephone you, Sylv. Trev, can you call her taxi?" He tossed a five pound note at Sylvia and walked towards Karla who stood with her hands on her hips. She glared at Sylvia, twirled on her stilettos and marched out of the club. Humiliated, Sylvia grabbed her coat. She needed to walk home, to clear her head. Were Sammy and Karla an item? He'd mentioned that she had a kid. Had Sammy just been lying to her? There could be no other reason she was so angry? Why, oh, why was life so complicated? The rude end to the evening left her feeling like a half-done hairdo, neither one thing nor the other, filled with both desire and humiliation.

As she crept into the guesthouse, she hoped Mrs Grimshaw wouldn't hear her return. But to her dismay, a lamp glowed from the lounge room. She tiptoed past the door, but a voice made her jump.

"How quickly the virgin Queen Sylvia turned into a slapper."

"Arthur?"

He was draped in an armchair, twiddling a piece of paper in his fingers.

"How did you get in here? How did you know where I'm staying?"

"You're not the only one with excellent detective skills. I'd love to chat, but I've been waiting for hours and it's been a long day. The pointy point I'm making is to give you a heads-up, dear niece. Despite today's," he looked at his watch, "yesterday's extraordinary success, the police have been informed of foul play. The models want some recourse from their ugly de-hairing. I would imagine they want to question you since you played such a large role. I do hope you cleaned up after yourself, Queen Sylvia. Wouldn't like to see the crown jewels end up in the Tower of London!"

Arthur stood and smoothed his jacket of wrinkles. He shrugged on a thick overcoat. "Anyway, must be off, toodle-oo!"

He pranced past her and gently let himself out. Sylvia felt sweat prickling the back of her neck and a lurching in the pit of her stomach. Not only could she feel trouble brewing, but now she knew he had tricked her. She hated herself for trusting Arthur, for hoping that they could be, if not friends, at least share some family ties.

19

Mrs Grimshaw banged on Sylvia's door at 7.00 am. She heaved herself onto her elbow and squinted at her alarm clock.

"It's Sunday Mrs Grimshaw, I need a sleep in."

Her head throbbed and her feet ached. Her stomach sank at the humiliation of the night before, first Sammy, then Arthur. She groaned at it all.

"I know, pet, but you made the headlines."

Mrs Grimshaw opened the door, brandishing a newspaper.

"Look, Sylvia, 'Turban Turbulence Shakes Up Fashion Week', you've started a new craze!"

Sylvia groped for her glasses and read the reviews. Karla had once again aced the opening night of the show and fashion gurus were commenting on the style of the turban. She dressed and hobbled into the dining room, unsure if her stomach wanted any food or a big plate of it. She was glad of the toast ration, although Mrs Grimshaw had splashed out with some tinned fruit salad. It was halfway through her breakfast, chasing a cube of pear around the bowl, when she heard the phone ring in the back office. Mrs Grimshaw entered the dining room with a big grin on her face.

"I've got another surprise for you. Mr Grimshaw and I put

our heads together yesterday, and we found your grandmother in Bournemouth. They just called me to confirm. Evie Fraughton is at the Sweet Dream Retirement Villa. I've got the address right here and a coach ticket to the seaside!"

Sylvia blew out her cheeks and stuck out her eyes. "You found her?"

"Yes, the bus leaves at 9.00 a.m."

"Wow! Oh, thank you Mrs G!" She jumped up and gripped Mrs Grimshaw in a fervent hug.

"Go on, go and pack a bag. I'll call you a taxi." Mrs Grimshaw shook her head but couldn't stop her lips lifting into a smile as she disappeared to get the ringing phone.

Sylvia went back up to her room and stood inside the door with her hand on her open mouth. A relative, a real live grandmother! She would actually meet someone from her own flesh and blood! She threw her scattered clothes into her bag and grabbed her toothbrush and toiletries. There was a knock at the door.

"I'm coming, nearly ready. That taxi came quickly!" She threw on a coat of lipstick and shoved her remaining belongings into her handbag.

"No, I've got a phone message for you." Sylvia let Mrs Grimshaw into her room. "Someone called Mandy, she said can you get to the salon. Straight away."

"Oh right, do I have time?"

"It sounded serious. You could make a quick stop, I suppose. Ah, that'll be the taxi honking now. You ready?"

Sylvia swept up her mother's brooch and dropped it in her bag.

"Yup, sure am!" She clapped her hands in nervous excitement, glad to leave her men problems behind.

Sylvia's conversation with Arthur the night before unnerved her. Once again, she felt her scalp prickle and itch. This time, she didn't ignore it. She instructed the taxi to stop at the end of Carnaby Street and wait for her. As Arthur predicted, there were two police cars parked by Crassoon's. She approached the salon with caution and peaked in the window. Inside, two policemen were dusting mirrors, basins and walls for fingerprints. Vitale sat in one of the chairs, looking even more serious and forlorn than the previous morning, and a man in plain clothes interviewed a pale and tear-stained Mandy.

She couldn't hear anything, but he showed Mandy a photograph. Sylvia squinted and held her hand to the windowpane. The picture was of her. She could see Mandy nodding her head and pointing to the phone. Now worried about being seen, she backed away. If Arthur was right and they were looking for someone to blame, she would be the obvious choice. But nothing was going to stop her from seeing her grandmother. She walked briskly down the street, noticing with surprise window dressings in the trendiest clothes shops already sporting turbaned mannequins.

The taxi dropped her off and Sylvia stamped her feet and blew puffs of visible breath as she waited for a coach at Victoria Station. She was jittery. Every siren made her sink deeper into her collar, and she jumped at a passing pair of coppers. Once on the coach, she was glad to leave behind the menacing square shapes of the city. Even though the trees were bare and the fields dark brown with mud, the hedgerows and gardens still teemed with life and lush greenery. The sky had cleared away the cloth of clouds and it sparkled blue.

After two hours, the coach arrived in Bournemouth. The air smelt sharp, like metal, and her nose took her to the coast. A long swathe of coarse sandy beach landed at the bottom of a steep incline, holding back a choppy sea. A pier stretched out into the water, inhabited by circling birds. Maybe she'd take a walk there later, but first she had to see Evie.

20

Sylvia found the Sweet Dream Retirement Villa perched up on a white cliff. There were wide lawns around the house with herbaceous borders, benches and chairs dotted around a croquet lawn. A lone gardener dug manure into a bed of twiggy rose bushes. Sylvia suspected the frosty air too harsh for the elderly residents. Once again, her scalp tingled as she walked towards a glossy blue front door. Inside, a large hall of the old country manor had been converted into a reception area. Sylvia could smell corned beef and furniture polish and, for a moment, she was back in the orphanage of her childhood.

"Can I help you, miss?"

A stout middle-aged woman manned the desk.

"Yes, I'm here to visit Mrs Evie Fraughton."

"Sign in here, please."

Sylvia signed her name.

"Matron will take you to her room."

Dressed in starched white and with an impassive face, matron reminded Sylvia of the nuns, invoking both a familiarity and fear. Her scalp prickled, and she scratched under her turban. Matron warned Sylvia that Mrs Fraughton had advanced dementia and these days she rarely spoke. Before she knew it, the door had opened and her legs carried her inside. A large room overlooked the sweeping back lawns and French doors which would open onto a stone balcony in warmer weather. It took a moment for Sylvia to locate Evie sitting in an armchair facing the windows. Her frail body flowed around the contours of the chair. A clock ticked on the mantelpiece, a fly buzzed determinedly at the window, unable to break through the invisible pane to the sweet world beyond.

Sylvia cleared her throat to announce her intrusion and tiptoed towards the veined hand that rested on the arm of the chair.

"Hello, Mrs Fraughton. Evie?"

Sylvia inched around the armchair and swung her eyes to the first, the only maternal relative she had.

The old lady was dozing, her mouth open wide enough for Sylvia to see a row of small teeth, surprisingly intact. Her wig of dark hair was slightly askew. It was Sylvia's second nature to reach out and straighten it. A hand whipped up and gripped Sylvia's wrist. Sylvia jumped with a sharp intake of breath.

"Get your rotten, bleeding palms off me."

Violet eyes pinned Sylvia. A beauty spot pulled at the papery skin on her cheek, and Sylvia could see she had once been a stunner.

"It's Sylvia, your granddaughter." She put her free hand over the old lady's, smoothed the grip and held her fingers. She knelt next to her.

"I'm a hairdresser, just touching up your hair, that's all."

Evie blinked; the briefest sign of recognition passed through her eyes. She sighed, turned her head, and dozed off again. Sylvia sat cross-legged at her grandmother's feet and wondered what to do. The fly had given up and lay on the generous carpet. It was stuffy; the sun shone through the window and the ancient chunky radiators filled the room with a dry heat that caused her eyelids to droop. She forced open the French door and stepped out onto the balcony, breathing in the crisp clean air. The peace of the countryside was a balm.

"Shut that frigging window, draw the blinds, the Gerries will find you, you stupid cow!"

The peace shattered with foul language. Sylvia rushed back in and closed the door.

"The curtains, draw the bloody curtains, you idiot."

"Evie, it's 1977. We won the war, the Gerries are gone. I'm Sylvia, your granddaughter, from Australia."

"I'm not a dim-witted shit-for-brains like your mother." Sylvia opened and closed her mouth. "Now give me the brooch." She swore like a hungover sailor with no rum. "It's taken you long enough to get here."

"But you..."

"Yes, yes, advanced dementia, I know. These idiots can't tell one old person from another. The whole of bleeding England thinks everyone over 70 has dementia."

Sylvia began to open the curtains again to let in some light.

"You cloth-eared wench, close the bloody curtains, I told you they're spying."

"Is that a code? Oh! For the nurses? Ah, OK, I got it." Sylvia winked.

"Stupid girl, what happened? You were a bright child once. Did they feed you nothing but sand in Australia?"

Not knowing what to say, Sylvia crossed her arms in defiance.

"Now give me my brooch or I swear I'll have someone dig up your mother's bones and swap them for yours."

"What kind of greeting is that for someone you haven't seen in over fifteen years?"

"Well, you shoulda come a bit sooner then, shouldn't you? Expect me to traipse all over the world, eh? You're all selfish, the lot of you. Blood sucking, shit stinking..."

There was a knock at the door. Evie gave Sylvia a hard stare before dropping her head, closing her eyes and pushing a glob of saliva over her lip. The nurse entered with a tray of tea.

"Everything alright, deary?"

Sylvia nodded, though everything was certainly not alright. The nurse set down the tray on the coffee table. She adjusted the pillow behind Evie's back and wiped her chin, giving her a condescending pat. As the door clicked shut, Evie's head sprung back to life. She yanked the pillow from behind her and threw it on the floor.

"Meddling, nosy old bitch!"

"Why are you pretending?" Sylvia asked.

"Shh! The Gerries'll hear us." The old lady's eyes scanned the room. "There are spies everywhere!"

Sylvia nodded and tapped her finger against her nose. "Spies," she repeated.

Evie held out a quivering hand and stared at the brooch on Sylvia's turban. Sylvia kneeled back down, unpinned it and handed it to her. Evie turned it over and ran her fingers over the back of the brooch. She nodded.

"Give me your hand, Sylvie," she said gently.

After a bizarre start, this was the moment Sylvia might at last find a loving relative. Tears pooled in her eyes. She shuffled closer and placed her hand in the old lady's. Evie turned Sylvia's hand over.

"I have something to tell you. Don't make a sound or those filthy spies will kill us both."

Sylvia swallowed and nodded.

"There are people, blood sucking creeps, who want this brooch."

She held it up in front of Sylvia's face, the pin dangling loose from its clasp.

"There's special information etched on the back, numbers to my bank vault."

Evie ran her thumb over the palm of the mesmerised Sylvia.

"There are secrets in that vault. And riches."

Now genuine spittle gathered around the old lady's lips, which turned the same shade of violet as her eyes.

She went on. "That's your inheritance, *yours*, you hear? Them swindling bastards will hunt you down, they'll grease you up good and proper, make you feel like a queen, and then they'll stab you." She raised the brooch and sunk the pin deep into Sylvia's palm. Sylvia screamed, but Evie slapped her across the face and grabbed her by the chin, the brooch still implanted in her hand.

"Bloody hell!"

"When the war is over, use it to escape. Never let it go and don't let those bastards get their hands on it."

She released Sylvia and flopped back into her chair and promptly fell asleep. Sylvia painfully pulled out the brooch and held her throbbing palm.

"You evil, evil cow," she muttered under her breath, scrabbling to her feet.

She ran from the stifling room, down the wide carpeted stairs and burst through the front doors, gasping for air, trying to make sense of what she'd heard. The receptionist followed her.

"You all right, deary? Looks like you've seen a ghost."

"She's mad!"

"That's what they all say," she sighed. "Do you need a drink of water?"

"No, no I'm OK, thanks."

She just wanted to get away.

Later that day, after she'd stuck a bandaid on her hand, Sylvia sat in a seaside café. She sipped hot sweet tea and picked at a dry crumbly cake they called a scone, whose only redeeming feature was a blob of thick cream and a dollop of strawberry jam. As she had done all her life, she examined the back of the brooch. She was astonished that the figures stamped crudely into the gold were a key, a location rather than a gold mark. Had the numbers been engraved in a fancy font, she may have questioned their meaning. She was naturally curious, had driven the nuns crazy with her inquiring mind, had uncovered anomalies in the salon and learnt many tricks of the trade by her questioning. But now she wondered what she had missed, by making assumptions, by taking things at face value.

Her grandmother was clearly as batty as a bald hairdresser, mad as a mohawk, crazy as a pair of clippers on speed, but at times she had been completely lucid. The way she slumped back into a gaga granny when the nurse came in, yet she seemed genuinely terrified of the Nazis. Sylvia had so many questions. Did she want to go back? Her stomach and its resident scone told her to never go back, to run as far away from her as possible. But there was something nagging at her, an itch she needed to scratch. She poked a finger under her turban and picked at the remaining scabs of her tattoo. She decided to sleep on it.

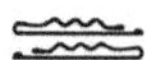

The eerie screech of seagulls woke her at dawn. She dreamt they were picking at her hand as she fed them, pulling pieces of her flesh away. Jabbing peck by jabbing peck, they ate her alive. Her palm throbbed. She winced as she dabbed it with water and changed the band-aid. Overnight, her need to know more about her mother had overshadowed the pain in her hand and her heart. She decided to revisit her grandmother, but she'd keep her distance this time.

She walked along the cliff side road that took her to the home, formulating questions and rehearsing her approach. The frost was thawing into sparkling dew as she crunched up the driveway. A man with a leather case was saying goodbye to the receptionist.

"Thank you, Dr Glover. See you again soon I'm sure."

Sylvia smiled and nodded 'good morning' as she passed him.

She went to the receptionist behind the desk.

"Hello, I've come to visit Evie Fraughton again."

"Oh my dear, I'm terribly sorry. The doctor has just left. You see... I'm sorry to tell you, Evie passed away in the night."

Sylvia's vision blurred. She felt like she was falling down a deep well, voices faded, cold wind wrapped around her.

"She was 87, dear, and although we made her comfortable..." The woman's voice faded back in and Sylvia was surprised to find herself still standing with both hands on the reception desk.

"... wasn't capable of much, rarely spoke. She's in a better place now."

"Oh." Sylvia felt like a brain pickled in a jar, a jumble of thoughts, words, emotions, but no means of organising them and letting them express.

"I've informed the relatives."

"Relatives?" the brain spoke.

"Yes, her two nephews. They visited about twice a year, I'd say. Lovely men, they seemed. You know them? Um..." She closed her eyes and remembered. "Colin and Donald, that's it."

"No, no, I haven't met them yet. What did she die of?"

"Old age, my dear. She was very frail."

Sylvia closed her hand over the yellow tinged band-aid, it ached.

"And... not with it... up here," she whispered, tapping her temple.

"When will the funeral be?"

"Next week, I'd imagine. We'll see what the family wants to do. Shall I pass on your contact number to them?"

Evie's words echoed, 'don't let those bastards get their hands on it'. But she was clearly mad, and now dead. And there was a family, cousins!

"Yes, of course."

She scribbled the number of the boarding house on a pad and slid it across the desk.

"Thank you. Is there anything I can do?"

"All taken care of. I'm sorry to give you the sad news. I'll call you when the funeral is arranged."

She patted Sylvia's hand. Sylvia sighed, dropped her shoulders and walked out of the home. The loss of a grandmother and the discovery of more family, sorrow and excitement all battled for dominion. Colin and Donald weighed in heavily, and the bitterness of Evie had no power over the sweetness of cousins. Hope won the day.

Sylvia rang Mrs Grimshaw to fill her in, and that she intended to stay for the funeral.

"And I found out I have cousins, Mrs G, imagine that?"

"Cousins! Well there you are, pet, always a silver lining."

"I thought my mum was an only child. I'm just trying to work out how I have cousins. Anyway, I guess I'll find out at the funeral."

"I'll keep your room for you here. Now, watch how you go, and stay in touch."

She supposed it was now a waiting game, but she had too much nervous energy to sit around in the boarding house waiting for the phone to ring.

21

Sylvia woke early the next morning, again the seagulls startling her out of an uneasy sleep. She dressed in a warm jumper and jeans. Her hand was too sore to wind her turban on, and she found a purple beret in the bottom of her suitcase. She hurried out of the stuffy boarding house, grabbing a croissant for breakfast. The winter beach was deserted, bar an old man with a metal detector. Slate blue sky met a slate grey ocean, a strong wind teased white horses out of the waves. Sylvia leaned into the wind and forced her way along the pier. She stood at the end, like the last person on earth, and let the gusts support her. The vast and wild ocean of the future roaring ahead of her. The brooch sat heavily in her pocket. She pulled it out and raised her still throbbing fist. The rolling waves hissed "Ssss" under the boardwalk. The gulls called "ylvia, ylvia" as they wheeled above, rearing with the gusts of wind. She wanted to be rid of her past, to throw the brooch into the ocean. She drew back her hand. The water and birds were calling her, willing her to let it go.

"Sylvia, Sylvia!"

Startled, she turned. "Sammy?"

He stood a few steps behind her, a helmet under his arm. She pocketed the brooch and her bandaged hand, and turned back to the sea, allowing the wind to knock the tears across her cheeks.

"Sylvia." Sammy's hot breath was in her ear.

She shivered.

"I'm sorry," he said.

She stared at the furious sea.

"Can I buy you a cuppa?" Sammy pleaded.

She held her breath, turned and nodded, relief and joy threatening to explode in a snotty mess. She contained the storm in her chest with an internal sob. They walked back along the pier. The wind took away any words, and so they waited until they had a pot of tea on the table in a seaside café.

"How are you, Sylv?"

"I'm just great," she said with cutting sarcasm. "I met my grandmother on Saturday and she was dead by Sunday."

"Bloody hell, Sylv, I'm so sorry."

"Not to mention the fact, I was left like a lemon on the dance floor. I was double crossed by my uncle and the police might be after me. Why are you here, Sammy? I thought I was just another of your hussies."

"No, Sylv. You are the most amazing woman. All the models or film stars I've met ain't got a patch on you. It's just Karla's way. I'm about the only person she trusts, makes her a bit touchy."

"I'd say!"

"Hang on. Why might the police be after you?"

"Don't worry about it. I haven't done anything wrong." She brushed the fact away with a wave of her hand.

"I mean it Sylv," Sammy went on, "you got brains, you got skills, and you can dance!"

Sylvia let out a long puff of air and folded her arms across her chest.

"Well, thank you Sammy for your sweet words, but I'm not some loose girl that has a two-week affair and then sails away."

"Do me some justice. I am a gent, you know."

"Well, you didn't act like one the other night. Why do you let that woman boss you around like that?"

"It's, it's complicated."

Sylvia raised her eyebrows and cocked her head, asking for an explanation.

"She's got this little kid. A boy. I look after him for her."

Sylvia laughed through her nose and shook her head. "You're the dad?"

Sammy opened his eyes wide. "NO, no. I'm not the dad. They, he doesn't have a dad. So I guess I fill in sometimes. She doesn't have any time for the little blighter. I know what it's like not having a dad. I feel sorry for the little bugger."

"Still, she's got no right to talk to you like that."

They sat in silence for a minute.

"How did you find me, anyway?" Sylvia eventually asked.

"I hounded Mrs G. She said you was in Bournemouth, lucky the place is deserted."

Sylvia huffed.

"Com' on, Queenie. I told Karla I had to take four days off to look after my sick ma."

"Karla acts like your wife, your mother, and your boss. How am I supposed to compete with that?"

"I'll quit my job, I'd do anything for you, Queenie." Sammy's twinkling eyes implored.

Sylvia pursed her lips and sighed.

"We can catch a flick, feed the seagulls, eat fish and chips," he pleaded.

"If you want to, I suppose I can't stop you. But as soon as the funeral happens, you're gone, OK?"

"It's a deal." Sammy grinned. "Ever been on a motorbike?"

She shook her head.

"Com' on!" He leapt up and took her hand, pulling her onto the street. Behind the supermarket, a car park held a smattering of cars, but the shiny silver motorbike with a deep blue leather seat stood out. He put his helmet on and unlocked the carrier, retrieving another one for Sylvia. She shoved it on over her beret, unwilling to let Sammy see her bald head.

They zoomed along Undercliff Drive that hugged the coast. The cold air stung her cheeks, but she was warm, snuggled behind Sammy, her arms around his waist. Crazy golf in Boscombe released much needed giggles. The ferry trip to Shell Bay and a picnic on the windy beach in Swanage made Sammy hug her inside his jacket. The sun pushed through the grey clouds, sending silvery slices of light onto the ocean. The wind still howled as they battled down the promenade, whisking words away. But Sylvia was happy to not talk. The wound in her hand throbbed. She avoided questions by keeping her gloves on outside, but in a café she struggled to keep her hand hidden, wincing with pain. Sammy was too busy staring into her eyes to notice. When she went to the toilet and came back, he held a newspaper he'd grabbed from the adjacent table.

"Bloody hell, Sylvia. Look at this!"

"What is it?"

"There was a small article on the second page reading 'Hair Horror' - Police are searching for a suspect in the shocking hair remover cream crime at the famous salon of Vitale Crassoon. A woman in her twenties is said to have fled the scene. Her whereabouts are unknown. If anyone has any information, please..."

A relatively inaccurate photo-fit picture accompanied the article, but the turban was enough to give her likeness away.

"Jiminy clippers! Do they mean me?" she said in a heavy whisper.

"We better get you out of the public view, Sylv."

Sammy dropped her at the guesthouse and promised to come by first thing the next morning. But by late afternoon, she was feverish. Her palm swelled and an unnatural yellow coloured her skin. The hand ballooned and her fingers would not bend without excruciating pain. Her hot head pounded and yet she shivered on her bed. She left a note for Sammy. It said she wasn't well and she wouldn't be coming out. By sundown, pain racked her whole body. She was too weak to ask for a painkiller and water from the bathroom tap seemed a universe away. As the clock blinked 6.00 p.m. on her bedside table, there was a knock at her door.

"Phone call for you, ma'am."

She groaned and heaved herself out of bed. The room slanted one way and the other. She held onto the walls as she wobbled down the stairs. The phone receiver felt like lead in her hand, so she ducked her head to speak into it.

"Hello," she croaked.

"Oh pet, so glad I got hold of you at last. It's been crazy here, what with the elephant people and... Oh hark at me, Sylvia love, are you there?"

Sylvia had dropped the phone and managed to drag its weight back to her ear.

"Yes, yes, Mrs G, I'm..."

"Oh good. Now listen, I had a visit from the..."

Sylvia collapsed.

"Hello, hello?..." Mrs Grimshaw's voice was left dangling.

Darkness fell and took Sylvia away. She slipped into a timeless plane of delirium. She dreamed the brooch morphed into a giant obsidian beetle that rammed into her. Then her hair grew down from her head, through her body and out of her feet, weaving down into the ground, tangling in on itself so she couldn't move, rooted. In the dream she wound her turban on to her bald head but it fought back like a boa constrictor and strangled her, howling with laughter like her dead husband Solomon.

Then warm voices, white light, a smell of disinfectant filtered through. She opened her eyes. They felt dry and full of sand. She opened her mouth, but only a croak escaped. 'I'm a toad' randomly passed through her mind. Who am I? Where am I? she thought. Then a familiar voice.

"Hey Queenie." It was Sammy.

"Where am I?"

"Bournemouth General Hospital. That cut in your hand was infected. You got blood poisoning."

"Blood poisoning," Sylvia echoed.

"You're gonna be fine. The doc cleaned your blood," Sammy pointed to the drip.

"Clean blood," she repeated.

"In a few days you'll be up again, right as rain."

"Rain," she moved her eyes to the window and, sure enough, rain splashed off the sills. She sighed. "What day is it?"

"Thursday. I've been here every day, right by your side."

She nodded. "Thursday," she murmured and closed her eyes, but opened them again. "Wait, Thursday? When did I come in here?"

"Monday evening."

"But the funeral!"

"I'm sorry Sylv. There was a message for you. I'm afraid the funeral was yesterday."

"I missed it?"

Sammy watched as Sylvia turned her face away. He couldn't hold her bandaged hand, and the other was full of tubes.

"I want to go home."

"I called Mrs G. She's really worried about you. She tried to warn you about the police. She wanted to come down, but the guesthouse is full with the Elephant Arthritis Prevention Society."

"No, I mean home, back to Australia. I'm sick of this place. I've had nothing but bad luck."

"Come on, Queenie, we've had a good time, ain't we?"

She said nothing. Sammy lingered. Sylvia closed her eyes. She wanted to be alone now. Minutes passed. She could hear his breathing.

"Look Sylv, I've gotta go. The boss is having kittens. I'll see you back in London, alright?"

She didn't reply—there were no words. Then his footsteps took him away. She must have fallen asleep because she woke up again as a nurse took her blood pressure.

"Good morning, Sylvia. How are we feeling today?"

"Better, I think," she croaked. "Can I have some water?"

"Here you go, dear. Now, you have some more visitors. Are you up to seeing them?"

"Who is it?"

"Two chaps. They say they are relatives."

"Oh, OK," replied Sylvia, perplexed.

The nurse helped Sylvia to a sitting position. She worried about her appearance, wanting to make a good first impression. But what little hair she had was a mess. She couldn't even run her fingers through it. Two men appeared in the doorway.

"Sylvia!" they both crooned together. "Our long-lost cousin. I'm

Colin, so pleased to meet you!"

Sylvia judged him to be around forty. He was as thin as the tooth of a comb and wore a beige polo-neck sweater under a dark brown suit jacket, chequered golfing slacks flared onto the floor. His wrists held chunky gold chains. A gold tooth gleamed. She wasn't impressed by his thin hair that dripped into a mullet. With no hand available to shake, he squeezed her shoulder.

"And I'm Donald, blessings to you my child in this so tragic of times. May our dear grandmother rest in peace, God bless her soul." Colin shot him a glance.

"Amen!" Donald finished.

Donald, in contrast to his devout words, dressed as one who had been praying at the feet of Jimi Hendrix rather than God. His luxurious Afghan coat couldn't hide the glow of a psychedelic shirt. Bright yellow corduroys finished the look with a faint aroma of patchouli that clashed with the sterile hospital. They spoke in an accent Sylvia had not heard before.

"I'm sorry I missed the funeral," she croaked.

"Och, don't worry about it. The old girl can finally rest in peace, safe in the knowledge her granddaughter is alive and well." Colin looked at the tubes in Sylvia's arm, "er, alive at least."

"Yes, she talked about you often," Donald added.

"Really? I thought she rarely spoke."

"Oh, that was before she went madder than..." started Colin.

"Before she deteriorated, dementia is a terrible curse," Donald broke in.

"Did she, er, make any sense when you saw her?" Donald asked.

The cousins leaned in. Sylvia's mind recalled the stuffy room, the ticking clock. Her hand throbbed, and a wooziness overcame her. She felt ashamed that a crazy old lady had put her in this situation with nothing more than a brooch pin.

"No, she... just talked about the Gerries, the Germans."

The cousins shifted away.

"She was mad..." Colin started to say, but Donald interrupted.

"...ly in love with life, dear, sweet Evie."

"I wanted to ask her about my mother. Did you know her?"

"Oh, she was a stunner, not much between the..." said Colin.

"Simply beautiful. She knew how to pull a good pint," Donald interjected.

Sylvia smiled.

"Was she happy? Did she like to dance?"

"Our dad, Mickey, he had to..." started Donald.

"His work took him away from Hackney," Colin continued.

"We live in Scotland. We lost touch with the Fraughton side o' the family."

"Oh." Sylvia tried to keep up, her mind still foggy with painkillers.

"Until recently, that is."

"Is that right?" she replied.

The men looked around the room. Donald shifted in his seat, Colin chewed at a hangnail. The sound of the nurses on the ward filtered into the searching silence, each willing the other to find something to say.

"When you're better," Donald broke the impasse, Sylvia and Colin let out a breath, "we'll take you out for dinner, and tell you lots of stories about, about... your ma."

"Yes, cracking idea," said Colin. The silence threatened again.

"Well, better be off," said Donald.

"Aye, och, is that the time?"

They handed her a business card with their name and number. The words mashed together on the card. Sylvia's mind drifted away from her body. She forced a smile and nodded in agreement. A nurse reappeared.

"Visiting time is over. You've worn the girl out. Off you go now." She shooed the men out. The cousins released themselves from the ward, bobbing their heads and waving goodbye.

Sylvia must have dozed off for a few hours because a different nurse woke her by pumping up her arm to measure her blood pressure again.

"Oh, hello there. Just doing a few checks. Glad you're awake, you got some visitors."

"More visitors? I only know about three people in this country."

"Two gentlemen."

"Oh? The cousins again?"

The nurse shrugged. "I'll show them in."

Two men appeared at the end of Sylvia's bed. She did recognise them, but they weren't her cousins.

"Good afternoon ma'am, I'm detective inspector Grouse and this is PC Bean. Are you Mrs Sylvia Scutlash?"

This was the man grilling Mandy in Crassoon's and Bean who was dusting for fingerprints. There was no way of avoiding them now.

"Yes, I am," she simply replied.

"In that case, I'm arresting you for suspicion of actual bodily harm..."

"This is nuts. I helped Vitale, I solved the case of the hair dye, I..."

"Mrs Scutlash, we have found depilatory cream in your room at your lodgings. Your fingerprints will prove whether you are responsible for this crime." He continued to read her rights.

"But officer..."

"You can make a statement at the station back in London. You'll be coming back with us. The doctor said you'll be good to leave tomorrow."

22

The police agreed that she needn't be handcuffed, but Sylvia's legs were weak and wobbly after a week in bed. Her hand was heavily bandaged, and she oscillated between tears, panic and nausea as they drove back to London in a police car. After the two and half hour drive, the detective sat Sylvia opposite him at the police station. They spent an hour combing through every detail of what happened. A policeman entered.

"Are you able to identify this case, Mrs Scutlash?"

"Yes, that is mine."

They took a mugshot of her naked head, made copies of her fingerprints, which was painful for the fingertips that poked out of the bandaged hand. And for the second time in her life, locked her up.

"I need to make my phone call," she called out.

"All in due course. We're a bit busy. There's a war out there; those bloody idiot youths, teddy boys and punk rockers fighting in the streets."

Sylvia sat in the cell and, for the umpteenth time that day, went through the series of events. First, who could she call? Vitale was as helpful as a blocked toilet. Mandy had clearly pointed the finger at her. International calls were not allowed, and besides, it was the middle of the night in Australia. She felt too ashamed to call Mrs Grimshaw. That left Sammy. He had scrawled his number on her bandage with a biro and the numbers remained like ghosts. An hour passed. And then another. A different policeman came in with a cup of tea.

"How long will this take, officer?"

"Sorry, love, we're at capacity. Sergeant Bugle is too busy processing punks."

"Well, can I make a phone call?"

"See what I can do."

She sipped the milky tea, which surprisingly did indeed make things seem better. Twenty minutes later, the lad returned and escorted her to the phone on a desk. She rang Sammy's number, not knowing what she would say.

Brrrp, brrrp, brrrp.

There was a kerfuffle as five or six policemen bustled in with handcuffed blokes. Most of them bloody and battered, shouting and swearing. Sylvia put her hand over her free ear.

Brrrp, brrrp, brrrp.

"Sylvia?"

It confused her because the familiar voice wasn't coming from the receiver, but from behind her, she turned.

"Sammy?"

"Bloody hell, Sylv, they caught up with you! How are you feeling?" he winced, as his swelling eye and cut lip moved. He moved towards her, but the policeman shoved him onward.

"Move along, sonny."

"Why are you here?" she called after him, but he was bustled down the corridor. He craned to look at her before the officer hoisted him away.

She replaced the receiver mid *brrrp.*

"No reply," she whispered to her accompanying policeman.

Another hour passed before the overworked police dealt with the brawling gangs and an investigating officer was free to attend Sylvia. Again, he questioned her about the events at the salon. Back in the cell, three other female inmates had arrived. She sat on the edge of a bench, picking at her bandage and chipped nails. The police had refused her turban due to its length resembling that of a rope, and for the first time her shaved head and nearly healed tattoo were bare. Her head was now covered in a number one fuzz of hair, giving her a menacing look. The women eyed her up and moved away. By evening, Sylvia became used to the constant traffic of policeman, arrestees and lawyers drifting in and out of the cells.

"Visitor, miss," an officer grunted and let a man through the door. "Five minutes."

"Arthur!"

He approached the bars of the cell and smirked.

"Get me out of here," she pleaded, "there's been a mistake. They think I swapped the hair dye for depilatory cream."

"Really Sylvia, I don't know what you have against Vitale."

"I don't have anything... I didn't do it, Arthur! You know that. You need to ring Wiz for me. They won't let me call Australia in here."

"Another jail bird in the family. Runs in the blood, doesn't it? Not even a bunch of saintly nuns could wash you clean."

"What do you mean 'runs in the blood'?"

"Your father, a convicted felon."

"I remember him being locked up a lot, but he wasn't a bad man, never hurt anybody."

Arthur raised his eyebrows. "Is that what you've told yourself?"

"Just get me out of here!"

"I'd love to help, but I'm afraid that once they discover who your father was..."

"What are you talking about, who my father was?"

Arthur heaved a weary sigh.

"Blood runs thicker than shampoo." He laughed at himself. "Frank Sprout was not only a common thief, but a murderer. He was in and out of jail so many times I lost count, not a very good thief clearly."

"A murderer? He never hurt anyone!"

"Ha, I felt the back of his hand more than once, I can tell you, but not only that. His final heist was a jewellers. The owner had installed an emergency button, and the bobbies arrived sooner than he expected. They chased him down the street and he ducked through his local barbershop, where he knew he could disappear through the back and get lost in the maze of lanes. But for good measure, he squirted shampoo all over the shop floor. Two officers came rushing into Giuseppe's. They skidded and slipped like drunken ice-skaters. One knocked his head on the basin, stone cold dead. The other knocked his teeth out but survived."

"Did they catch him?" Sylvia whispered.

"Of course, he was a loudmouth and a clumsy criminal. The only reason he didn't get put away for manslaughter was because Giuseppe swore he spilt the shampoo himself by accident." Arthur stood proud. "Hairdressers will do anything for a good customer. But the police, they knew the truth. They never forgave him, your idiot father, for killing that young copper."

Sylvia collapsed onto the hard bench.

"Why didn't you ever tell me this?"

"You think I'm proud? You think I wanted to brag about his dirty little exploits? Besides, I was trying to protect you. What good is it knowing you came from a messed-up family?"

"Protect me? You couldn't stand the sight of me!"

"Look, I had my own issues to deal with. I washed my hands of this family and escaped to Australia, banished the whole bloody lot of them from my mind until you turned up. What did you expect… a happy little family reunion?"

"Yes, I did, as a matter of fact. But you had to make it into a war!"

"Perhaps if you weren't so sickly nice, sugar and spice. Yes Sol, sir, no Sol sir. Freaking nuns ruined a perfectly good urchin. Euch!"

"You hate me because I'm too nice?"

"Yes, you're the most irritating, eager little sneak that got under Sol's skin. You took away my man and now my business. I built that place up with Sol. I deserve it."

"Sol made that salon, Arthur, you just hung around for the champagne and a shampoo. And you know what? That place took off when I was managing the books, keeping things going, when you two buggered off on a jet plane every five minutes. I swept the floors, washed the towels, paid the bills, ordered the product. And yes, I was friendly and happy and nice because I loved it. And if I hadn't married Solomon, you two would have been run out of town. I have never had a holiday or a boyfriend. I never even danced until last week. All I ever dreamed of was a proper family and all I ever got was a selfish, jealous pig."

Arthur let out a dramatic sigh.

"It's a shame you won't be able to continue your amazing work at the Wavy Lady, then, isn't it, Miss Perfect?"

"What do you mean?"

"Wiz has signed the papers for the shop over to me. I won, Sylverella."

"But I solved the case!"

"Enjoy your holiday from cleaning the floors, washing towels blah blah blah. Hopefully, it'll be a nice long one."

"Leave me alone. You're a monster, an evil, nasty double-crossing creep!"

"Ah! There she is. I knew there was a dark side in there somewhere."

"Get out, OUT!"

"Music to my ears. The room service here is terrible."

She screamed at him. The words she had pushed far down the plughole of her mind rose to the surface and gushed out. "I hate you, you pig. You were never good enough for Sol. He carried your lazy backside and you killed him. You made him sick. I hate you!"

The women in the cell shrunk back against the wall and looked at the floor. Arthur turned to leave, but then swung around on his patent heels and advanced back to the cell.

"You want to know something about your fam-il -y?" he inched out the word with menace. "Your father was quite a catch, excuse the pun... for your mother, I mean." He put his face close to the bars. "You have no idea the evil in *her* side of the family. Your Dad was a saint compared to that mob." He gave her a nasty smile. Sylvia looked at her hand and winced.

"Toodle-oo, must dash. I'm meeting Vitale at the Prunier for dinner."

Sylvia sat in shock, cradling her sore hand. Nobody could be more evil than that man. How could he leave her here? Steal the salon from her. She'd done nothing wrong, nothing. But she would not let him bring her down. She refused to feel the hurt, refused to be beaten. A policeman came to give her the medication for her hand. She was grateful it included a sleeping pill. Eventually, she dozed off. Sounds of clanging, yells of inmates and the management of midnight crime filled the long night as she fitfully slept.

Another day followed another night. This time, she had no visitors and no chance to make a call. The cell guard told her it was Sunday, so she might as well give up expecting anything to happen. Sylvia heard Arthur's words over and over in her mind, devastated that her ancestors, her roots, were so twisted. She couldn't even find the heart to strike up a conversation with the other women. Normally by now she would have known their life history and given them hair advice.

An unappetising flabby ham sandwich heralded Monday morning. Its smell alone was a strong motivation for her to change her circumstances. She needed help; she needed to talk to Wiz. She'd last spoken to him from the phone box. The phone box... a memory struck her. She squeezed her eyes closed and brought to mind the advert for 'Wiggles On Clipper Street'. Below the massage parlour and above the Indian restaurant, the hairdresser's number floated up through her subconscious to her mind. It was a long shot, but the fifth UGH commandment was: 'Always help another hairdresser in need.'

"Excuse me," she called out. "Hello!"

The sandwich delivering officer returned.

"Please officer, I need to make my call."

He rambled off to check with his senior. Permission was granted, and he led her to the phone booth. She dialled the number with trepidation.

"Good morning, Wiggles on Clipper Street, Jez speaking."

"Hi Jez, my name is Sylvia. I'm a hairdresser from Australia. I don't suppose you are familiar with... Nihil mali capillos...?"

For a second, Sylvia held her breath where there was an agonising silence.

"Blow me! That's what's written above our door. I ain't no idea what it means, but yes I am familiar with it."

Sylvia raised her eyes and thanked Mother Mary.

"I need to ask a favour. Can you make a call for me? It's to Australia I'm afraid, but I'll repay you."

"Of course, us hairdressers need to gel together. Give me the number."

Sylvia relayed the number.

"You'll speak to Wiz. Tell him 'Solomon's queen is in chains. Send in a wig.' Did you get that?"Jez repeated, and Sylvia thanked her with a blast of relief.

"I'll come and see you soon. Thanks again, Jez, I owe you."

Feeling calmer and more composed than she had for the last two days, Sylvia return to her cell and hoped the message would filter through and help arrive. Many dull hours passed when a uniform collected Sylvia and placed her in a room with another cup of milky tea. The tired and unkempt looking detective slouched in the chair opposite her. He lit up a Marlboro and slid the packet across the table.

"Detective Inspector Grouse," she said.

Sylvia waited for him to speak. He smoked and watched the corner of the interview room, motionless.

"Help yourself," he nodded towards the pack.

"No thanks."

"Mrs Scutlash, tell me about the events that happened at Vitale Crassoon salon last week. That is Friday 18th November 1977."

"I've already been through this twice," she said.

"Third time is the dream then, Mrs Scutlash."

Sylvia told them what had happened.

"And did you pick up the dyes used on the victims?"

"Yes, I did."

"Is it true you disappeared into the lavatory before returning to the salon on Friday afternoon?"

"Yes, but..."

"Can you explain the presence of depilatory cream in your possession?"

“I use it on my legs. Sir, I have quite dark hair and...”

“Yes, er, quite,” he coughed and cut her off mid-sentence.

“It’s not looking very good for you Mrs Scutlash, or should I say ‘Sprout’?” He put his hands on the table and leaned across at her. Bean shook his head at her in disgust.

“The name is Scutlash. There is no reason for me to put that cream in those poor girls’ hair. I’m trying to help Monsieur Crassoon, not ruin him, or anybody.”

“Then can you explain, young lady, why you have been consorting with Humphrey Lebonne, Crassoon’s sworn enemy?” He pulled a Polaroid out of a manila envelope and slapped it on the table. It showed Sylvia and Humphrey embracing outside his salon the day she had interviewed him.

“I had just met him, I, I...”

“I’ve been in this game a long, long time, young lady. I had been promoted to Sergeant in 1960 but I didn’t get to celebrate that auspicious occasion. Shall I tell you why, Miss Sprout.”

“As I said, it’s Mrs Scutlash, but carry on.”

“Because my best mate died that week.”

“I’m sorry to hear that, detective, but...”

“And a little birdy tells me it was your dad that killed him.”

“That little birdy was his brother, so go and find him!”

“Mrs Scutlash,” he shouted at her and stood, his hands on the table as he leered towards her. There was a knock at the door. Grouse nodded at the officer, who let in a gangly man dressed in a pinstripe suit.

“Good morning. Sorry for the delay. I’m Jeremy Pointer-Smith, Mrs Scutlash’s lawyer. Now, Mrs Scutlash, you are not obliged to say anything. These gentlemen should have waited for my arrival. I have bail papers here.”

With few words and even less fuss, he magicked her out of prison, hailed her taxi and galloped off to save another fly that had been caught up in the judicial system. All Sylvia wanted was a hot bath, a good feed and sleep. But there was something she needed to do first.

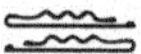

As usual, the London streets were slick with rain, but the deluge had reduced to a drizzle which settled on her purple beret. Sylvia ducked into the shop on the corner and changed a five-pound note for coins. She thanked mother Mary that the phone box was vacant and called Australia. There was no reply. She wondered what was happening over there. Where was Wiz?

The Underground train was empty apart from a pack of punks who were scratching slogans on the walls of the carriage. The feeling of dread that had clutched at Sylvia's heart and guts faded a little as she arrived at Wiggles on Clipper Street. It was a small hairdressers lost in a row of shabby shop fronts. She pushed the door and entered. A buck-toothed girl with a messy beehive read a magazine in a chair. She jumped up and stubbed out her cigarette as Sylvia entered.

"How can I help you?"

"I'm looking for Jez."

"I'm Jez," she replied, looking like she might do a runner any minute.

"Hi, I'm Sylvia. You made a very important call for me to Australia."

Recognition spilled across Jez's face.

"Oh yes, hi! Did everything get sorted? I sent you Mr Pointer-Smith. He always gets me off."

"You sent...? But didn't you call Australia? You spoke to Wiz, right?"

"I did call Australia, 'cept no one answered at first. I tried a few times, then a lady answered with a funny accent and said she didn't know what I was talking about and could I kindly stop calling."

Sylvia relayed the number again, checking it against the one Jez had written down.

"How strange. Well, then I have even more to thank you for." Sylvia paused and replayed Jez's words. "Gets you off? For what?"

"Ah, just a bit of shop-lifting."

"Oh, I see."

"And once I accidentally broke a lock and ended up in Tesco's."

"Right..."

"I was hungry, you know, after..."

"After?"

"After my brief career in prostitution."

"Flicking fringes, Jez, I'm glad you have a good job now. How long have you worked here?"

"Five weeks. It's the longest one I've had."

"Where did you train?"

"Longshot Secure Youth Training Centre."

"I've not heard of that school."

"Well, it's a good job. It's a hellhole. Shall I put the kettle on?"

The women chatted like old friends. Jez was eager to hear about Australia and what 'nihil mali capillos' meant. When she found out Sylvia knew Vitale Crassoon, her teeth seemed to jut out even further with astonishment.

When it was time for Sylvia to leave, she promised that she would visit Jez again and headed back out into the street. The mantle of questions threw layers over her mind, fogging her thinking. A horn blared and a steady stream of cars trundled past, spewing out exhaust fumes to add to the sludgy city air that was now choking her. She longed to throw off the suffocating cloak of this place, heavy with the shadows of mystery, and return to the blue, clear skies of Perth. She made her way home to the guesthouse where Mrs Grimshaw came out of her kitchen to greet her.

"And where do you think you've been, young lady? I thought you were coming home! Then not a word from you."

"It's been a long..."

"I've had the boys in blue here asking about you. I have never had a criminal staying in my guesthouse. Look at the state of you. If you're in trouble, you need to come clean with me, or find somewhere else to stay."

Sylvia's knees wobbled and the walls pulsated.

"Mr Grimshaw hasn't been able to eat a sausage since last week with the worry."

Fatigue and emotion surged.

"Even Mr Brown from table 2 has been concerned about you!"

Sylvia's body folded onto the bottom step of the staircase. Her eyes filled and overflowed.

"Oh dear, oh pet, come here." Mrs Grimshaw softened and took her in her arms. She guided Sylvia to her room and sat with her, rubbing her back and handing her tissues.

It took Mrs Grimshaw an hour to console Sylvia, who wept noiselessly. It was a skill learnt from her days in the orphanage. The nuns did not tolerate self-pity, and although tears and snot flowed, Sylvia never made as much as a hiccup. When the floods of tears ran dry, Sylvia's words took over, and she relayed the events of the last few days. Mrs Grimshaw took pity and even though it was now mid-afternoon, she cooked Sylvia her breakfast with an extra-large pot of tea.

"Thank you, Mrs Grimshaw. You've been so kind."

"No worries, pet. I'll run you a nice hot bath and get you an early night."

23

The chirpy breakfast call from Mrs Grimshaw dragged Sylvia from a dream of nesting prison cells. Each one smaller than the last until she was curled up with her knees under her chin, barely able to breathe. She was grateful for the release from its clutches. Another breakfast piled high with bacon, sausages, eggs, toast, tomatoes, beans and potato cakes arrived on the table. But it only served to remind Sylvia of the myriad of problems she had to solve. Along with the news that her father had, in effect, killed a man, and her mother's side of the family were evil, and she'd lost the salon and the police falsely suspected her of actual bodily harm. Bite by bite, she made her way through her breakfast, but the pile of unsavoury problems remained.

Sylvia returned to her room and stared at herself in the mirror. Her hair had grown fast, thick and black and spiky, looking more like a punk than one of Sammy's beloved Teddy Boys. She opened her case for her scissors to trim the sides so she didn't look like a fuzzball. As she clipped around her left ear, she thought about Vitale and the salon. She gave her head a blast with the hairdryer to blow away the loose hairs. She knew it was Arthur who set her up. It was him she needed to investigate and quick too, before he left the crime scene. She recalled the night he waited for her here at the guesthouse. He must have planted the depilatory cream as evidence in her case that night. She dashed down to the parlour and prayed Mrs Grimshaw hadn't been too thorough in her cleaning. Sylvia looked under the armchair, then felt down the sides. Bingo! She pulled out a receipt which gave her just the information she needed. She forgot all about her half snipped hair and grabbed up her case and coat. The taxi driver took one look at her and shook his head, mumbling something about 'yoof these days.'

The curtains of Crasson's salon had been replaced with an angry pink fabric. New matching towels and large vases of bright flowers added a forced cheerfulness to the salon. Mandy came rushing up to Sylvia.

"Sylvia! What are you doing here? I was so worried about you. Vitale refused to let us see you or even mention your name." She grabbed Sylvia's arm and pulled her out of the salon.

"He'll burst a pipe if he sees you. He has been impossible. Oh, you have hair! I love that look!" She spun Sylvia around, admiring her lopsided haircut. "That looks wicked!"

"Oh, ah, thanks," Sylvia replied, only just remembering her hasty exit from the guesthouse.

"Listen, I need to ask you some questions. Can you meet me on your break at the coffee shop?"

"OK, I'll see you in half an hour."

When Mandy got her tea break, she joined Sylvia at one of the cafés on Carnaby Street.

"I can't stay long. Monsieur is being interviewed by Tittle Tattle about the turbans. That's all the clients want at the moment. It's more like the rag trade in there these days. He's not happy."

"Did Thames Water come and test the water?"

"Yes, you were right. It was contaminated with lead. They reckon the pipes dated back to the 1800s!"

"And there's been no more disasters with the dye?"

"No, they're all working fine. Even Lalula Von Crump came in yesterday!"

"Is Arthur still around?"

"Yes, he's leaving tomorrow. He gives me the creeps. Be glad to see the back of him."

"Yes, me too. I know he set me up."

"Look, I don't know anything about that. The police have been sniffing around. I'd better go. And don't come into the salon if you want to keep your life. Monsieur knows you were consorting with Humphrey."

"But you know, I just went to interview him about the dye."

Mandy shrugged, "Sorry, Sylv, I gotta go."

Sylvia walked away from the coffee shop. She wandered along the street. Punks littered any available low wall or car bonnet, strutting their eccentricity for public view, inviting and rejecting attention. She noted with a sense of irony a couple who had shaved their heads in black and white stripes. The winter wind slapped across her face, but for once the sky was not covered in a grey blanket. It was dotted with clouds that allowed moments of dazzling sunlight darts to arrive on earth.

Sylvia was effectively banned from the salon, and Arthur kept Vitale close by. Any ideas of waltzing in and proving her innocence were gone. She needed more proof that Arthur had set her up. He must have had inside help to get to the dyes. Her training had taught her the rudiments of surveillance. It was time, she decided, to put it into practice. She needed a disguise, and the punks had given her an idea. She ducked into a second-hand shop and picked out a black miniskirt and a faded black t-shirt. Across the road, a shoe shop provided her with a pair of Doc Martens and fishnet stockings. She got changed in the toilets of a pub and applied long slicks of black kohl below and beyond her eyes. A dark mulberry lipstick finished the look. All she needed now was a leather jacket, but her dwindling pounds were never going to stretch that far. She ordered a brandy and black at the bar and took it to a window seat. Outside, a group of punks were laughing at one of their friends, messing up his hair. The guy was young and gangly, acne splattered his face. He swore at them and jutted out his chin along with his middle finger and stomped off. He sported a huge mohawk, except the spikes flopped to one side and then the other. What she wouldn't give to get her hands on that hair! Or that jacket, too, she thought. Bingo! She dashed out of the pub and pursued him up the street. He stopped to light a cigarette and she caught up with him.

"Hey, mate! Excuse me!"

He slid his eyes to her and inhaled deeply on his fag.

"I saw you arguing with your friends back there."

Expletives peppered his response about so-called friends.

"You know, I could give you some advice about your hair. I have a secret tip on keeping it in place."

"Just leave me alone, you bleeding wacko," he responded. Yet he still stood there, looking at her.

"Listen, I'm a hairdresser, I can give you the best mohawk in London. I'll make it stand up for days, weeks on end, and all I ask is if I can borrow your jacket."

He looked down at his black leather jacket decorated with safety pins and chains. His eyes widened.

"What have you got to lose? Meet me at Wiggles on Clipper Street in one hour."

An hour later, she finished her third a cup of tea with Jez. The door shoved open and the spotty, angular punk came in with an exaggerated swagger.

"I'm so glad you came! I never asked you your name."

"Shaun," he grunted.

"Nice to meet you, Shaun. I'm Sylvia, this is Jez. Take a seat here."

He nodded at them, mumbled, "Yep," and slouched in the chair. He folded his arms while the women poked at the crumpled mohawk. Sylvia took him to the sink and washed out the stale hair spray, lumps of glue and even twigs that Shaun had used to scaffold the spikes. She then twisted the long hair on top and shaved the sides of his head. Now the sides were even, she tackled the mohawk. She chatted to Shaun as she worked. His answers began with monosyllabic grunts, but by the time she had separated the spikes, he had told her about his apprenticeship at a factory. As she applied the gel, he told her about the crush he had on a girl called Patsy. Sylvia had to interrupt his flow to tell him how to use potato starch to keep the mohawk stiff. As she sprayed the spikes blue (she already knew his favourite colour) he told her about his mum who'd been depressed for years.

"There," said Sylvia and she placed her hand on Shaun's shoulders and looked at his reflection. Shaun laughed.

"You wait until the lads see this! Sylvia, you are the fricking queen of hair!"

Sylvia gave a regal bow.

"A fair exchange for the loan of your jacket?"

Shaun shrugged it off without hesitation.

"Give me your address, and I'll drop it to you when I'm done."

Shaun wrote it down and handed it to her. He removed a few coins, keys and his fags from the jacket pocket and transferred them to his jeans. He lit one up and strutted out of the shop, catching himself in the shop windows as he swaggered down the street, his blue mohawk erect and proud.

"Thanks for your help, Jez."

Sylvia put on the jacket.

"How do I look?"

"Like a right rebel." They laughed.

"Right, I'm off to find out who's been messing with Vitale Crassoon, and with me."

The women said goodbye and Sylvia took the tube back to Soho. She walked up and down Carnaby Street, seamlessly blending in with the eclectic shoppers and sightseers. At 4.00 p.m., she saw Mandy head home. She was grateful that the Doc Martens were so comfortable, and that she was used to standing, because another hour passed before Arthur left the salon at 5.00 p.m. along with Vitale and Ronaldo, who walked in the opposite direction to Arthur after saying goodbye. She kicked away from the wall and bent over to tie a lace as Arthur passed her. Fixing her gaze on his back, she set after him. Sylvia feared he would take a taxi and she would have to follow him in another, but instead he walked fast and loped into a Tesco supermarket. He navigated the aisles while Sylvia flicked through a magazine. He bought a tub of ice cream, chocolate topping and a bottle of whisky. With a most inelegant carrier bag, he was swallowed by the Underground. The pedestrians gave Sylvia a wide berth, and she dived down the steps, craning her neck to keep him in view. No one seemed surprised or gave chase when this female punk jumped over the barrier to the platform without paying. She daringly boarded the same carriage, using his reflection to watch him in the window. After twenty-five minutes, they disembarked at Cresswell. It was quieter than the Inner London blast. Blocks of flats blotted out the darkening sky. Scruffy kids occupied the playground with smoking mums jiggling prams. Arthur turned into one of the blocks and started up a dark, peeling, pee-drenched stairwell. She could hear his breath puffing by the fourth floor. She tiptoed behind him as quietly as possible, just catching his jacket tails as he turned the corners. He slowed and retrieved a hankie, wiping his brow. He cleaned his hands and inhaled its freshness, then stepped over a dried turd, gagging into his hankie. He left the foul stairwell, but Sylvia could not follow him along the exposed walkway. She peeked around the blood-streaked wall, punched in several spots, and watched him bang on a door. The door opened.

"Hi Mandy, sorry I'm late..."

Mandy? He was visiting Mandy? Sylvia rushed to the door. Crouching, she inched open the letter box and just glimpsed Arthur disappearing into a room. She put her ear at the door... nothing. In shock, she backed away and lent over the railings. She saw a gang kicking up the gravel with their BMX's, taunting an old lady as she walked past with her shopping trolley in the street-lamp's glow. So, Mandy was in on this too. The sense of betrayal permeated her; Wiz, Vitale, Arthur and now Mandy. It cut like a blade, each one, all the people she had trusted one by one slashed at her heart. She didn't know what to do. At least she still had Sammy, Jez and the Grimshaws. Sylvia waited, chewing her nails, wondering what to do. She watched the unruly boys harassing the locals. The London drizzle set in again, and her fishnet knees were jumping up and down in protest from the cold. She traipsed with heavy boots back down the filthy stairs. The boys were still hooning their bikes, laughing like kookaburras. As she walked past them, a wiry teenager glared at her, snorted and spat a sticky blob of phlegm on the pavement.

"Oi, show us your tits!"

Sylvia ignored him but instead of fear, she felt a pang of anger shoot up and down her spine. The lad stepped up to her and grabbed her arm.

"Hey, I'm talking to you, cow."

She shrugged him off.

"Leave me alone," she snapped.

The boy laughed.

"Ha ha, what kind of accent is that, 'lave may aloan!' Weirdo!"

Sylvia carried on walking but the boy followed fast right behind her and jumped in front, blocking her path.

"Nice jacket... hand it over."

He pulled a knife and pressed it to the side of her neck, a manic smile on his face. She felt the prick in her skin and her fury broke free. She whipped her scissors out of her pocket and elbowed her attacker under the chin. He fell back, and she flung her right Doc Marten into his crotch. The other kids scattered to a safe distance and watched as Sylvia grasped the boy's hair in her fist and held the scissors to his face.

"Ninth commandment of UGH: Never mess with a hairdresser who's had a bad day." She slashed at his hair with abandon and lastly snipping under her hand to release him from her grip. His head fell with a thud against the pavement and she dropped the hair clippings on his face.

Sylvia couldn't remember how she got back to Elephant and Castle, but once back in the familiar street, her heartbeat lowered to a regular rhythm. But as she approached the door of the guesthouse, her heart stopped, her knees went dippy and her mouth dry. Sammy was waiting for her. Night was well and truly upon the city and the street lamps cast a smoky light.

"Sammy!"

She ran up to him, relieved to see a friendly face. A face she really liked. A face she wanted to see more of. Sammy stood up, stuck his head out and squinted at her.

"Sylvia? Jesus, what have you done?"

She put her head on his arm. But he recoiled with a look of disgust.

"How could you do this?"

"Do what, Sammy?"

"Go punk on me."

"I haven't. It's just a..."

"Why do you think I got this black eye, eh? Why do you think I got arrested? There's a war out there between us."

"Between who?"

"Between us and the punks. Jeez, don't you read the newspapers? You're not the person I thought you was." He pushed past her.

"Sammy, I can explain."

He backed away from her, looking her up and down with contempt, shook his head and turned his back on her and loped down the street.

"Sammy," she called after him, "Sammy!"

If Mrs Grimshaw was around, Sylvia didn't see her. She ran straight to her room, tears streaming. She dropped the crumpled jacket over the Doc Martens she'd kicked off and curled up in the torn fishnets, mini skirt and T-shirt. She didn't care that her makeup bled black rivers onto Mrs Grimshaw's crisp white pillowcase. She stayed in her bed all night and right through breakfast.

24

At lunchtime, Mrs Grimshaw tapped at the door. When she got no reply from within, she gently let herself in. She sat on the edge of her bed and put a hand on Sylvia's back, patting her softly as one would a baby.

"Tell me what happened, pet."

"I blew it with Sammy. He took one look at me dressed like this and ran."

"If Sammy can't see the gem you are on the inside, then he's not worthy of you."

"And Mandy, I thought she was my friend, but she's not. She's in it with Arthur."

"You've had a rough time, but you're not in prison now, and I believe in you. You'll sort it out."

Mrs Grimshaw stood up with a sigh to get on with her myriad of tasks. Sylvia gave her a weak smile.

Sylvia stayed in bed, going over the events of the last two weeks. Later that afternoon, Mrs Grimshaw tapped on Sylvia's door again.

"Those coppers are back. Hop up and get dressed. They're waiting in the parlour."Sylvia dressed and padded down the stairs, her heart beating with her footsteps. Mrs Grimshaw had shown DI Grouse and his junior into the parlour and offered them tea.

"Thank you very much, ma'am. A couple of biccies wouldn't go amiss neither," he asked with a raise of his eyebrows.

"Right you are. Sylvia'll be down shortly. She's had a rough patch, go easy on her. Ah, here she is!"

She bustled off and passed Sylvia in the hall, giving her shoulders a squeeze. Sylvia took a deep breath and entered.

"Hello."

Sylvia hovered in the doorway.

"Good morning, Mrs Scutlash. Take a seat, won't you?"

Sylvia perched on the edge of the chair. Her injured hand cradled in the other.

"I'm happy to inform you that all charges of actual bodily harm have been dropped."

She let out a long puff of relief. "Thank Mother Mary and Joseph for that!"

Mrs Grimshaw arrived with a tray. She set it on the table.

"Did I hear right? Charges dropped?"

Sylvia nodded.

"Well, finally the London Constabulary have come to their senses! As if this girl would've harmed anyone."

"We've brought you your case back as it's no longer needed for evidence."

Sylvia gratefully took her leather case back and stroked the lid. "Do you know who did it?" she asked.

"When we re-interviewed the driver, he admitted that you had not had access to the hair dye the afternoon you picked them up and, in fact, had handed them fully sealed to Amanda Makepeace." D.I. Grouse explained.

"Mandy?"

"Yes, Mr Crassoon's receptionist. We have her in for questioning. All evidence is pointing toward her. Have you got anything to add, Mrs Scutlash?"

Sylvia recalled how she followed Arthur to Mandy's flat. How betrayed she felt. But what did it really prove? Arthur was the mastermind. If Mandy had anything to do with this, it was at Arthur's bidding. Putting Mandy in jail was like colouring hair after it had been cut off.

"Mrs Scutlash?" DI Grouse waited for her response.

"No, nothing to add."

"Oh well, we'll keep investigating," he said as though Sylvia might have saved him the trouble. Sylvia bit her lip. She couldn't let Mandy take the blame, end up in prison or have a record.

"Actually, there is one more thing, Inspector."

"Oh yes, what's that?" he brightened.

"Did you question Arthur Sprout?"

"Arthur Spout? Let me see." He rifled through his miniature note book.

"No, the name is Sprout, S P R O U T. He was in the salon that day. He is the brother of Frank Sprout, my father."

His junior whispered something in his ear.

"We had an Arthur Scout talk to us, very helpful he was. You say he's your uncle?"

"Yes, and he had a good reason to frame me for this."

"And why would that be?" asked Grouse.

Sylvia hesitated. "It's... it's an old family feud."

"I see. There was something familiar about that man. Bean, make a note to look into this Arthur character."

"What will happen to Mandy?"

"If Mr Crassoon decides to press charges and we have evidence, then she'll be arrested."

"It's not her. It's Arthur you need to be looking at. He's trouble that man. I mean, who would turn in his own niece?"

"Yes, well, you can rest assured that we'll do our job, Mrs Scutlash, and I can see you are still rather unwell. You should thank your lucky stars you're off the hook. Thanks for your time."

He nodded to Mrs Grimshaw.

"Cheerio, come on Bean, you can bring the biccie with you."

Mrs Grimshaw let them out the front and returned to the parlour where Sylvia was staring through the window.

"What's the trouble, pet?"

"Arthur bloody Sprout, he's the trouble, Sammy Lock, men, they're all bloody trouble!" she shook her head. "I'd better go, Mrs G, I've got to see a few people."

"I don't think that's wise. You're still as weak as a southern cup of tea."

"I'll be fine Mrs G."

Sylvia stood but tambourines went off in her head and the table seemed to slant in the opposite direction to the floor. Mrs Grimshaw caught her elbow and steadied her.

"Right, young lady, back to bed. I'll bring you up some tea."

Sylvia surrendered and trudged back up to her room.

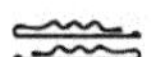

Later that afternoon, Sylvia woke from a deep sleep and wandered down to the dining room. Mrs Grimshaw was delighted to see some colour had come back into her face and sat her down with a glass of orange juice and a Club biscuit. Sylvia held the brooch in the palm of her good hand.

"What's up, pet? You still seem down. Aren't you happy the charges are dropped?"

"Yes, except the wrong person is getting the blame." Sylvia felt terrible that Mandy was in that awful place.

"I'm sure the police will clear that up." Mrs Grimshaw patted her on her knee.

"There's something else. Why so glum?" The force of Mrs G's unfettered maternal instinct was released on Sylvia.

"I forgot my birthday on Monday. And I don't have a single person to celebrate it with."

"Flipping 'eck, lass! Why didn't you say? Right, I'll get a cake on. We'll pretend it's today!"

"Don't go to any bother, Mrs G, smells like you are already busy in the kitchen." The smell of fried onions wafted into the dining room.

"Is Mr G making sausages?"

"No, I wish! It's the Onion Enthusiasts, they pay me in produce. Do you think there is an onion porridge recipe? I must ask them. So, what are your plans for tomorrow?"

Sylvia turned the brooch over. The inscription read OCB 0703. She showed it to Mrs Grimshaw.

"Evie said this was the number of a bank vault, but there was a strong chance she was speaking nonsense. What do you think OCB means?"

"OCB? It could mean anything."

Mrs Grimshaw looked into the distance and chewed her lip.

"Ah, hang on! The Old Capital Bank. Yes, Mr G's grandfather had one for his sausage recipes. He won awards, you know, best Yorkshire sausage for ten years in a row."

The doorbell rang.

"Who could this be? We're full of Onion Enthusiasts and I've got the Hoover Hounds coming tomorrow. Can't take any walk-ins. Hang on a tick."

At the reception desk, two men stood waiting. Sylvia gazed into the black onyx jewel; veins of silver ran through it.

"Sylvia, two men are here to see you. They say they're related."

An instinct told her to pocket the brooch. Mrs Grimshaw ushered Colin and Donald into the dining room.

"Hey cuz! Good to see you looking better!" Colin held out his arms, as if expecting a hug.

"Hello Colin, Donald, what a surprise!"

Having a family was a surprise for Sylvia. Two in one room was a miracle. It was a dream come true, so why didn't it sit right? She dismissed the jagged feeling. This was what she'd been waiting for, finally, to find out about her ancestry, about herself.

"Would you like some tea?" Mrs Grimshaw was still standing in the doorway.

"Smashing, ta," said Donald.

They sat at the table, smiling at each other awkwardly. Sylvia wanted to ask a million questions but she didn't know how to start.

"Nice place," "nice day," "nice of you to come," they said in unison. They chuckled and fell into silence.

"How are you feeling?" Donald ventured.

"Oh, much better, thanks."

"Good, good," he said. "It was a bit touch and go there."

Birds chirped about their business outside the window.

"What..." "When..." "Who...?" they chorused together again.

To their relief, Mrs Grimshaw arrived with a tray of tea and more Club biscuits.

"Do you live in London?" she asked.

"Och, no we're from Scotland."

“Beautiful part of the world. Are you in the city for long?” Mrs Grimshaw was good at small talk.

“No, just a few more days. Getting Grandmother’s affairs in order.”

“I’m so sorry to hear about your loss, must be hard being so far away from her.”

“Aye, it’s no been easy.”

“Nothing was ever easy with Evie.” Colin spoke for the first time, laughing at his joke.

Donald gave him a stern stare. He glanced sideways at Mrs Grimshaw.

“Aye, well, we can’t stay for long. Sylvia, we came to ask if you would join us for dinner tomorrow night?”

“Aye, a family dinner, for old times’ sake,” added Colin.

Sylvia agreed and took down the address of the restaurant. She was frustrated. She still had no more information on her mother or grandmother. The cousins left with their strange Scottish words. Mrs Grimshaw joined her at the front door.

“I see all sorts in this boarding house, but there’s something not right about those two.”

Sylvia nodded. “I never trust a man with more hair around his neck than on his head.”

They closed the door.

25

Sylvia was thrilled to feel her former strength on waking the next day. The previous evening, Mrs Grimshaw had baked a big cake and asked all the guests to the parlour to sing 'happy birthday'. They presented her with a catering size pack of Yorkshire tea and lifetime VIP guest status. Mr Brown from table 2 gave her a purple chiffon scarf and a stiff hug.

She removed the bulky bandage and replaced the healing puncture hole with an ordinary Band-Aid. With her beret at an angle and her new matching scarf, she set off.

The Old Capital Bank dominated the street. Sylvia stood in front of the gigantic bronze doors. She entered the huge foyer, feeling unworthy of its grandness. The ornately tiled floor served as a gulf to cross between her and the teller. Her footsteps echoed as she made her way to a desk, each step magnified her insignificance. The clerk, another woman yet one of an utterly different species, asked how she could help in a superior tone.

"G'day Miss..." Sylvia looked at the gold label on the desk that said 'C.F.B. Forsyth', "Forsyth. I have a number."

"Yes, well, we all have a number, don't we? God gave us that the first time we committed a sin and bled our way into this world."

Sylvia had never agreed with the concept of sinning. She couldn't see why little babies were sinners, and had grown tired of the nuns' constant battle with sinning, then reckoning with penance and prayer. For a second, she wanted to flee, to leave the institution that loomed over her. But her tough nugget of determination, a muscle she had flexed often in the last few weeks, stopped her feet from moving.

"I believe my grandmother, who has recently passed, has a bank vault here."

The clerk eyed Sylvia from across her massive desk and visually scanned her body for firearms.

"Would you mind checking OCB 0703, please?"

"What is the name of the vaultee?"

Miss Forsyth said 'what' as if she was blowing out a candle.

"Evie Fraughton."

The clerk rose.

"Please take a seat whilst I locate the paperwork."

"W-h-ell thank you very much." Sylvia clipped to a leather chair that swamped her.

After fifteen minutes, Miss Forsyth returned. A forefinger signalled Sylvia over to her desk.

"The paperwork states that the vault can only be accessed by Mrs Evelyn Fraughton or by a Sylvia Sprout who shall be identified by a birth certificate. It also states that she must produce a specific item to further prove her eligibility."

It was a surprise to hear her name pronounced by C.F.B. Forsyth. She dug into her bag and pulled out her birth certificate. Miss Forsyth looked over the paperwork with pursed lips and through glasses that perched on the end of her nose.

"Splendid. And do you happen to have this specific item in your possession, Miss Sprout?"

"Do you mean this?"

Once again, she delved into her Mary Poppins bag. But the magic seemed to have gone. No matter how many crevices and pockets her fingers explored, the brooch was not there. Miss Forsyth looked on with her haughty stare. Sylvia turned her bag out onto the desk to the clerk's dismay.

"It was in here this morning." She checked her pockets. "It's a brooch. It must be back at the guesthouse. I've had it all my life."

"Indeed, the item is an Elizabethan onyx brooch."

"Elizabethan?"

Miss Forsyth raised her eyebrows in condescension. "I'm afraid access is only granted with the item described therein. I wish you a good day."

"But you've seen my birth certificate. You know I'm Sylvia, Evie's granddaughter."

"The terms are very clear, Miss Sprout. Good day to you."

Sylvia stuffed everything back into her handbag and stalked out of the bank. The short journey took an age, as she panicked on the whereabouts of the brooch. She rushed into the dining room of the guesthouse. But it was full of vacuum cleaners and their sellers. The leader was donned in a pink apron, demonstrating the newest features of the latest model, the Sucker 76. Mrs Grimshaw stood by the kitchen door, beaming.

"Ey up, pet, never seen my carpet so clean. How did you get on?"

"It's missing, the brooch. It's not in my bag. I had it in here this morning. I need to search the room."

"There isn't a speck of dust left in this room. I'm sure one of these gentlemen would have said something if they found it."

Sylvia rushed over to the sales rep by the window. The vacuum cleaner roared as he waltzed around the table. She had to get his attention, but the noise in the room was so loud he didn't hear her. Sylvia went to tap him on the back but he sidestepped as he navigated the machine around the furniture. His bottom lip clenched in his teeth. He was obviously passionate about this model, sliding it along the contours of the dormer window. In desperation, Sylvia dropped to her knees to search the floor. She crawled under the table, groping for the heirloom. The vacuum cleaner rounded the corner, the rep adeptly pulling the head back and forth. Sylvia scoured the floor, crawling further under the table. The noise was deafening. It lifted the carpet as every molecule of ancient dirt disappeared up its nozzle, along with the end of Sylvia's scarf that trailed on the carpet beside her. The greedy machine whipped it up, and Sylvia was yanked towards its hungry mouth. She yelped, her glasses flew off as she got whip lashed into the caw. The Sucker 77 made an ugly grunt as the side of her head blocked any further entry. The salesman's ecstasy interrupted, but he opened his eyes to see he had a major blockage and flicked off the switch. Sylvia choked, her eyes watered. The room grew quiet. "Help!" she wheezed.Mrs Grimshaw squawked and rushed over. She pulled the scarf from the jaws of the vacuum cleaner and loosened it from Sylvia's neck. The reps, having silenced their hoovers, gawked in astonishment.

"You all right?"

Sylvia nodded. "You should get one of these, Mrs G, very good suction," she croaked.She retrieved her glasses that had flown under the curtains. And there it was, her brooch. The pin had caught up in the fabric, hanging at an angle in the folds.

"I've found it!"

"How on earth did it get there?"

"Cursed thing! Search me. I don't have time to go back to the bank now, I've got to go to the salon."

Sylvia left to get dressed. She pinned the brooch onto her blouse, but took it off again. She already associated it with pain, and now choking. Instead, she pinned it onto her handbag.

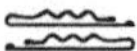

Sylvia had not spent her days recovering idly. Her mind had followed every twist and curl of the case until she worked out exactly what must be done, and what she must do for her own future. Arthur had been right about one thing. London was a tough place to be, but she had met some people who had found a place in her heart.

First stop, Clipper Street. Jez was in front of a mirror, back-combing her beehive. She tossed the comb down and greeted Sylvia with joy. "Where have you been?"

"It's a long story. How are you?"

"Been better, got the sack again," said Jez.

"Why, what did you do?"

"I told a customer to eff off when he tried to put his hand up my skirt."

"Bloody hell, Jez. Fair call." Sylvia shook her head in shock.

"You just don't get the right clientele around here. I bet that sort of thing never happens at Crassoons."

"Nobody deserves to be treated like that. Anyway, I've been thinking." Sylvia sat down and Jez followed suit. "Why don't you come to Australia? We could work together. Open a salon somewhere, Sydney, or even stay in Perth. What do you think?"

"Australia?" Jez blew out her lips. "That's a long way away."

"What have you got to lose? No funny business, mind. Neither of us needs any more time behind bars."

"But how can I afford it?"

Sylvia handed her an envelope. "Take this. It's all the pounds I have left, it'll be enough to get you to Oz. Come with me. I leave on Friday night. What do you say?"

"Tomorrow? I'll think about it," replied Jez with luminosity shining in her eyes.

"Oh, I do hope you come. Call me at the guesthouse. I've got to go to Vitale Crassoon's now to clear my name."

"Thanks Sylv, you're the bomb. Good luck!"

"There's one more thing. Can I buy a gift voucher for someone?"

"Sure. How much do you want to spend?" asked Jez.

Half an hour later, Sylvia arrived at the council estate address written on the scrap of paper and knocked on a shabby door. A woman opened it.

"G'day, is Shaun home?" Sylvia asked.

"Don't be daft. That snotty little shit ain't never home. Who are you?"

"I'm returning his jacket. He lent it me the other week."

"Did he now?" She looked Sylvia up and down.

"Yes, as a favour, it's a long story. I don't have time to explain."

"Oh, give it over then."

"Tell him, thank you. I left a note in the pocket. And a bottle of starch."

"A bottle of Scotch?" The woman's face lit up.

"No, starch."

"Oh, well righto. Ta ra."

She went to close the door, but Sylvia stopped her. "But I do have something for you. He's a good lad, you know. Cares about you a lot."

"What are you, his new girlfriend or something?"

Sylvia chuckled. "No, though I could do worse! He helped me out, and well... this is for you."

The woman looked suspicious, but Sylvia thrust an envelope in her hand.

"A voucher, for a haircut at Wiggles on Clipper Street. You'd be amazed at what a little pampering can do. Treat yourself—you deserve it."

Sylvia left before the woman could respond and headed back into the city centre. She ducked down a small street in Soho. Wigwag was open and offered a full display of wigs to buy or hire, and now also ready wrapped turbans. The owner remembered her and they chatted. She dropped Vitale's name in the conversation and mentioned how she was involved in the KKK fashion show. Suitably impressed, he was happy to furnish Sylvia with answers to a couple of pointed questions and a copy of a receipt he had issued less than two weeks earlier.

There was one more stop before Crassoon's.

"Hey, Humpo!"

"Hey! How you hanging?

"Like a ponytail on a Saturday night. You?" Sylvia joked.

"Cruising along, you know?"

"It's time you and me sorted things out with Vitale. Tell him what happened to Mimi," she explained. "And we have to buy him a gift on the way."

Humphrey looked uneasy, but Sylvia tilted her head to one side. "Please!"

"Sure, anything for you, Sylvia-Sue. Guys, look after the shop, I got business to attend to."

Humphrey crooked his elbow for Sylvia to take.

"What's this gift?" Humphrey asked.

"Guess!"

"Are you thinking cuff-links?"

"No."

"A pair of platforms? He sure needs the height."

"No," Sylvia giggled.

"Um, an electric moustache groomer? Or a monkey that understands French?"

"No," she laughed, "but you're getting close. Here we are."

The pet shop gathered together an eclectic mix of beasts. Terrapins rubbed shoulders with budgerigars and kittens.

"Monsieur needs another dog, we're here to buy him a Fifi!"

Humphrey rubbed his hands together in glee.

"You're a genius!"

There was a pen of squirming hairballs, tying each other in knots as they tumbled and tottered around. After much deliberation, they picked out a pure white poodle with soft brown eyes.

"He's going to love her." They bumped shoulders and grinned at each other in excitement.

"You ready?"

"Sure am!"

Carnaby Street was its usual buzz of colour and crazy. She'd grown used to the clamour, might even miss it. Another gust of icy wind blew rain drops down her collar. She wouldn't miss the cold, though. Sylvia hesitated before she opened the door of Crassoon's. She was as nervous now as the first time she came here.

"Can you stay out here with Fifi? I'll come and get you," she asked Humphrey.

"Don't be long, I don't want Fifi to cark it from being wet and cold."

The bell tinkled and, as usual, Vitale was remonstrating Ronaldo.

"Mon Dieu!" Vitale collapsed in a chair when he saw her. "Get that mole out of here!"

"Wait, Vitale, let me explain..." Sylvia chimed.

"Mandy, call my lawyer, the police. This girl 'as tried to ruin me."

"Actually, she saved your derrière, Monsieur," Ronaldo piped up. "She came up with the turbans, remember?"

"But zee hair remover cream, I still 'ave nightmares."

"That wasn't me. *Please,* let me explain. The police have dropped the charges," said Sylvia.

Mandy looked terrified, ready to dial the police.

"Monsieur?"

Vitale waved his comb at her. "Non, non, no more blue bodies in here. What do you want to say, Sylvia?"

"When I tasted the tap water, I realised there was something wrong with it, it was contaminated with lead."

"I know all this, Sylvia. Zee plumber 'as fixed up zee pipes and zee colours are working like a perfectly cooked souffle."

"And I believe the depilatory cream was planted by Arthur. He was setting me up."

"Nonsense! What proof do you 'ave for this?"

"What evidence?" She paused. "I noticed Arthur was distressed at my discovery of the water contamination that Thursday evening."

She paced up the salon floor.

"When Mandy prepared the Black Velvet Hole from the batch I picked up, Arthur managed to 'obtain' the key to the cupboard. Mandy?" Sylvia swivelled to Mandy, who was frozen.

"Yes?" she whispered.

"Am I right in saying that the key to the dye cupboard was missing that Friday morning, but when you checked the cupboard, it was, in fact, unlocked?"

"Yes," Mandy barely said the word.

"Non!" Vitale shot Mandy a glance of contempt and disappointment.

“Yes, Monsieur. I have reason to believe Mandy was an accomplice.”

“Why didn’t you tell me?” he wailed to Mandy.

“Arthur asked me for the key to investigate the dyes. Then I thought it was all OK, because it was the water. But when the... the incident happened, I was scared I’d get the blame. I’m not an accomplice. I wouldn’t. Sylvia, why are you saying such a thing? She’s lying, Monsieur, you know I wouldn’t do anything to hurt you!”

“Then why did I see Arthur going to your flat in Cresswell? I followed him there, Mandy.”

“I don’t live in Cresswell! I don’t know what you’re talking about. I’ve already been at the police station for hours.”

“Where do you live then?” Sylvia asked, her flow broken.

“In Finchley, look, here’s my address.”

She rummaged around in her handbag for proof. Sylvia barely contained her surprise. If Mandy didn’t live there, then who did? Mandy handed her a gas bill.

“Finchley, yes, I see that now.” Sylvia winced.

“For heaven’s sake. Sylvia, I could ‘ave told you this!”

Sylvia was confused, she stammered. “Right, sorry about that, Mands, my mistake.”

“Really, Sylvia. You are not making any sense!” Vitale reprimanded.

“I saw Arthur visit a woman. He called her Mandy. I assumed. I’m really sorry, Mandy. But this is all on Arthur, I assure you. May I continue?”

Mandy nodded. Sylvia felt rattled by the mistake. She ran over events in her mind.

“I believe Arthur broke into the salon that night and laced the dyes with depilatory cream.”

“Objection! That is not proof, merely circumspection,” Vitale yelled.

"When Arthur readily had a solution for the disaster, what was it?"

"Wigs!" Vitale exclaimed.

"And were there any wigs to be had in London on the morning of Friday 18th November?"

"Non, there were no wigs! You looked for them and there were no wigs."

"And, ladies and gentlemen," said Sylvia, back in her stride. "I have here an invoice from Wigwag, a local shop that supplies wigs, dated 18th November 1977, in the name of Arthur Sprout, who hired all 25 wigs."

She pulled the invoice from her case and waved it in the air. Everyone gasped.

"In addition, Arthur was waiting for me the night of the fashion show at my lodgings. He left behind him a receipt from Boots..." She pulled the scrap of paper from her case. "For depilatory cream, purchased on Monday morning when I was here at this very salon!"

She let the facts sink in for a moment.

"Arthur Sprout attempted to sabotage Vitale Crassoon and blame it on me so he would inherit the Wavy Lady Hair Salon. I rest my case."

The salon staff looked on wide-eyed. Mandy put her hand to her mouth.

"I apologise, ma cherie. I don't know why I doubted you. Arzur can be very charming sometimes."

"Apology accepted, Monsieur."

"Zee police, 'ave you told them?"

"I'll be sending my report to D.I. Grouse, but I suspect Arthur is long gone by now. There is one other thing to clear up."

She signalled for Humphrey to come in. He raised his eyes, as if to say 'about time', and manoeuvred the dog carrier into the shop. The staff gasped.

“I’ve come to say sorry, Vitale, about Mimi,” said Humphrey.

Vitale’s moustache quivered and tears sprung to his eyes.

“It was your dodgy water that killed Mimi. I only gave her a drink. I didn’t kill her on purpose,” Humphrey continued.

“You didn’t?”

“No, Monsieur, of course not!”

Vitale looked at Humphrey, then Sylvia and to the sink.

“Mon Dieu, I ‘ave been getting a lot wrong these days.”

“We wondered if you could find a seat in the salon for…” He opened the carry case at his feet. “Fifi?”

A little black nose peaked out. Vitale shrieked and shrunk down to the floor. He crawled towards the warm white body curled up in the case.

“Fifi?” he whispered.

He put his tools into his breast pocket and with candy floss soft hands, picked up the puppy and held her to his cheek. The puppy whined and then licked Vitale’s face. The staff erupted into laughter, the little dog chewing on Vitale’s moustache. Humphrey and Sylvia smiled at each other.

“‘Umphrey, I forgive you.” Vitale kissed him on both cheeks and hugged him with his free arm, “Let’s celebrate!”

Vitale took everyone to the pub and bought drinks. But Sylvia’s night was not over. She said her goodbyes and walked the short distance to Soho.

26

Sylvia paused outside the Roasted Rook in Soho. It had been a long day, and she was tired in her still weak state. Her scalp tingled and wondered if this sensation was a premonition. She took a big breath and stepped inside. Donald and Colin were already seated. They both stood up and pulled out a chair, fussing over her with 'och's' and 'ayes'. The waiter poured fizzing wine into a flute and before she could say a word, they were toasting Evie Fraughton.

"So, I'm sure you mentioned it in the hospital, but I was a bit out of it. How are you related?"

"We're brothers, see?" They smiled, showing identically crooked teeth.

"No, I mean, related to Evie, to me? My mother was an only child."

"She had a brother, don't you know? His name was Denny."

A hot prickle ran up the back of her neck.

"Take a peek at the menu, lassie. What do you fancy?"

"How did she have a brother?" Sylvia pursued.

"Rolled herring? My favourite. Or a salad... girls like you ought to watch their weight."

"He was more of a half-brother," said Donald.

"A half-brother?"

"Well, more of a step-brother. Denny was Mickey Manic's boy."

"Who's Mickey Manic?" asked Sylvia. The conversation was taking a nonsensical, nightmarish feeling.

"And for main? Grilled chops or stuffed duck, duckie?" Colin roared with laughter.

"Och, I'm surprised Evie didn't mention him." Donald rubbed his chin.

"She didn't."

Sylvia's mind was churning, along with her gut. This wasn't what she wanted, what she'd imagined as a family reunion, a patched together, jumbled lineage. She'd come for bloodlines, to find her people, her roots.

"Who is Mickey Manic?"

"Och, he and Evie went back years," Colin said.

"Went back? You mean they were together? Married?"

The waiter approached.

"I'll have the golden glazed lamb with fries, he'll have the lucky duck stew also with fries. She'll have the twice roasted pigeon with mash." Donald instructed the waiter and snapped the menu shut.

"Where were we? Oh yes, the family tree. Mickey and Evie..."

"Mickey and Evie were sitting in a tree, K I S S I N Gee!" Colin sang.

Sylvia's scalp itched. Colin's high-pitched voice gave her a headache. She poured a glass of water and drank it.

"They were... lovers?" Donald and Colin nodded vigorously.

"And Denny? Was he their love-child?" She was clutching at hairs.

"Of course, Evie loved Denny," said Donald.

"Aye, worshipped him," Colin winked and Donald stared at him hard.

"But he wasn't of her loins, no. Denny arrived at the Lively Lady at the same time as Mickey. Denny was about ten, I reckon."

"Never walked out though, did he?" Colin folded his arms. "Aye, carried out most nights."

"They fell in love, see," Donald continued. "And lived happily ever after."

"Happily?" Colin winced.

"So Denny wasn't Evie's son?" Sylvia struggled to follow.

"Not by blood, but beer is thicker than blood, aye!" Colin cackled at his joke.

"Fer God's sake, shut your trap, Col! Forgive this blithering eejit, love. Thinks he's funny. Your dear grandmother took that boy under her apron like she'd squeezed him out herself."

"How old was Angie, my mum, then?" She needed to know about her. The conversation was slipping out of her hands like a freshly caught trout.

"Your Mam was born a few years later, before Mickey pickled every swimmer he possessed!" Colin leered. He didn't seem to be able to say a word that wasn't coarse or nasty.

"That makes him your granddaddy," Donald added.

"Is he still alive, uncle Denny, your dad?"

"Our Pappy? Och, no, lassie, He wasn't actually our daddy. He died of gout a fair few years ago."

She was losing the thread, their strange words sending her off course.

"Not your Pappy? but I thought ... your mother...?" Sylvia desperately wanting to untangle the threads.

"Aye, he married our Ma when we were 6 or 7."

"So you're not related to my grandmother, and neither was my uncle who was not related to my mother?"

She stood up. This was not what she had imagined. This raggle-taggle, tied together mess of a family tree, all scraped up and pinned together like a rushed up-do. The pieces were falling out. This wasn't a family reunion as much as a family disunion. The brothers jumped up as the waiter arrived, balancing three plates on his arms.

"Sit ye down, lass, don't be upset."

"I'm not hungry. I'm sorry, I made a mistake coming here."

"Don't be daft, wee girl. Sit with us. Besides, we have some family business to discuss."

"What family? I don't have a family, never have, never will."

Sylvia allowed anger to suffocate her sorrow. She snatched up her bag and pushed back her chair. But Donald placed a heavy hand on her arm and pulled her back.

His voice hardened. "I said sit."

In that second, the situation became clear. These two wanted something.

"It's the small matter of your, *our*, grandmother's estate."

Sylvia's thoughts clarified, unlike the food on the plates that congealed into slimy blobs.

"How big is this small matter?"

"Och, it's just a trinket, not worth much except sentimental value. We believe your mother gave it to you to safekeeping, but Evie's will states she left it to her grandsons."

Sylvia knew a lie when she heard one. It was in his over-exaggerated shrug, the slimy sincerity, the nodding head. The trinket was the key to Evie's vault, and now she was more curious than ever to see what it held. She glanced at her bag. The edge of the brooch peeped from under the flap.

"But you're not her grandsons! I want to read the will."

Colin leaned back. "She doesn't trust us, Don. What sort of cousinly love is that? We visited the old bat year in, year out."

"Calm down Colin, the young lady is merely being cautious." He turned to Sylvia. "Of course you can read it. We can organise an appointment with our solicitor. But just let me confirm that you do indeed have in your possession an onyx brooch?"

A moment of silence hung in the air while a lifetime of memories sped through Sylvia's mind. Her father pressing the brooch in her hand at the port. Running her fingers over it in the convent, gazing into its depths in private moments, imagining her mother's face. The picture above the Lively Lady, Evie pressing the needle into her palm, standing at the pier in Bournemouth, her hand raised, so close to delivering it to the ocean. She then knew what she must say.

"I did. But it's gone. I threw it into the sea after Evie died."

Colin leapt up, swearing. Donald dropped his head in his hands.

"You stupid, selfish little bitch."

He slammed his fist onto the table, making the other diners and cutlery jump. Sylvia had to get out of there. She grabbed her bag; the brooch hidden by the flap, and pushed her chair back. She lurched for the door and bumped into a startled waiter, who dropped his plates of food on to seated customers. The bag flew open and exposed the heirloom."Colin!" Donald pointed to the bag, and they jumped out of their seats.She had to escape from the poisonous remnants of her family. The scattered rotting leaves of a family tree. The detritus left on the salon floor at the day's end. Disconnected hair cuttings that could have belonged to anyone and now no longer wanted.

Sylvia evaded their grasp and rushed out onto the street. She threw her bag across her body and yanked out a hairbrush. Looking left and right, she chose right. She dodged the many people that inhabited the night streets of Soho, slowing her down. Scuffles of footsteps and complaints behind her alerted her to danger. She ducked down an alleyway. Hard looking girls in short skirts lounged sleazily along the wall. Sylvia dared to glance behind her. Colin appeared at the mouth of the alley.

"What's your fancy, love?" one of the women pouted.

"Oh knots!" Sylvia muttered and kept running down the side street. She came out at another brightly lit thoroughfare. Her instinct was to get back to the guesthouse, but Colin and Donald knew she lived there. She would have to find somewhere else to stay until the Old Capital Bank opened in the morning. It was only eight o'clock now. Where could she spend the next twelve hours? The graveyard passed through her mind, but she soon dismissed the idea. She needed a safe, warm place. Then she had an idea. She picked up her pace and ran towards the Underground and jumped on the line that would take her to Clipper Street.

Wiggles was of course closed, Clipper Street deserted. Drizzle left globules of moisture on Sylvia's shoulders. She walked down the street, counting the terraced doors until an alleyway split the buildings. She doubled back behind the block, recounting until she arrived at the backyard of Wiggles. The gate was locked, but some crates gave her a stepping stone to scale the wall and she dropped down into the small yard. She retrieved two bobby pins from her bag and bent them into a key shape. With little effort, she tickled the lock and the door opened.

The familiar smell of shampoo, clean towels and hair spray soothed her raised follicles. Her heart beat slowed. She slid into a chair and took several deep breaths. She took out the brooch. Its cold weight she once cherished now felt chilling and cumbersome. Once she'd gained access to the vault, she wanted rid of it. Did the cousins know about the vault? Why else would they want the brooch? She made herself a cup of tea in the kitchenette. Sylvia paced up and down the shop. Cousins! She scoffed. They could be anyone. But Evie must have known them. She scanned her memory of her time with her grandmother, what she had said to her.

“Don’t let those thieving bastards get their hands on it.”

But she had clearly been mad, harping on about the Gerries. A connection then fired in Sylvia’s brain, and she rummaged around in her bag for the card Donald had given her. It read Donald Michael Geraldton. Geraldton! Is that what Evie meant by the Gerries? Perhaps she was, as she had appeared for moments of their meeting, completely sane. Was she warning Sylvia off the impostor cousins? Did they believe she had discarded the brooch? And what did Evie’s will really say? What else did she leave and how would Sylvia get access to it? Did she even want anything? Perhaps the only thing worth having was tied up in the brooch. How did the cousins know about the Elizabethan brooch then? Questions looped around Sylvia’s mind until she dozed off.

27

Street noises woke her. She had dreamt she was being chased and shot at by Germans, but it was rain pelting the shutters. Sylvia grabbed her glasses, put them on and looked at herself in the mirror. She looked pale and puffy eyed. She washed her face in the sink and gave her armpits and nether regions a wipe. Once she had slipped on a fresh pair of undies (a tip Emmy-Lou had given her, always be prepared), she pulled out a range of makeup and painted her face, finishing with a thick coat of frosted pink lipstick. She wrote a note for Jez, thanking her for the tea and explaining that she borrowed a cape and would post it back to the salon. Glad of UGH's advice to dress appropriately for adventure, she scaled the wall with ease in her pantsuit. She dropped the cape over her head and ran to the Underground station, keeping dry in the squall.

At 7.50 am, she disembarked the tube. The bank opened at 8.00 a.m. and it was a five-minute walk. As she approached, her scalp prickled. With an urge to run, she slowed down and looked around her. She clenched her fingers around the hairbrush in her coat pocket. Suddenly, a hand covered her mouth and yanked her into a side alley. She screamed, but the hand muffled any noise. She pulled her arm out of her pocket with an elbow to the ribs of the attacker. Swinging her hand around with the hefty brush, she connected to a helmet protected head.

"Bleeding hell, Sylvia. Calm down!"

His grip loosened, and Sylvia broke free and turned to face him, ready to swipe again.

"It's me," the helmeted man hissed, "Sammy."

"Jesus mother and Mary, Sammy! What are you playing at?"

"I'm sorry, Queenie. Better me than those two."

"What two?"

"Look."

He crept to the corner of the wall and pointed to a car parked across the street from the bank.

"Donald and Colin," she hissed.

"That's right."

"How did you know where I was?"

"I don't know what trouble you're in, Sylv, but Mrs G rang me yesterday afternoon. Told me you were meeting these two at the restaurant. I turned up just as you were running away. So I figured I'd stick to them, just in case they tried any funny business."

"I'm a big girl, Sammy. I don't need your help."

"I don't want to see you getting hurt, Sylv, and neither does Mrs G."

"You think those two morons can hurt me? You have no idea Samuel Lock. When your mother dies at your birth, when your father ships you out to the other side of the world, when you have a bunch of nuns raising you, when your uncle hates you." She took a breath, "when someone you love dies, when your grandmother is a crazy hag that stabs you, when your boyfriend dumps you because of how you look..." Her voice rose and rose.

"Shush, Queenie, I'm sorry."

"And you're concerned that a pair of nitwits like that can hurt me?"

Sammy opened and closed his mouth.

"Goodbye, Sammy."

She sidestepped him.

"Wait, Sylvia, I love you!"

He ripped off his helmet and dropped to his knees and grabbed her hand; the hairbrush sticking out at an angle. There was a booming crack of thunder that rattled their bones. Lightning lit up the dingy alleyway. A cat frozen by the sudden light scarpered away in fright. A downpour followed that almost flattened them. Thunder boomed again.

"Sylvia, will you... will you marry me?"

"What?" She thought he had asked her to marry her, but couldn't be sure over the noise.

"Will you marry me?" he shouted, competing with the rain that ricocheted off the dustbin lids. She never understood why she reacted the way she did. But she pulled her hand away from his grasp, raised it, and smacked him across the side of his head with the hairbrush. She made a dash on to the road, sprinting the last few hundred yards to the mighty doors of the Old Capital Bank. The two cousins leapt out of the Ford Cortina and jogged across the street. After gaining entry, she fumbled around in her bag and pulled out the steel UGH embossed comb. She slid the comb into the two handles. Feet scuffled up the steps behind the bronze doors, which soon rattled, opening a crack until the comb caught the handles. She pushed them closed and searched for a bobby pin. A brief resolution to keep her bag tidier passed through her mind as she pulled one out with some crumbs. With her shoulder against the door that was now being banged on with Scottish expletives, she jammed the pin into the lock and twisted. The lock slid with a satisfying swish. She whipped the golden comb out of the handles and slipped it back into her bag.

The same clerk, Miss Forsyth, sat at the desk across the ocean of tiled floor. Sylvia scissored her legs towards the desk, her eyes lasered onto the woman. They eyed each other, the clerk sensing that Sylvia was not to be messed with. She unhooked the brooch from inside her bag and deposited it on the desk with a thump.

"The brooch."

The clerk lifted it up and viewed it through a magnifying lens she held to her eye. Banging on the door and muffled shouts distracted her attention. Sylvia put both hands on the desk, leaned into the clerk and said in a low voice, "First commandment of UGH - never keep a hairdresser waiting."

She put out her hand for the brooch.

"Yes quite, er Miss Sprout. Have you had it insured?"

"I am not here to buy insurance, dove, I just want access to the safe deposit box that belonged to my grandmother."

The furore outside alerted a security guard who ambled across the desert of floor towards the doors.

"Can I ask our valuer to take a look at it?"

"The bloody doors are locked," the guard exclaimed.

The guard rummaged through his jumble of keys. Voices shouted outside, thumps rained on the door.

"Just a tick, I'm opening up now," he yelled.

"No, not today, thank you. I'm here to have a gander in that safe..." Sylvia looked behind her to the guard who selected a key and put it in the lock. "... straight away."

"Miss Sprout, I can assure you that..."

The key refused to work. "Ah, buggering keys!" The guard pulled it out and picked through his bunch one by one.

"Open the fecking doors!" *Bang, bang, bang.*

"Look, I appreciate your suggestion, but I have a flight to catch and I'm in a terrible hurry. Would you mind showing me to the vault?"

"Ah! There you are, you bleeding bugger."

Sylvia snatched the brooch out of the woman's grip.

"Shall we? Lead the way, Miss Forsyth."

Miss Forsyth reluctantly rose from her seat and led Sylvia to a door that said 'vault access'. She pulled her own set of keys from her waist and Sylvia looked heavenward as she heard the lock click in the main doors. The clerk opened it and ushered Sylvia through as she turned to see the guard open the two heavy doors to a kerfuffle of feet.

"Oi, oi lassie!"

"Hurry up, Miss Forsyth."

"This door automatically closes after thirty seconds, very James Bond."

Sylvia watched in horror as Donald and Colin slid across the glacier of floor towards her.

She counted under her breath, "27, hairdresser, 28 hairdresser, 29 hairdresser..."

The door finally swung closed, and the clerk let Sylvia into a small dark room.

"Wait, wait, stop!" The reinforced door muffled the cries.

Sylvia let out a held breath and dropped her shoulders. In this antechamber, Miss Forsyth unlocked a safe and took out yet another key. She then led them through a door that opened to a long spiral of steep steps. Miss Forsyth explained how the private vaults were below the gold vault in case anyone tried to tunnel through and steal the gold. She noted the door that lead into the gold vault and told Sylvia it required a key three feet long. Sylvia wondered how many bobby pins she would need to break in. When they arrived at the private safe vault, the key was less impressive but still a hefty six inches.

Inside, small metal doors lined the walls of a vast carpeted room. Its eerie silence made Sylvia think of Solomon buried in his coffin. Miss Forsyth walked along the walls briskly, stopping at 0703 and unlocking it with a miniature key.

"I'll be at the desk by the door waiting for you. You have fifteen minutes."

She bustled off, her nylons crackling.

Sylvia could hear her own breath disturbing the still air. With trepidation, she hooked her finger in the steel door and pulled it open. She placed her hand inside the gloomy interior and touched a wooden box. She slid it out and held it, rubbing her fingers over the lid inlaid with mother-of-pearl. Her own grandmother had stood right here in this spot and put it inside the safe once upon a time. Sylvia knelt down and placed it in front of her. She cleaned her glasses with the hem of her sleeve. The box was smooth and polished, a tiny key protruded from the front of the lid. She turned it and opened the box, inching the lid open under stiff hinges. A Venetian style mask looked back up at her, causing a startled intake of breath. She lifted it out, its long nose made it grotesque. She unpacked the box item-by-item, a bundle of Italian lira, a bone with a ring on it, a small silver pistol. Then a silver box with her grandmother's initials that contained a baby's brush and comb. At the bottom was a dry piece of paper. She unfolded it, afraid it would disintegrate. It was a birth certificate dated 7th of October 1915, the name Evelina Frattini. The rest was in Italian, but she understood the name of the mother 'madre', Contessa Maria Capelli of Sicily. A hefty envelope left in the box bore her name, simply Sylvia. Her heart skipped a beat to see it emerge from a wooden box buried deep below the city of London. She opened the flap and gasped as a thick wad of money neatly slept inside. She pulled one out. It was a fifty-pound note and there were hundreds of them. She shook her chin from side to side and pulled out the letter.

'Dear Sylvia,

If you are reading this, my plan has worked. If you are not Sylvia, go to hell and rot. I curse you.'

Sylvia believed her grandmother could successfully curse someone from her grave. She read on.

'I was born in Italy in 1915 to a daughter of a count. My mother, Contessa Maria Capelli, disgraced herself by becoming pregnant with me, a love affair with a boy from a Mafia family. They sent her to England to have me in secret and she left me there when they brought her home. I made a life for myself here in London, but many years later I heard my father was furious and his family took revenge on the Capelli's. Who knows what became of them? What do I care? All I know is they paid a foster family to take me on. The Fraughtons, poor, dim-witted, and mean, from the east of London. They dragged me up by the scruff of my neck, but they couldn't control my Mafia blood. With a little help from some associates, I outlived them all. But I didn't let that miserable childhood stop me. When the blood of heartless nobility and murderous Mafioso runs through your veins, as it does yours girl, you survive, and you survive well. The way to get on in this world is to give as good as you get, and you won't find no good. I will not waste any ink writing about your grandfather. He turned my head, but he was a gutless wretch and looked only for the bottom of the glass. By now you know the value of the onyx brooch. A mourning brooch that belonged to Queen Elizabeth the First. A lock of her hair is embedded within. It has passed through the hands of pirates, traitors and thieves. Along with the cash, it is your inheritance. Use it well.

Your grandmother,

Evie Fraughton'

Sylvia picked up the brooch. She looked into its inky depth and saw images in its flawed veins. She saw tears flowing over a cheek as they cut off a lock of their loved one's hair, a flash of a sword slicing off a head, a dagger in the heart, a highwayman wrenching it off a woman's breast, her own mother screaming in agony and finally the searing pain of the pin into her own hand. She let it drop into the box and snapped the lid shut. Feeling sick, she leaned her cheek against a cold metal safe door. Her grandmother had also been abandoned but ended up a bitter and vengeful old woman. She had died wealthy, lonely and paranoid. Sylvia now knew where she was from. She suspected her nameless grandfather in the letter was Mickey Manic, an alcoholic bully. Her own father a petty criminal and her mother a beautiful but simple pawn for Sylvia's life. Her uncle Arthur a narcissistic queer. She threw the box back into the safe and shoved it in hard, but it got caught on something else. A small bound journal blocked the box. She pulled it out. The smell of stale tobacco smoke invaded the neutral air of the vault.

Miss Forsyth rang a bell.

"Time's up, Miss Sprout. We need to leave now."

Sylvia glanced at the box inside the safe. 'Good bye' didn't seem like a fitting word to sever herself from her roots, to bury them in this tomb forever.

"Excuse me, Miss Forsyth, if no one accesses this security box again, how long does it stay here?"

"One hundred years."

Not quite forever, but long enough. She carefully folded the letter and slipped it into the unopened journal and put the envelope of cash in the bottom of her bag..

"OK, I'm ready."

Miss Forsyth locked the box and let Sylvia back into the stairwell.

"Now, about that brooch, I believe it's an extremely valuable piece..."

"It's gone."

"What do you mean it's gone?"

"I've left it in the safe."

"Miss Sprout, you do understand that you need the brooch in order to access the safe?"

"Yes, I understand perfectly."

"But it's like locking your keys in the car. Now I really shouldn't do this, but we can go back in and get it out."

"That's very kind of you, Miss Forsyth, but it's a broken car that will only bring me grief. I've made my decision. It's for the best."

Miss Forsyth stared at her for a moment before turning back towards the staircase. They arrived back in the antechamber and waited for the automatic door to open. Sylvia surveyed the bank. There were several customers being served, a low murmur of voices, no sign of the cousins.

"Well, thanks very much Miss Forsyth, g'day."

Sylvia stuck out her hand, which Miss Forsyth shook limply. She marched across the vast savannah for the last time and released herself from the grandiose building. The rain had ceased. Sammy was waiting for her on the steps. A police car pulled away, and she glimpsed the face of the furious Donald in the window.

"What happened?"

"They punched the guard. Not a very clever thing to do. The Old Capital Bank has a direct line to the police force. They arrived in seconds."

Sammy had a swollen bruise forming on the side of his head. He put on his helmet, wincing.

"For protection," he said, giving it a knock with his knuckles.

Sylvia bit her lip in shame.

"I'm sorry, Sammy. Does it hurt a lot?"

He shook his head and dropped to one knee. The wind blew a moment of light through the clouds of the still stormy sky.

"Sylvia, you are the best girl I ever met, smart, brave and," he paused, "you throw a mean punch."

She winced and looked apologetic.

"I'm asking you again, Queenie. Will you be my wife?"

"Yes! Oh Sammy, yes I will."

For the first time in her life, Sylvia felt the cords of her past sever. Now she could tap into a source of her own making. She drank from the deep well of love for Sammy as they embraced and, for a moment, life was perfect.

28

Sammy took her to lunch. They walked through Hyde Park, holding hands, stealing kisses, not knowing what to say to each other. Sylvia pulled away.

"Sammy, I need to say goodbye to my dad."

"Do you want me to come with you?"

"No, thanks. I'll meet you at the guesthouse later, before I leave for the airport."

"Why don't you stay, Sylvia? I've got a job, we can find a flat, you'll get work easy with Crassoon."

"I'll miss you so much, Sammy, but there is unfinished business in Australia. Plus, it's my home; I like it there."

"Where will we live then, when we're married?"

"Well, come over and see if you like it in Perth."He leaned in and nuzzled between her shoulder and cheek.

"I'll catch you later," she whispered.

He held onto her fingers for as long as possible as she walked away.

Sylvia trod the now familiar path to the graveyard to where her father lay.

"Hi Dad, I understand why you sent me away now. You loved me. I wasn't safe with that crazy mother-in-law of yours and someone would have taken me away from you. You tried to buy me a better life. I can't say if you pulled it off or not yet, Dad, but I won't let you down."

A shaft of sun broke through and landed by her foot.

"You must have been so sad when Mum died. At least you knew her, got to hold her and kiss her."

A tear escaped, and Sylvia chewed her bottom lip.

"I just wish I could, could see her face."

She sniffed and settled on the nearby bench. The corner of Evie's journal poked out of her bag. She slid it out and put her hand on the cover. She expected it to be filled with vitriol and debtors. She wasn't sure if she wanted to open it or not. But she did.

'8th June 1956

Today is my wedding day. I'm so happy. Frank is a real gent. He says next year we'll buy a house and give me a proper kitchen with an oven. Don't tell anyone, but I think there will be three of us then. Have to keep it a secret from Evie, she'll kill us both.

Later

It was a smashing day. The sun shone and Frank looked so handsome. We'll leave our honeymoon for a few weeks, wait for Frank to save up some money. He doesn't want me working in the pub anymore and Evie is not happy. Why did I end up with such a wicked mother? Is money all she cares about? Didn't even splash out on a big reception. Had it in the Lively Lady, old Ian played the piano, we had a bit of a knees-up. Back to work tomorrow. I think Evie knows I'm with child. Can't get much past her.'

It wasn't Evie's journal; it was her mother's! She flicked through some more pages to make sure, and a photo fell out of the book. It was a picture of her mum and dad on their wedding day. Frank smiled like he'd struck gold, and her mum, the mystery of Sylvia's life, was there on the page beaming at her. Sylvia put a hand to her heart and let out a breath she had held her whole life.

"Mummy."

She pushed up her glasses to muster their full power and scrutinised the picture. Her mother's dark hair was set in the voluminous 50s bob of the era, black and thick, just like her own. She wore a simple white frock and her father dressed in a suit with slicked hair as neat as a ballerina's bun.

"I was in your tummy," she whispered.

There were more pictures; Angie pregnant, holding onto her round belly, taut with baby. Angie and Frank at the beach, maybe a honeymoon. There was no time to study them closely; the afternoon was drawing in.

"Thanks Dad, goodbye."

She kissed her fingers and rested them on the gravestone. An impulse rose in her to walk beyond her father's grave, and she allowed her feet to take her. It was as if her dad guided her to another grave; that of her mother. Sylvia dropped to her knees and let a sob escape, for once an out loud cry, followed by another and another. The sobs faded to weeping and then stopped. She laughed.

"I love you Mummy, rest easy. I'm fine now. I love you."

Sylvia left the cemetery and found a post box. All the evidence against Arthur and a letter explaining what happened was inside an envelope addressed to D.I. Grouse. She balanced the envelope on the lip of the slit. Her head tingled, her heart contracted. No, she couldn't do it. He was family, after all. She put the letter into the bin at the bus stop and boarded the bus. It trundled past the Lively Lady, and one last time she beheld her grandmother swinging for eternity on the sign above the door.

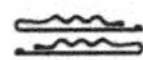

There was one thing still gnawing at Sylvia. If Arthur hadn't visited Amanda Makepeace, then who had the power to lure him to the filthy, dangerous, down-at-heel suburb of Cresswell? There was only one way to find out. She read her mother's journal on the tube, turning the pages with care, tracing her handwriting and staring at the photo. Scrutinising every detail, she nearly missed her stop. Left out of the Underground, she remembered, but which of the concrete block of flats? She walked along the pavement looking for clues, then she saw the playground, the Mums with prams, pushing toddlers on swings. She entered the festering stairwell. Up past cigarette butts, broken glass, past pools of dried vomit, past graffiti insults to a blood-stained wall to the fourth floor. Sylvia hesitated. She took a breath and knocked on number 44. She waited, knocked again. There was a shuffling, banging.

"Who is it? I'm not bloody interested and I don't know nothing."

"Hello, my name is Sylvia," she called.

There was no response.

"I, I'm looking for Arthur Sprout."

After a few seconds, the door opened as far as the chain would allow.

"How do you know Arthur?" the woman asked, eyeing her suspiciously.

"I'm his niece."

"Well, blow me down with a bleeding feather."

The door closed and opened again, released from the chain.

"You better come in."

The old woman led them down a shabby hallway. Cat hair covered the threadbare carpet and the rank smell of cat pee permeated the air.

"Git off the bloody table, you mongrel, shoo, shoo."

The small kitchen housed five or six cats who weaved around their legs, mewing.

"Have a seat."

"Thanks."

"Tea? Ain't got no milk though."

She filled a saucepan up with water from a juddering tap and turned the ring on an old stove. She tossed a foot at a cat curling around her leg.

"Git out of it, bloody pests."

"How many cats do you have? Mandy, is it?"

"Five, last count, people dump 'em on my doorstep."

Sylvia had no response and so cut to the chase.

"How do you know Arthur?"

"Haven't seen him for twenty years, little shit. He buggered off to Australia. None of us ever heard from him, not a peep. Then he's banging on my door like it was yesterday."

"So, you're an old friend?"

"He's my brother, you daft bint."

"Your brother? That means you're my aunt. I'm Frank's daughter, Alfred Frank Sprout."

"I know that. Why do you think I let you in? Honestly, it's like an episode of 'This Is Your Life', first Arthur, now you. I expect Eamonn Andrews'll be knocking at my door next. You're the spit of your grandmother, evil bitch and clearly empty between the ears like your mother."

"I wish people would say nice things about her," Sylvia sighed.

"Don't mind me, been on me own too long."

She patted Sylvia's hand.

"Can you tell me about her and my dad? Look, I found this."

Sylvia slid the photo out of the journal. Mandy gasped.

"Weren't they a picture? Your dad was a rascal, true enough, but no one made him happier than your mother, Angie. It was love at first sight. The day he walked in the pub and she was pulling pints, she must have been sixteen. I remember he came home with an idiot smile on his face. Promised her the world, he did. He'd bring her round when Evie wasn't working her to the bone. She was a good girl, your mum, wouldn't harm a caterpillar."

"What was it like in, in our family?"

Her heart smiled at the words. Mandy poured a good glug of whisky in Sylvia's black tea, then her own.

Mandy told Sylvia about her family, her father and his exploits, how she had married herself before the bugger had run away with another woman. She described Sylvia's grandparents, working class Londoners who had survived through war and poverty and more war.

"They never forgave your dad for sending you away, being the only grandchild. Or me for failing on the kiddie front, and Arthur for being the way he was."

"Arthur! I don't understand what he has against me. He did some terrible things, you know."

Mandy puckered her lips and tutted. "He never did fit in here. He got bashed more than once and his sweet little heart just froze over. Maybe you bought it all out of him, like a big vomit. No one likes to vomit."

Sylvia felt sick at the analogy and took a sip of her whisky-laced tea, feeling its warmth trickle into her stomach.

"He left me this." Mandy retrieved a cheque from one of her cupboards.

"Two thousand pounds!" Sylvia read.

"That'll keep me in cat food and liquor till I die!" said Mandy, with a sparkle in her eye.

"Wow, I'm really happy he did that." Sylvia couldn't find words for a moment, both hurt and happy mingled in her chest.

"So there are no more relatives hiding away?"

"We're it, love. But look at you, good healthy girl, you'll keep the line going."

Sylvia smiled. "I hope so, Mandy." She glanced at her watch.

"It's getting late and I'm flying back to Australia tonight. I'd better go." She hugged the frail bones of her aunt and promised to write and visit again when she returned to London.

"Thank you, Mandy. You have no idea how much this has meant for me."

"Time I feed these pesky little critters, anyway. Off with you, I can't abide tears."

Sylvia saved them for the cab ride home when she let them pour over her cheeks.

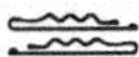

There wasn't much time to spare once she arrived back at the guesthouse. Vitale waited with his car and driver to take them to the airport. Humphrey, now reconciled with his patron, also came. Mrs Grimshaw fussed as if she was entertaining royalty, refusing the Teabag Traders entry into the dining room and the kettle, despite them suffering withdrawals. Sammy hovered as close to her as possible, stealing glances. Everyone squeezed into the car to head to the airport, along with Fifi, who chewed on whoever's foot was closest.

Once she checked in her luggage at the airport, Sylvia turned to the group to say goodbye. Mrs Grimshaw had tears streaming down her face. Sylvia went to her first and buried her face into the familiar scent of sausages and clean sheets that clung to her sweater. Mrs Grimshaw hugged her tightly. She pulled away and took Sylvia's face in her hands.

"Now you write me, OK? And take care of yourself, make sure you eat properly."

She let another wave of tears break free and pulled Sylvia in close again.

"Rightio, away with you now, pet, or I'll run out of hanky. You're a good girl."

Sylvia couldn't speak and put her knuckles to her mouth, holding in her emotions, already too many tears for one day.

"Come here, sister. If you ever write that article, be sure to send it, and if you need some inspiration, keep your eye on Lebonne International."

"Ooh, I like it, Hump, keep thinking big. Goodbye."

They hugged.

"Sammy, where have you been?" a voice shrieked from beyond the group.

"What time do you call this? I expected you here an hour ago. My jet is leaving. I told you I have a meeting in Paris first thing."

The woman recognised Vitale."Vitale, monsieur, quelle surprise! Where are you off to?"

"Karla," they air kissed. "I'm just saying au revoir to a friend. You remember Sylvia?"

Her eyes swept from Sylvia's feet to her head and to her feet again.

"Yes, quite. Sammy, we're leaving, immediately."

"Sylv, I've got to go, I," he looked around, embarrassed in front of an audience and stepped in close, "I love you, Queenie. I'll come soon, to Oz, and I'll write."

He kissed her, briefly, tenderly.

"SAMMY!"

"I love you too," she replied, but he was gone, chasing the queen of couture through the airport.

For a moment, they all watched his back recede.

"Mademoiselle, ma petite fille, I wish you luck and 'appiness. If you ever need a job, Crassoon is always 'appy to 'ave you."

"Monsieur, I don't know how to thank you..."

"Non, ma cherie, I thank you from zee bottom of my heart. You saved my scalp."

"Mon pleasure," she attempted in a terrible accent. "Right then, I'd better go."

She walked away, giving one last glance at the new friends she had made. They waved and blew kisses and cried. A tear fell from each eye and she removed her glasses to wipe them away. As she made her way through the baggage check, she felt alone. The security guard glared as she let out an ugly sob. She wondered why she was leaving, leaving those four people who had become family to her. Going back to Perth for what? She had no one there anymore, no salon, no friends, nothing. A wave of panic rose in her chest. She tried to turn around, but the flow of bodies trapped her, like a barb.

"Wait, let me through. I don't want to go."

"Sorry miss, you can't go back through this way." A beefy guard with a too tight shirt blocked her.

"I've changed my mind; I'm not leaving."

"You'll have to go back through the gates over there and wait for security to take you through."

"But..."

"Keep going please, miss."

She turned and craned her neck. Vitale was talking to Humphrey. Mrs G blew her nose and picked up Fifi. Sylvia waved, but they didn't see her.

"Who am I kidding? I don't belong here," she thought she said in her head.

"Belong where?" a voice piped.

"Jez? Jez!"

Sylvia threw herself at the surprised girl.

"You came? I'm so happy!" And she burst into tears again, which confused them both.

"How could I refuse? Shall we get a drink?"

29

The plane trip was as full of wonder as the first time. Jez clipped and unclipped the seat belt for the first ten minutes, then put her seat back and forth until the lady behind complained. She clung to Sylvia as the plane rumbled along the runway and took off. She put her tray up and down and ordered drinks. Once they were above the clouds and Jez had marvelled at the view, she went to the back of the plane for a cigarette. They talked like old friends until boredom and too much champagne sent them both to sleep.

Jez's beehive and Sylvia's turban were both tilted at dangerous angles when they arrived in Perth.

"Right, into the dunnies. We can't arrive home looking like we're disappearing down a sinkhole."

They spent a quarter of an hour rebuilding the structures on their heads, applying lipstick and smoothing eyeshadow and blusher across their puffy faces.

After watching the entire plane's worth of suitcases rattling around, their luggage appeared.

"Hoo-bleeding-ray! Where to now, Sylvia?"

"That's a good question, dove. I don't know. Let's find some lodgings in the city."

As they emerged through customs, overheated officers paid little attention. Summer had arrived in Perth, their shirts stuck to their backs, and flies to the shirts.

"Sylvie, Sylvie, over here!"

A blast from a hairdryer cut the air, and Wiz pushed through waiting friends and family of other people to the two women.

"Wiz! What a surprise!"

She jumped into his arms, quite forgetting his highness.

"Welcome home, my dear. You have so much to tell me, and I you."

"Wiz, this is my friend, Jez. She has immigrated to Australia, another hairdresser."

"Jez, may I introduce you to Wiz, head of..."

"... head of the crowd!" he interjected. "Come along now. I have news."

They opened doors into a wave of heat that resembled a hairdryer. Jez's beehive visibly slumped.

"Bleeding hell! Where's the off button?" she said.

She pulled out a tissue and dabbed at the sweat on her forehead. Wiz's car drew up, and the driver loaded the boot with their cases.

"Where are we going, Wiz?"

"Well, my dear, talking of heat..."

"Wiz, I know Arthur is inheriting the salon, but he didn't solve the mystery. He tried to set me up and..."

"Yes, dear, I am acquainted with the facts of the mission."

"You are? How?"

"My dear girl, I am in the loop of every salon in the world. Did you think Arthur would get away with such a low deed?"

"You knew he put the hair remover cream in the dye?"

"I did."

"And that I spent two nights in prison, falsely accused?"

"Not at the time, Sylvie, I'm so sorry you had to go through such an ugly experience."

"But Arthur has ended up with the salon. He said the paperwork had gone through and..."

"This is what I'm trying to tell you, Sylvia. Please cease interrupting me."

"Sorry, Wiz."

"I'm afraid I had to go to America. N.A.S.A. had to fix my computer, so information wasn't incoming. I made the mistake of trusting Tatyana. As soon as the deceit came to light, I halted the proceedings. You succeeded in your mission. Vitale is extremely pleased and sung your praises. Well done. I knew you wouldn't let me down."

"What do you mean 'trusting Tatyana'? Halted what proceedings?"

"Tatyana and Arthur planned to win the salon together. Once I discovered their sneaky plot, I expelled them both. The salon is now in your name, my dear."

"Jiminy clippers! True? Did you hear that, Jez? We have the salon, the Wavy Lady salon!"

Sylvia clapped her hands together and tears stung her jet-lagged eyes. Wiz took a deep breath and stared out of the window as they entered the suburbs of Perth.

"I'm so happy to be home. Look at that blue sky. I thought those clouds would choke me in London."

Wiz allowed her some time to enjoy the moment.

"Sylvia, my dear." He leaned across the gap between their seats in the limousine and took her hands. "There is something I haven't told you... oh dear, we're here."

"This is it Jez, we're on Rosella Street, see the trees like I explained, and the salon, it's so..." they drew up outside the Wavy Lady. "... so gone."

She got out of the car, disbelief freezing her mouth into a large 'O'.

"I'm sorry, my dear, I was trying to explain..."

What was left of the salon had uneven planks of wood boarding up the window. Black smudges decorated the once lilac paintwork, the rank whiff of smoke hung in the air.

"What happened?"

"There was a fire, the police suspect arson."

Sylvia walked up to the front door, broken glass crunched underfoot by the doorstep. She pushed the door.

"It's dangerous in there, Sylvia, be careful."

"But who would do this?"

"Arthur and his accomplice, Tatyana Streekz."

"Why Wiz, why?"

"As I said, it was Tatty who convinced Arthur to go to London to attempt the mission. Or at least make sure you didn't succeed. You see, Tatty wanted one thing from the salon... the Hairflet 700. She promised to help him win back the salon if he gave her the Hairflet. Tatty advised Arthur to lace the dye with depilatory cream and dump you in it. Once they knew I was onto them, they came to Perth and torched the salon after removing the chair. I'm so sorry, my dear."

"Do the police know they did it? Where are they now?"

"They made it back to Moscow. If they ever set foot in this country again, the Feds will nab them. Arthur will have to get used to the taste of vodka instead of whisky."

He gave a wry smile. "You can stay at my city apartment until you work out what to do, as long as you like, both of you."

"Thanks, Wiz. You know what? I went halfway around the world to find out who I was, only to find out this is where I belong. I'm planting my own roots right here."

She linked arms with Jez and Wiz. They gazed at the empty shell of the salon; a blank slate awaiting to be washed out, brushed up and styled by Sylvia Scutlash and her Wavy Ladies.

The End...?

EPILOGUE

Three months later.

Jez turned the sign around to 'open' and wiped the inside of the glass door. Above the door, 'Nihil mali capillos' was embossed in gold.

"That's great news, monsieur, so happy for you both. Send my love to Hump. And again, thank you so much for everything..... Yes, we've been open a couple of weeks. The salon looks amazing. I'll send you some Polaroids... Au revoir!"

"Was that Vitale?"

"Yes, he and Humphrey are now partners. Watch out London!"

"Did you tell him how busy we are?"

"Yes, he's thrilled."

"What time is our first booking of the day?"

"Any minute now, Mrs Butson from across the road."

"We'll hear all about the..."

The phone rang. Sylvia picked up the receiver.

"G'day, Wavy Lady Hair Salon, how can I help you?" Sylvia's eyes lit up, a smile stretched her lips from ear to ear. "Hi Wiz, how are you?... Already?... I'm sure Jez can hold the fort for a few days..."

PLAYLIST

Pure seventies nostalgia!

Go to Spotify https://tinyurl.com/yw3capw5to enjoy!

Chapter 1 It's Your Life – Smokie

Chapter 2 Don't leave me this way – Thelma Houston

Chapter 3 Boogie Nights – Heatwave

Chapter 4 Don't Give Up on Us – David Soul

Chapter 5 Sunny – Boney M.

Chapter 6 Go Your Own Way – Fleetwood Mac

Chapter 7 Moody Blue – Elvis Presley

Chapter 8 Black is Black – Belle Epoque

Chapter 9 Oh Daddy – Fleetwood Mac

Chapter 10 Chanson D'amour – Manhattan Transfer

Chapter 11 The Crunch – the Rah Band

Chapter 12 Dance Little Lady –Tina Charles

Chapter 13 Remember Then – Showaddywaddy

Chapter 14 Whodunit – Tavares

Chapter 15 You Gotta Get Up and Dance – Supercharge

Chapter 16 Blinded by the Light – Manfred Mann's Earth Band

Chapter 17 Dancin' Party – Showaddywaddy

Chapter 18 So You Win Again – Hot Chocolate

Chapter 19 Sound and Vision – David Bowie

Chapter 20 Help is on its way – Little River Band

Chapter 21 Good Morning Judge – 10cc

Chapter 22 Pretty Vacant – Sex Pistols

Chapter 23 Name of the Game – Abba

Chapter 24 I Feel Love – Donna Summer

Chapter 25 Bye Bye Baby – Bay City Rollers

Chapter 26 When – Showaddywaddy

Chapter 27 Daddy Cool – Darts

Chapter 28 Ain't Gonna Bump No More With No Big Fat Woman – Joe Tex

Chapter 29 Never Going Back Again – Fleetwood Mac

Reviews for Dying Roots

"I'd never think you could find such an amazing story set in the world of hairdressers, but here it is."

"Laughed out loud and was at the edge of my seat several times egging the lovable protagonist on. Bravo!"

"I really loved this book! What a treat to get back to the 1970s, and get to know the heroine of this story, Sylvia!"

"A fun book full of twists and turns, as Sylvia is sent on a mission from 'Down Under' to London to rescue another hairdresser's salon. I love the constant play on words for the names of the people in the story! Sylvia is also searching for information about her family, and the father that sent her to an Australian convent at a young age. Read along as Sylvia makes new friends and uncovers a few enemies in Britain. An interesting read full of Aussie expressions and London lore!"

LETTER TO MRS GRIMSHAW, 1987

To: Mrs Nancy Grimshaw, Come Again Guesthouse, Elephant & Castle, London

November 1987

Dear Mrs G,

Thanks for your last letter. I hope Mr G has recovered from the flu. How did you go with the Cuticle Cream & Nail Varnish Remover Association? I bet they 'polished off' all your breakfasts!!

Things are going well at the Wavy Lady Hair Salon; business is booming, and Jez is the best friend and assistant I could wish for. I have big news, she is engaged! Clive finally proposed over a schooner of beer and fish and chips. She's as happy as a nit in a wig. I'm so pleased she's found a bloke that treats her right. I don't know where my prince in shining hairspray is. I'm beginning to think I'm going to end up a lonely spinster with good hair and no one to show it off to. Every Saturday I have a bride or two in and I have to keep a chirpy face while making them look all pretty for their big day. Maybe I'm just married to the salon!

I'm still doing missions for the United Guild of Hairdressers, though I haven't been on one for ages. It's amazing how much UGH has grown in the last 10 years. When I joined, they only had members in a few salons in a few countries but now nearly every hairdresser in the world is signed up. Wiz (you never met him, he's the head of UGH—remember me telling you about him?) sends out a newsletter every quarter with all the current news, views and latest hair hues that he collects from all the data the member salons give him. Next week it's the Golden Scissors Awards in Las Vegas. I really wish I could go!

Remember my first mission with Vitale Crassoon? It was so flicking exciting going to London, a bit hair-raising, but it turned out alright in the end, and I got to meet you and Mr G. Not been much on the go recently. Last month I went to Albany and sorted out a feud between hairdressers with businesses on the opposite sides of the street. They'd had a parting of ways a few years ago, but I managed to smooth things out. I'd love to get my hands on a real case though, something to distract me, being nearly 30 and still single.

Anyway, I'd better go and hang these towels out to dry. I'll write again soon. Send my love to Mr G.

Yours,

Sylvia

Dear Reader

This is me super-stoked that you've read my book!

I hope you enjoyed reading about Sylvia's first adventure in 1970s London as much as I did. If you did, it would be flicking brilliant if you could leave me a review. This really helps me get the book into more hands, which makes for happy story lovers (and a very happy author!).

It need only be a sentence or two.

Now, you know there's more to come, don't you? The next time we meet Sylvia, she is ten years older and heading off to the bright lights of Las Vegas In book 2 'High Lights'.

If you would like to keep up to date with my writing, please join my newsletter email list:

https://www.subscribepage.com/dyingroots

Until next time, may you have many good hair days,

Karen X

About the Author

Karen is originally from the UK but has lived in sunny Perth, Western Australia since 2008, which practically makes her a local. With a writerly father and a lifetime with her head and heart stuck in books, Karen has aspired to be an author for as long as she can remember.

After writing her 'experimental first book', (a fantasy novel) in 2015, she has moved on to the fun genre of cozy mysteries. Still working on becoming an overnight success, she continues to carve out a creative life whilst working as a freelance copyeditor and mothering her two teenagers and a fluffy white cat.

For more information head to:

www.redfeather.com.au

or

www.karenperadonauthor.com

Follow her on socials at:

www.facebook.com/karenperadon
www.instagram.com/redfeatherpublishing

Also by Karen:

High Lights – book 2 in the Wavy Lady series

About High Lights

All that glitters is not gold at the 1987 Golden Scissors Hairdressers competition.

Amidst the shimmer of the 1987 Golden Scissors Awards, Sylvia Scutlash, special agent is tasked with unearthing missing communication crucial to the United Guild of Hairdressers.

Yet as her mission unfolds at the lavish Pharaoh's Palace Hotel, a murder by scissor blade is committed. Amid foul play, rigged rounds, and greedy sales tactics, Sylvia must race to untangle the hairstylists' data mystery and help the dishy detective uncover the murderer before someone else is killed.

Will Sylvia cut to the chase and save UGH from extinction? Can Detective Danny Dreamboat unravel both the murder and Sylvia's heart? And in a world where vanity and greed reign, who will claim the coveted Golden Scissors trophy?

A punny, funny cozy mystery, where there is more backstabbing than backcombing set against the extravagant backdrop of Las Vegas.

Reviews:

"Delicious and all-women worthy! Great book and now I am a fan."

"Sylvia is a one of a kind, but in the best way. She's loyal, emphatic and brave. I just love her! This is an entertaining and suspenseful story that I just devoured over the weekend. The story is good and as it's set in the eighties there is a lot of fun details here and there."

www.ingramcontent.com/pod-product-compliance
Lightning Source LLC
Chambersburg PA
CBHW061029120726
47910CB00006B/2169

* 9 7 8 0 9 9 4 2 8 4 5 4 9 *